CAPTIVE PRINCESS

CURSED THRONE

BOOK TWO

ALEXA B. JAMES

Captive Princess
Copyright © 2019 Alexa B. James
First Edition

Published in the United States by Alexa B. James and Speak Now.
Cover design by Fantasy Book Designs

ISBN: 978-1-945780-67-7

TRIGGER WARNING

This book is a dark romance that includes coercion and other dark themes of captivity and consent. Reader discretion is advised.

ONE

Itzel
Princess, Ocelot Nation

I CLUNG TO SHADOW'S BACK AS HIS MOTORCYCLE rocketed along the endless, cracked pavement toward an old hangar on the edge of the city. The road itself looked like a runway. If only we could fly, I could be by my sister's side already, our squabble forgotten, defending her from Shadow's fellow panthers.

Silently, I urged him to go, go, go faster. I searched the nearby trees in the swamp for a glimpse of Balam's spotted fur as he ran alongside the bike, but I didn't see him. He probably couldn't keep up with the speed with which we were shooting along the road.

Suddenly, the hangar appeared in the distance, and relief flooded through me. I would get my sister on the private flight King Ocelot had booked for her. I would make sure of it. If anyone got in my way, I'd kill them with my bare hands.

My heart hammered so loud in my ears that I barely heard the motor beneath me, the wind rushing past my ears. I had to get there. I had to protect Camila. I closed my eyes, saying a silent prayer. If she was okay, I'd be agreeable and never argue with her again. I would meekly go back home if she told me to, would say nothing more than "Yes, Ma'am."

As if sensing my terror, Shadow gunned the engine even faster. I should probably not have trusted him to get me here, or anywhere else for that matter. But somehow, I knew that he was an honest man. When he'd kidnapped me, he'd made no pretense about it. He hadn't lured me. He'd dragged me off to his trailer in the swamp and told me exactly what was coming. Now, he'd told me the panther clan was pissed. They didn't want my sister to take their mating amulet, and they'd gone after her despite the fact that she was the princess of the Ocelot Nation.

As we drew closer to the hangar, my heart sank. A chain-link fence surrounded the place, and only a keypad allowed entrance. The hangar sat back from the gate, and outside it...

I swallowed. There were at least half a dozen vehicles, and was that... a body on the ground? Bile rose in my throat, and I clutched Shadow's leather jacket. "Go through," I said.

"Are you sure?" he asked, turning to speak to me over the roar of the engine. "You're human. It might hurt."

Ahead, I heard an ear-splitting shriek, and my heart stopped dead in my chest. "I'm sure," I screamed, my arms clenching around Shadow's thin build.

He gunned the engine, and the bike roared like a beast and leapt forward, speeding toward the twisted metal links of the fence. I closed my eyes and pressed my face to his back so I wouldn't get my eyes ripped out by stray wires. The bike lunged at the fence, ripping through in a screech of tires gripping the pavement and metal protesting as it was shredded and snapped. We hit the ground and skidded before Shadow righted the bike.

"Go," I screamed, lifting my head and pointing to the cars ahead, a haphazard handful of dusty sedans and faded pickups all parked around a sleek, black SUV. A small plane sat on the runway behind them, the ladder lowered to the ground from the door.

Shadow's bike leapt forward, eating up the distance in seconds before skidding to a stop in a swirl of dust and smoke. The smell of the burning tires filled my nostrils as I leapt from the bike and sprinted for the cars. My heart froze in an instant when I saw the doors to the SUV hanging at odd, twisted angles. One of them had been ripped off altogether. A dozen cats were fighting, screaming and snarling, tearing at each other with teeth and claws. Half a dozen human bodies littered the pavement. My stomach lurched as I saw a panther swipe its powerful paw at an ocelot that snarled with its long teeth showing. It was no match for the oversized panther, which raked claws through its spotted fur, leaving furrows of torn and bloody muscle exposed.

"Camila," I screamed, charging forward, not knowing if that was my sister. Maybe she was safely on the plane already.

I tripped over one of the many piles of clothes strewn across the pavement from where the shifters had stripped before changing to animal form. I flew forward, my feet tangling in the jeans, cursing my damned human fallibilities. A cat would never trip. I landed hard but scrambled to rise, my adrenaline fueling my fear and masking any pain. My hand landed on something hard beneath a stack of neatly folded clothes, grinding along the pavement.

I was already on my feet before I realized what I'd touched, and my heart somersaulted as I snatched up the navy-blue guard uniform. Heat and terror shimmered through my chest.

Gabor.

Gabor. Fuck, yes. I tore through his clothes and yanked out the pistol he had once tried to give me so I could protect myself. I hadn't taken it then, but I was damn sure taking it now. Blood rushed in my ears at the thought of what this meant, this abandoned pile of clothes. But the fall and the discovery had knocked sense into me. I was no longer an animal driven by blind panic and fear, rushing into a fight unarmed like a death wish.

I scanned the dwindling fight. Six panthers and two ocelots remained. The mangled ocelot was leaping out of the way of the panther who had backed it against the SUV. Another panther was swiping a long, sleek front leg under the SUV, trying to get what I assumed was another living ocelot. One panther stalked around the SUV to get to the other side, and another two panthers were snarling and leaping at Shadow, who had shifted and joined the fight behind me. I trusted him to keep them occupied as the last panther stalked toward me, its gleaming fangs bared.

"Not today, fucker," I said, clicking off the safety, taking aim, and popping it right between the eyes. As it fell to the ground, I turned to the one who had clamped its jaws around the skull of the mangled ocelot who had so bravely fought a hopeless battle.

"I may not have big teeth and claws, but I've got years of target practice under my belt," I muttered, steadying my right hand in my left. I knew the mangled ocelot had precious seconds, if that, but shooting the SUV wasn't going to help it any. I took careful aim and put a bullet in the panther's eye. Its body tensed, and it dropped the ocelot to the bloody pavement. Its head swung in my direction, but it only managed one step before crumpling to the ground.

"Little sister don't miss when she aims her gun," I said, swinging in the direction of the next panther. The one I'd just shot was still twitching, and to my horror, it began shifting into a human. What I'd just done hit me then. I hadn't just shot panthers, but people, too.

I fought the urge to fling the gun away from myself in horror.

A roar sounded behind me, and I spun to find Lord Balam charging at the two panthers who had leapt onto Shadow. Balam knocked one away, rolling across the pavement in a blur of claws and fur. I wiped one trembling palm on my pants at a time, switching the pistol from one hand to the other. My brain was still in shock, and for a second, I didn't know what to do. A breathless whimper sounded from somewhere nearby, and my head shot up, my horror forgotten. Whatever I had to do was worth it if Camila was alive. To save her, I would have killed all the people in Florida.

"Camila," I cried, racing around the SUV. Two panthers were swiping their razor claws at something in the undercarriage.

"Back off or I shoot," I said, my voice coming out firm and loud. Its strength seemed to steady my hands, and I cradled the pistol, taking careful aim.

One of the panthers lifted its head, staring at me with unblinking green eyes that shone out of its sleek black coat. The intelligence behind them made me want to drop the gun, but I didn't. I might not be able to shoot now that the panic had subsided, and my mind had cleared to what I was doing. But he didn't need to know that.

Lord Balam ran straight for the SUV, leaping through the open doors. His powerful front and back legs stretched out straight, and he came soaring through and landed between me and the panther. He whipped around to face the panther, snarling with his huge incisors on full display. The panther snarled back, and Balam dove for him, slamming into him. They both rose onto their hind legs, their front paws batting at each other as they each tried to grab their opponent's throat.

I turned to the last panther, the one who had crawled halfway under the SUV. It snarled, and I heard a hiss and then an animal howl of pain. Rage slammed through me, and I lowered the pistol to aim at its hind leg. I pulled the trigger, and the bullet pierced through his leg and buried itself in the pavement. Blood splattered the ground, and my stomach lurched.

The panther squirmed out from under the car and turned to snarl at me, its fangs sending an instinctual flood of adrenaline through me. For a second, I was reminded of the tiger that had ripped Tadeu's head off, and my legs nearly gave way. Even with a gun, I was no match for a direct attack.

"Go or I'll shoot," I said, my hands shaking as I aimed the gun.

It sprang at me.

I squeezed the trigger instinctively. The bullet missed by inches, and before I could get off another shot, the beast barreled into me. I hit the ground, the breath crushed from my lungs. The panther snarled, sinking his teeth into my shoulder. A scream of pain tore from my throat as he ripped through skin and muscle. My head swam with dizziness, but I gripped the gun, pushing it into the panther's side. Before I could shoot, another panther sailed through the air, slamming into my attacker. My shoulder popped as it was wrenched, and then he tore free. I screamed again as blood splattered the ground around me. Rolling over, I gripped my shoulder, holding back my screams. Blood oozed between my fingers. A second later, a bloody panther head landed beside me.

Two

A minute later, I'd wrapped my shirt around my shoulder as well as I could and sat up to take in the damage. Human and feline bodies littered the ground all around us. My heart leapt into my throat. Were all the ocelots dead? A mewling cry came from under the SUV. I dropped to the ground and squirmed under on my belly. A bleeding ocelot huddled against the inside of the back tire.

"Camila," I said. "Thank the gods you're okay."

She hissed, baring her teeth. They looked small and fragile compared to the saber-like canines of the big cats. Having never seen an ocelot in real life, I hadn't realized how small they were next to the big cats. Fury charged my veins—fury at Father for keeping us in our little utopian country where no one shifted out of necessity, where they only shifted at exclusive parties as a symbol of wealth and status. Fury at him for sending Camila on this crazy mission, and at her for insisting she was a match for the other cats. Fury at the panthers for attacking the ocelots in what was so clearly an unfair fight.

"Hey, it's me," I said, keeping my voice soft and soothing, the way Camila liked. I snaked toward her on my belly. "How badly are you hurt? Can you shift?"

She hissed again, batting at my hand as I reached for her. I drew back, sucking in a breath, and stared at her. She might have been a medium cat, but she was an animal. An animal who, if rumors to were to be believed, ate humans on occasion. I was certainly no match for her, and as I looked into her round, ocelot eyes, all I saw was a wild, trapped animal. For the first time in my life, I was actually afraid of my sister.

She knew me down to the very innermost desires of my soul, but all my life, I'd only known half of her. I was surprised by the depth of pain that realization caused.

"Camila," I said again, drawing back. Blood soaked through my t-shirt bandage, and my heart suddenly fluttered in panic inside me. Would she smell the blood and attack?

I hated myself for the thought that she would ever hurt me, but I couldn't help the fear rolling through me. As a human, she loved me. As a cat, I didn't know what she felt, didn't know what she'd do. I wasn't even sure she could understand my human words when she was in cat form. I was trapped under a car with a cornered, terrified predator.

I began to back toward the edge of the vehicle, shaking with adrenaline. I didn't know this side of my sister. I didn't know if I could trust her.

She hissed, backing against the tire again as I retreated.

Frustration twisted through me. I couldn't help her. I'd failed her.

"Itzel," Lord Balam's barked. He hauled me back the last foot and yanked me to my feet, his gaze sweeping over me. "What the fuck are you thinking?"

"Camila's under there," I said. "I don't know how to get her out."

"Are you crazy?" he demanded. He was back in human form, his swarthy, brown body scratched and bleeding from a dozen places. His jaguar cloak hung on his shoulders, shredded on one edge.

"But she's—." I broke off, the words choked in my throat.

"Ah, fuck, don't cry," Lord Balam said, pulling me into his arms. His muscles bulged and bunched under my hands as I clung to his powerful body. He wasn't a tall man, but he was built like a tank, and it was all muscle. Somehow, somewhere along the way, he'd become my comfort and safety.

"I'm not crying," I said. "But I can't get her out."

"Gabor," Lord Balam ordered. "Get the princess."

A panther loped around the back of the SUV, and I almost screamed.

"It's Shadow," Lord Balam said. "Want me to finish him off, too?"

"No," I said, pulling away from him. "What the fuck, Shadow. You're lucky I didn't put a bullet in you."

He shifted into human form, and my eyes skimmed over his tall, lean figure, landing on his stoic, angular face. His long hair was wild and tangled as it hung around his shoulders, blood and dust mussing his usually silky locks. "We should go," he said, his voice low and raspy. "Now. The panther clan is much bigger than this little group. They got here first, but the rest of the clan will be close behind them."

He picked up a canvas jacket from the ground, ripped the sleeve off, and dropped the rest of it as he strode toward me.

"We can't leave without Camila," I said, dropping back to the ground. Lord Balam hauled me up, keeping a firm grip on my upper arm. He held my elbow while Shadow tied the canvas sleeve tightly over my bandage.

"Let Gabor deal with Camila," Lord Balam said, turning me to face him. "You can't approach a frightened shifter in animal form. A human has no natural weapons to defend herself."

I wanted to protest, to tell him I didn't need to defend myself against my sister. But the truth was, I didn't know anymore.

The ocelot who had sustained the injury when I'd arrived, the one I'd saved from the panther's jaws, crawled under the SUV from the other side. When I realized that was Gabor, something settled inside me in the most disturbing way. I really didn't want to think about it, so I turned and examined Lord Balam instead. His broad, thickly muscled shoulders both bore deep, jagged wounds, but already they seemed to be closing. Blood trickled over his bulging pectorals and down the ridges of muscle in his abdomen. Instead of being horrified, some primal part of me found the sight of him—bloody but victorious—more irresistible than I ever had before.

He grinned when he finally caught my eye. "I'll fuck you in the bathroom on the plane."

"What?" I asked, pretending to be busy checking the gun.

"It's a normal reaction to battle," he said. "All those endorphins from surviving combined with the adrenaline from the fight and relief at knowing your mate is safe. Don't be ashamed."

"I'm not ashamed," I said. "And you're not my mate."

"Aren't I?" he asked with a smug smile.

Before he could answer, Shadow spun around, scenting the air like an animal. A growl rumbled through him, his shoulders shifting into a forward position, his knees slightly bent as if crouching to spring. Three-inch claws extended from his fingers, and his green eyes rounded as he stared at the trees outside the fence. The animal way he moved still made me uneasy. Even in human form, I couldn't be sure how much of his animal nature ruled him. Unlike ocelots, or even Balam, Shadow seemed always in some state of transition between animal and human.

"They're here," he said.

"Where?" I asked, looking around, my heart fluttering at the thought.

"The swamp is full of them," he said. "They're all around us."

"Fuck," I cursed as I spotted black forms slinking from the trees, materializing out of the swamp like shadows. Fear punched through my chest, and I swayed on my feet.

"Gabor, let's go," I yelled, leaning down to see him lying on his belly, still in ocelot form, his nose to Camila's. "There's no time to talk sense into her. We need to get out—now."

He looked up, his eyes so intense and so like his human gaze that it startled me. I drew back a little, and after a second, he turned back to Camila and lunged at her throat. I stifled a scream as he grabbed her by the throat. She snarled and scratched, raking her claws through his fur, slicing open more crimson gashes. I winced, turning away as he backed from under the car, dragging the future queen of the Ocelot Nation by the throat. She dug her claws into the pavement and into Gabor, scratching and hissing all the way, until she was free.

The first wave of panthers was climbing the chain link fence, sliding smoothly up it in a way that sent chills racing along my spine.

"Where's the amulet?" I demanded.

"Grab her bag and let's get the fuck out," Lord Balam said. "I'm not anxious to die today."

"Not before Camila," I said, but Lord Balam grabbed my arm and pulled me toward the waiting plane. Shadow fell in on my other side, marching me like a condemned man entering Father's stadium of death.

"Fuck your sister," he said. "You're getting on the plane."

I dug my heels in, but they dragged me forward. "Looks like some things run in the family," Lord Balam muttered, glancing back over his shoulder.

I was turned halfway around already, watching Gabor drag Camila from under the SUV. The first panther leapt from the fence, racing across the grass toward Camila.

"No!" I screamed.

Shadow dropped to all fours and shifted smoothly into his fur. "Don't hurt her," I yelled, grabbing the skin on the back of his neck and digging my fingers in. He yanked away and dashed back to join Gabor. Shadow grabbed my sister by the back of her neck like a kitten and charged toward us.

"Up the ladder," Lord Balam barked, boosting me halfway up with one push. I lurched to the top and tumbled in, Balam rolling over me. He hauled me up and pushed me into a seat, yelling for the pilot to go. The plane started moving, agonizingly slow and impossibly fast at once.

"Camila," I screamed, diving for the door. Lord Balam shoved me roughly back into my seat, but I was up in an instant, almost on his back as he blocked me and hung out the door. A second later, an ocelot appeared, her four legs splayed out as she gripped the doorframe, refusing to be shoved inside as I had.

Shadow was behind her in panther form, and behind him, another ocelot wobbled down the runway, trying to keep pace as the plane picked up momentum. A swarm of black panthers closed in on him.

"Gabor," I cried, my heart seizing in my chest. He looked up, and for one second, our eyes met, just as Tadeu's eyes had met mine in the moment before his death. A sob choked my throat, and I covered my mouth to hold it in.

Lord Balam wrenched my sister in, hurling her back into the seats.

Shadow hesitated, looking ready to pounce. Instead, he dropped from the ladder to the ground.

"No," I screamed, reaching past Lord Balam, finding nothing but thin air.

Shadow grabbed Gabor, and together, they raced for the ladder, just a pace behind, then two, as the plane picked up speed. "They won't make it," I cried, tears bursting from my eyes.

"You owe me for this," Lord Balam said, and then he was a long, powerful jaguar flying out the door. He hit the ground, his huge form dwarfing Gabor as he closed his jaws around him. He raced the plane and grabbed the ladder, his back paws scrabbling along the runway for a second before he heaved himself up. Moments later, he was bounding up the ladder, heaving Gabor inside. Lord Balam landed on top of him, toppling into the cabin with the two ocelots.

"Shadow," I called, holding out an arm. The panthers pursuing us had closed in, falling in with him as he fell another step behind the plane. My eyes locked with his, and something twisted between us, a knowledge as certain as a goodbye.

No.

I refused to lose him.

"Shadow, you can make it. I know you can." My eyes burned into his, and a power swelled inside me, a feeling I'd only felt before when he'd chained me up and fucked me over and over all night. At some moment in that long night, I'd looked at him and realized he couldn't help it. He would do literally anything in the world to have me, that he would die to fuck me just one more time. He'd made me helpless that night, but he was helpless to resist what I did to him just by living and breathing and being a woman.

As the power coursed through me, Shadow paused, his body bunching, and he fell another step behind. But then he was soaring through the air, his powerful leap propelling him all the way to the ladder. He clung on, only to be joined by another panther a second later.

"Pull up the ladder," I yelled, and the ladder began to rise as Lord Balam obeyed my command. Shadow scrambled up a few steps, but the other panther sank his teeth into his hind leg. Shadow screamed in pain, a horrible snarling sound that filled the cabin and sent a stark flash of terror through me. What if the other panther got on the plane with us? I grabbed the pistol and tried to get a good shot, but Shadow was before the panther, and I couldn't risk hitting him. They twisted on the ladder, the panther below Shadow losing his footing and hanging from Shadow's legs. Shadow clung to the ladder, unable to let go and defend himself as the other panther ripped a chunk of flesh from his hip.

Lord Balam reached down, his hands closing around Shadow's front legs. He dragged him inside, giving me the perfect shot as the other panther's head appeared through the door with Shadow's back half. The bullet buried itself in his temple, and the panther jolted backward, disappearing instantly. Shadow scrambled the rest of the way in, and Balam reached out, slamming the door shut as the plane lifted off the ground.

THREE

"Why aren't they shifting?" I asked, regarding the ocelots with suspicion. Since we'd taken off an hour earlier, Camila had huddled in the back of the plane, baring her teeth and hissing if anyone even looked at her. Gabor had crawled behind a leather couch and lay motionless. I wanted to check and make sure he was alive, but when I stepped in that direction, Camila snarled so fiercely I shrank back next to Lord Balam. The pilot had notified us that we were at full altitude, and that everything had gone smoothly since our rough start. Now we were flying above an endless expanse of blue with another one overhead.

No way to escape if Camila lost her shit completely.

"They heal faster in feline form," Lord Balam said.

I wondered if that included healing from mental trauma. Camila had escaped the brawl without so much as a scratch. Shadow sat silent as his name, clutching the armrests of the plush leather recliner that faced the back of the plane. Since shifting into human form half an hour earlier, he'd alternated between staring out the window and watching my sister with distrust. His wounds seemed to have healed, as had Lord Balam's. The jaguar was bigger and stronger than the other cats on the plane and was apparently an excellent warrior. He'd barely spent ten minutes in his feline form before shifting back to human, fully healed.

Lord Balam had patched up my shoulder to stop the bleeding, but the pain seemed to be getting worse, not better. I moved over to the chair next to Shadow, cradling my arm at my side.

"I don't suppose you have any magical healing potions," I said, offering him a smile. I barely knew the guy, and what I'd known of him had been pretty scary, but he was in this with us now.

He shook his head.

"No, I guess you wouldn't," I said with a sigh, closing my eyes and leaning my head back against the seat. "Considering you weren't planning on flying to Africa today."

He shook his head again.

"Sorry about that," I said. "I guess it was that or die. Not much of a choice."

He shrugged and turned back to the window. Okay, then. Apparently he wasn't feeling chatty. I wracked my brain for something to say to him. I'd spent one night chained to his bed after drugging him. We'd talked a bit the morning he'd taken me back, but I didn't know much about him. He'd been celibate before our night together, but I didn't know why or for how long. He lived alone in the swamp and seemed to have trouble staying fully human, but I didn't know why he was that way, either. Maybe he preferred a life of solitude.

"I'm sorry all this happened," I said, resting a hand on his forearm. "I know you were trying to do the right thing by warning me the panthers were coming after the amulet. You didn't have to do that, and you didn't sign up for this. When we get there, we can fly you back home."

"I can't go home," he said, his voice low and raspy. The sound of it still did strange things to me, even though I didn't blame him for what he'd done to me while drugged. If I hadn't forgiven him before, I would have now. If it weren't for him, we wouldn't have known the panthers were going after the amulet until it was too late.

"I'm sorry," I said yet again, the word sounding worn out now. "I don't know how to thank you for what you did. You gave up everything for us. You fought your own clan, and now... Well, let's just say I understand how clan loyalty works. Our clans may not have anything else in common, but they have that."

A soft, incredulous exhalation was his only answer. I didn't know how to relate to someone who wouldn't talk. I didn't know if he blamed me for this—I had given the amulet to Camila, after all—or if he was always so surly.

"So, what do you want to do?" I demanded, frustration building inside me.

He shrugged.

"And you can't go home because your clan thinks you're a traitor."

"I am a traitor," he said, swinging his head around to face me. "I killed someone back there."

"Me, too," I said softly, sliding my hand down his arm to his hand. I covered the back of his hand with my palm, letting my fingertips rest between his knuckles. "I know it's not the same for me. I didn't know the person, and I'm not a panther. Thank you for helping us protect Camila. If it weren't for your warning, she'd be dead right now."

"I wasn't protecting her," he said, casting a withering look at the pathetic ocelot hunched in the back of the plane. Her wild eyes moved to us, and she hissed, the sound filling the plane and making a shiver coil around my spine like a snake.

When I turned back to Shadow, the intensity shimmering in his eyes fanned the flames of my fear even higher. I wasn't sure which one terrified me more—knowing that he'd done all that, become a traitor to his nation, to protect me, or the fact that he was, essentially, my responsibility now. I already had one unpredictable, unstable person under my watch. Camila was challenging enough, and she was usually meek and non-violent.

Shadow? I had no idea. I slid my hand from his, wondering what I'd gotten myself into. Had I read this all wrong? Did it actually speak to his mental state that he'd taken our side against his clan? I didn't think he was weirdly obsessed with me or anything, but he'd killed one of his own people for me, a girl who had drugged him to get what she wanted. Maybe I shouldn't be thanking him quite yet. We were about to visit the Cheetah Clan, a newly prosperous member of the Feline Nations. How would Shadow handle being thrust into a court full of wealth and privilege? And how would they react when I brought a half-feral panther into their territory?

Gabor and my sister were naturals at putting on their cultured airs, and even I could play the royal part if needed. Lord Balam had a prestigious position in his own court, and because of his diplomatic role with other nations, already knew most of the royal families around the world. Until now, Shadow had lived in abject poverty and would quite possibly kill anyone who messed with me.

Holy fuck. My life had just become a whole new level of crazy.

Four

I woke suddenly to the sound of snarling and screaming. For a second, I was unable to comprehend where I was or what was happening. The noise around us was horrendous, a constant drone below the commotion, and a dagger of pain pulsed in my shoulder with every heartbeat.

I blinked in bewilderment, and then it came crashing back. The noise was the plane, and apparently Camila, who was dashing up and down the center of the plane, screeching like a banshee. Lord Balam, whom I'd fallen asleep beside, was shielding me with his body while Shadow crouched on the leather couch in panther form.

"Don't hurt her," I cried, seeing him about to spring.

She scrambled onto a recliner, her claws shredding the leather, and leapt to the front of the plane. The tiny metal door to the cockpit flew open, and Camila disappeared inside. A shout of alarm came from within.

"Fuck," Lord Balam yelled, dashing for the cockpit. If Camila attacked the pilot...

Shadow leapt, knocking Lord Balam aside and racing into the cockpit before the shaman reached it. Shadow had been just waiting for a chance to take my sister down, and when he dragged her out of the cockpit by the back of her neck, I almost lost it.

"If you hurt her, I swear to all the gods in creation I will make you suffer," I said through clenched teeth. "Let her go."

He pressed her to the floor, and Gabor slid past me in human form, wearing the tightest pair of capri pajama pants I'd ever seen and a pink T-shirt that barely stretched across his broad chest and ended just above his belly button. Obviously he'd had to dip into Camila's bag, the only one we'd saved from the SUV before the panthers arrived.

Camila's eyes squeezed shut, her lips pulling back to reveal her teeth as a horrible growling scream tore pitifully from her throat. Tears stung my eyes even as I held back, not wanting to get in the way. Gabor knelt at her side, his face set in its iron mask as he uncapped a syringe with his teeth, gripping her leg with one hand and stabbing the needle into her with the other. She lunged forward, her teeth sinking into his hand. He finished injecting her, biting his lips together against the pain of her bite. When he finished, he dropped the syringe, but she refused to unlock her jaws.

Gabor stroked her head with his free hand, murmuring to her so softly it made the tears spill from my eyes as I stood watching what felt like an intimate, private moment. It was hard to believe this man was one of Father's brutish henchmen or the guard who had held me up and told me to watch my best friend's death in silence.

Even the hardest man could be softened by love.

I wrapped my arms around myself, my eyes flitting to the cockpit. Lord Balam still hadn't emerged. Finally, my sister slumped to the plane floor, and Gabor drew open her jaws and extricated his mangled, bloody hand. Shadow picked her up by the scruff of her neck and deposited her unceremoniously on the couch. I quickly swiped my cheeks dry so they wouldn't notice my emotional reaction to the horrible scene.

"Don't treat my sister like a commoner," I said. "She's a princess."

Shadow shifted smoothly, straightening and turning human in one motion. "She's a danger to us all," he snapped.

I leveled him with my best stink eye. "Yeah, well, she's going to be queen, so it's our job to keep her out of danger."

"She's no more fit to be queen than I am," he said, turning away in disgust.

I opened my mouth to protest, then looked at Gabor. He must have taken my look as needing help, because he fixed Shadow with a blood-chilling glare. "She's my queen," he said. "I will ask once that you not speak ill of her."

Tension crackled in the air between them, and suddenly, I was scared for Shadow. Moments ago, I'd had trouble believing Gabor was a man who would assassinate a threat to the king with no remorse. Now, I didn't believe he could be anything else.

Lord Balam stepped from the cockpit and gave a grim shake of his head. My stomach lurched sickeningly.

"Are you fucking kidding me?" I blurted in disbelief. "So, we all die anyway?"

"I can land it," Gabor said, breaking his stare-down with Shadow and pushing past Lord Balam into the cockpit.

I nearly collapsed in relief, but Balam moved to my side, sliding a thick arm around my waist. Scraping noises came from the cockpit, and a body thudded to the floor. I shuddered, pressing myself against Lord Balam's strong, solid form.

Suddenly I wanted to kiss Father for his paranoia. Because he had made so many enemies, he required Ocelot palace guards to train in more than the art of cold-blooded murder. Of course Gabor knew how to make quick getaways in case anyone invaded our tiny, defenseless nation. For all I knew, he could perform spells of illusion to disguise Father should he ever need to escape right under the enemy's nose.

"How about that entrance exam for the mile-high club?" Lord Balam purred in my ear, his hand caressing the bare skin of my waist.

"What's the entrance exam?" I asked.

"First I examine your entrance, and then I fuck it."

He was still naked except for his jaguar-skin cloak, and I was still in my bra after using my shirt for a bandage. My skin sang against his familiar warmth, my body craving his touch and what it did to me even as my mind was scandalized by his filthy words. He always gave me exactly what I needed—pleasure that obliterated all pain.

When he took my hand, I let him pull me into the claustrophobic bathroom. I didn't know if he loved me, but he was the closest thing I had since Tadeu's death. Already, that seemed to be fading into a constant but distant ache. I would never forget Tadeu, my first love. But it had been an innocent, childhood love. So much had happened since then. So much had changed, and I was not immune to it. I'd never even seen a shifter in its fur when I knew him. I barely knew about the amulets, and I'd never been with a man. I would always cherish the purity of my love for him. It would remain forever simple and true.

Any relationship after him would be much more complicated. Still, I clung to the simplicity of what I had with Balam even as I felt it changing every day. He meant more to me than I wanted him to. In the bathroom, I spun and pressed him against the door, wrapping my hand around his cock with no pretense. It swelled, hardening deliciously for my touch.

"Damn, you are ready," he said, burying a hand in my hair and pulling me close, rubbing his nose across mine and inhaling my scent. His other hand grabbed my ass, massaging my soft flesh as his cock throbbed into my palm.

"Just be careful of my shoulder," I gasped as he drew my head back, his full lips caressing my skin.

"I will," he growled, hitching my leg up. I wrapped it around him, rocking against him as my hungry mouth found his. I slid my tongue between his teeth, tasting his tongue as it plunged into my mouth, thrusting into me in a rhythm that made my thighs slick with anticipation. Gripping his massive girth, I squeezed his cock until he groaned into my mouth, thrusting his hips against mine.

He undid the button of my jean shorts, forcing his hand down them until his fingers sank between my slick lips. I grabbed the waistband and shimmied out of them, dropping them around my feet. Balam grabbed me and hoisted me onto the edge of the sink, opening my knees and dipping two fingers into me, twisting them together and swirling them against my walls. Ripples of pleasure ran through me, and my juices dripped down his hand as he continued thrusting his fingers into me in rhythm with his tongue claiming mine.

When he pulled away to dip his face to my neck, I gripped the edges of the sink, leaning back and spreading my thighs as wide as I could. Balam chuckled, drawing back and smearing his thumb through my folds, parting my pussy lips and pulling them so wide a twinge of pain tugged at my flesh.

"God, your cunt is a masterpiece," he said, circling my opening with his fingertip until I was panting for more. He wrapped a thick arm around my waist, lifted me, and slammed me down on his cock. I cried out in surprise as his entire massive length rocketed into me at once. He lifted me again, then slammed me down, stuffing me with so much of him that I cried out again, calling his name each time he buried his cock to the hilt in my tight flesh.

I didn't know if I was begging for more or begging for him to stop. All I knew was I was gasping his name, gasping for breath, gasping for relief. He pressed my back against the door, driving into me so powerfully that my back slammed the metal with each thrust. My pussy clenched around his rigid cock, aching from the roughness of his entry but slick with wanting more. Lord Balam growled, slamming harder into me. With a metallic screech, the lock gave, and the door flew open. We went with it, stumbling back against the door as it banged against the wall. Instead of stopping, Lord Balam gripped the top of the door while he continued driving into me over and over.

After a second, my head cleared to what was happening and where we were. My sister, in ocelot form, lay sleeping across the shredded leather sectional that ran along one side of the plane. Shadow, in human form, sat in one of the seats facing the back of the plane, his cock rigid, his eyes drinking us in like an intoxicated man. When my eyes met his molten gaze over Balam's shoulder, an inferno of heat erupted inside me. My core clenched, my walls clamping down on Lord Balam so hard he growled ferociously and drove into me so hard my feet left the ground.

Crushing me to the door, his cock swelled as cum coursed through that bulging vein, spurting into me. He came with a guttural cry, grinding his pelvic bone against my clit. A chocked scream twisted in my throat, and pleasure whipped at me, gripping my body in a helpless spasm. My toes curled, and my nails cut into Lord Balam's shoulders as I came. The orgasm rocked through me so hard I lost sight of Shadow behind a wall of black spots swimming over my vision.

When my vision cleared, Shadow was standing right behind Balam.

His green eyes tethered to mine, and he growled, "My turn."

FIVE

Sir Kenosi
Entrepreneur, Cheetah Nation

I HEADED DOWN THE ROAD THROUGH THE CHEETAH village, tossing things from my bag to the kids running out to see me.

"It's Sir Kenosi," they crowed happily to each other, running out to see me. Once, this had been the projects, but I'd spent a lot to fix up the place, and now it made a decent home for the remaining cheetahs in the world.

I slapped palms with some of the kids, tossed a ball to one, and kept walking. I had an audience with the king today. The thought cracked me up. The king was the last person who would want his presence to be called an audience.

I stopped at his door and knocked, though I knew he didn't stand on such ceremony. When he didn't answer, I strolled in. His house was hung with colorful tapestries, the kind you could get at local markets. I pushed aside the strands of beads hanging in a doorway and made my way out to the greenhouse, where the last cheetah king sat cross-legged on a mat in meditation pose.

He cracked one eyelid and then a big smile. "Ah, my favorite billionaire," he said in a voice that was both rich and rusty with age.

"You hate billionaires," I pointed out.

"I don't hate anything," he crowed. "I simply choose not to focus on worldly possessions."

The king had chosen not to marry or have kids, which made him the last cheetah with royal blood. He'd shunned all that in favor of becoming enlightened. He had no money and very few possessions, and if anyone wanted anything he had, they just took it. Having spent my childhood eating out of garbage cans, I figured I'd paid my dues. I'd earned every penny I had, and I wasn't ashamed of it.

As a kid, it had looked to me like the king had turned a blind eye to all our suffering. But over the years, I'd come to respect him despite our opposing views, and I knew that he actually wanted to help people as much as I did. He just believed in doing it with prayer instead of cash.

"I got a call for you," I said.

King Cheetah opened one eye again, peering at me from under a bushy white eyebrow. Tufts of white, fuzzy hair topped each ear, but his brown head was as bald and wrinkly as a raisin.

"Who ever would be calling me?" he asked, as if it were inconceivable that someone would want to speak to the king of our nation. Whether he wanted the role or not, he had it.

"King Ocelot," I said. "Apparently, his daughter is now old enough to take the throne."

"What wonderful news," King Cheetah crowed.

"She needs the amulet," I said.

"Oh, I'm sure it's around here somewhere," the king said, glancing around him at the greenery, as if it might be sitting in the dirt next to one of his plants. That wasn't actually unlikely.

"We're supposed to make a bargain with their nation for it," I reminded him.

"Eh, I don't want anything they have," he said, waving a hand. "Let her have it."

I ground my teeth, thinking of how much we had needed something like that when I was a kid. How much it could have helped if we'd had a king who had the wits and cunning to bargain for his people's treasures instead of handing them off as if the ancient traditions meant nothing.

If it hadn't taken any effort, he probably would have pulled out of the International Council of Feline Nations altogether. He'd have preferred to stay off the radar, like the Lynx Nation, who had chosen not to join the ICFN when it formed. But I knew how much we needed it. If not for the aid the ICFN had given us, we'd be extinct by now.

I didn't know a lot about the Ocelot Nation, but they had joined the ICFN despite not being big cats. I knew they were looked down upon by other nations. What little I knew beyond that, I could barely comprehend. Hearing about their ways was like hearing a history lesson in reverse. When shifters came out to humans, cheetahs had been persecuted and worse. Humans had committed genocide against our people, nearly obliterating our entire species.

The Ocelot Clan had done the opposite. They had taken the country from humans, made them lowly peasants in their nation compared to the esteemed shifters. Ocelots were considered the superior race. They'd never been spit on and mocked, used and coerced and threatened, their very existence a cause for hatred. The spoiled princess coming our way knew nothing but privilege and luxury.

"Tradition dictates that we make some kind of trade for the mating amulet," I told the king. "Or challenge them in some way."

"They're welcome to come and trade for it," he said. "Anything they like."

"Maybe I could come up with something," I offered.

"Of course," he said. "That would be fine. I think it's in a drawer in the kitchen. I know I saw it recently. Take it with you."

"Thank you," I said, not knowing what else to say. It saddened me that the king could be so careless. I tried to understand him, to see the world through his eyes when I came here, but it wasn't easy. There was more to life than what went on inside one's own mind.

I said my goodbyes and found the amulet in the kitchen, holding the lid closed on a box of tea. I slid it into my pocket and left the king, who told me to have the ocelot royals come for tea anytime. I knew that was all he'd be able to offer them. It was up to me to come up with a suitable challenge for the ocelot heir.

I took out my phone as I walked, scrolling through to find some information on the Ocelot Kingdom. Unlike some other feline nations, they were isolationists and shied away from the media. I couldn't imagine a life of quiet luxury any more than I could imagine their politics.

From the pictures, it looked as if their small kingdom belonged in the middle ages. They didn't allow vehicles inside the walls of the huge palace grounds. The surrounding city was tiny, with almost all the shifters living in the area. They had technology, but kept it largely hidden, keeping up appearances that they lived in much simpler times.

By contrast, we lived in an enormous, modern city. I was a celebrity, known around the world for my killer smile, my godlike riches, and my abundance of women. I owned an entire city block, including a skyscraper in which a lot of the cheetah shifters lived.

At last, I found some pictures of the princess. She looked as pale and appealing as a dead fish. In the most recent photo I could find, she was wearing a pantsuit and standing between two guards who had similarly lifeless eyes. I couldn't think of a less fun job than challenging this woman.

I was about to close the screen when I scrolled to the next picture and did a double take. The woman beside her, now she looked alive. All curves and wild hair, with eyes that begged for a challenge. I read the caption of the photo twice, trying to comprehend how this vixen could be related to the bland heir. But there it was. Her sister.

Well, fuck me. That was a woman who looked like she was ready to challenge *me*. Maybe this wouldn't be such a tiresome obligation after all. I had everything money could buy, enough women to warm my bed every night for the rest of my life, and fame that made me a star to the entire world. I was ready for a challenge.

SIX

Itzel
Princess, Ocelot Nation

AT SHADOW'S CLAIM, LORD BALAM PULLED AWAY from me and spun to face Shadow. Quick as a snake, Shadow's hand shot out and grabbed my arm. He yanked me in front of him, his razor clawed hand wrapping around my throat as he secured my back against his chest. I stared at Lord Balam, my breath still coming quickly and my heart racing. I could feel the heat and hardness of Shadow's cock against my ass, and a tremor of desire fluttered through me, turning my thighs liquid with fear and anticipation.

Before I could speak, Shadow turned and bent me over the back of one of the fancy leather seats and knocked my thighs apart. His deadly claws rested just under my chin, threatening to puncture my throat if I moved. His hot cock throbbed against my opening, and I gasped, my legs going weak at the memory of him ripping into my unyielding flesh the first time. This time, I was so slick with Balam's cum and my own juices that Shadow slid in easily, a helpless groan escaping his throat as he sank his cock to the hilt inside me.

"I'm sorry," he rasped, pumping into me with quick, sharp movements. "I can't help myself. Your pussy smells so fucking good, it's this or eat you alive."

I expected Lord Balam to yank him off and rip his throat out, but his sharp claws against my throat made sure that wouldn't happen. I searched the cabin for my lover and found him standing a few paces off, watching with a strange expression on his face. As I realized what that look was, a gaze of pure, shockingly raw lust, an erotic charge shot through me. I arched my back, my lips parting in a gasp of pleasure as my slickness coated Shadow's cock. He growled, thrusting harder, his cock slamming into me faster and faster.

His claws pressed into my throat so hard I was afraid they'd break the skin, and I tensed, drawing a strangled cry from Shadow as he pounded my hips into the back of the couch even harder. My thighs trembled at the power inside him, the power he was hammering into me with inhuman force. Because he wasn't human. He really might eat me alive if I stopped him. Any person on this plane could snap and rip out my throat at any moment, not just Shadow.

Balam might protect me, but he wasn't going to stop Shadow. He loved watching him fuck me, his hips slapping my ass with each quick thrust, his own cum dripping down my legs, wetting me for Shadow's pleasure. And I loved it, too. Not just the feel of Shadow's cock punching into me, but the sight of Balam watching, the fact that he loved watching, that it turned him on. His arousal fueled my own, which fueled Shadow's, all of it building inside me until I couldn't hold back. My walls clamped down around Shadow's cock, and he roared as he buried himself to the hilt inside me, cum shooting into me with painful force. Orgasm gripped my body, and I went rigid, my toes curling, my eyes falling shut, a cry tearing from my lips as wave after wave of pleasure rocketed into me.

A cry of yes.

Yes.

Yes, I wanted this. I wanted every last inch of him straining inside me, his hot cum spurting into me, his cock throbbing as he came with me. Yes, I wanted him to want me so much he couldn't help himself. I wanted him helpless with lust at seeing Lord Balam fuck me. And yes, I wanted my lover there watching, wanting me even more as another man fucked me—loving that another man fucked me. Loving that I wanted it so much I couldn't help myself from crying out his name as my pussy squeezed every last drop from his cock.

At last, Balam stepped toward us. "That was hot," he said. "Think you're ready for one more time?"

I glared. "There's still a man inside me. Think you could give it a rest for five minutes?"

"Five minutes?" he asked with a smirk. "I think I could manage that."

I pushed up from the back of the couch, twisting away from Shadow. "I don't know which of you is worse," I said. "You can't just take turns fucking me all the way to Africa just because it gets you hot and bothered watching someone else fuck me."

"We can't?" Balam asked. "You sure looked like you were enjoying it to me."

"I was," I growled. "But that doesn't mean you can just treat me like your blowup doll. I'm a human being, too. I have things going on above the waist."

Balam ogled my chest and ran his tongue across his upper lip. "Yes, you do."

"I'm not fucking either of you again on this flight," I said. "So you can put your dicks away unless you want to use them on each other."

Shadow eyed Lord Balam, whose massive cock was again standing at attention. Balam just grinned and flopped down on the couch, not bothering to cover it. "Too bad we don't have any clothes."

"If Gabor can squeeze into something of Camila's, you can, too," I said.

Fuck. Reality smacked into me, and I turned to retrieve my shorts. My sister was passed out on the couch, subdued by whatever tranquiller Gabor had used. Gabor was up there flying the plane. I could only hope all the engine noise had kept him from hearing our sex sounds.

I pulled on my shorts, fixed my bra, and went to Camilla's bag. Even though I'd helped her dress during most of our trip, I felt like a snoop as I rooted through her bag. I pulled out a shirt and tugged it on, aware that it strained over my curves much tighter than it did on Camila's thin frame. I was thinking about changing when my eyes fell on a little zippered pouch. She'd left it unzipped, and little tubes of neon yellow liquid spilled out. I paused, then picked up one of them.

It wasn't Camilla who had left the bag unzipped. It was Gabor, in his haste. I read the label on the little tube, but I couldn't make sense of the medical terms on it. What had Gabor injected into my sister? And why did she have this, whatever it was? I rolled it between my finger and thumb, my heart nearly stopping when I saw a tiny skull-and-crossbones symbol on the other side of it. Even an idiot like me knew what that meant.

I snatched up the bag and marched toward the cockpit. Fuck Gabor. If he'd heard what went on between me and my lovers —now plural—I'd deal with that later. Right now, he owed me answers. Answers like, where did his allegiance really lie? With Father or Camilla? I didn't honestly think Father would kill his own daughter to keep the throne. But he might hire someone else to do it—someone unquestionably loyal, close to the throne, and obedient. Someone exactly like Gabor.

SEVEN

GABOR DIDN'T LOOK UP AS I STEPPED OVER THE naked pilot and dropped into the empty copilot seat. Camila's pink pajamas lay neatly folded at my feet, and Gabor had dressed in the dead pilot's uniform. It was not helping make him less attractive. Not at all.

Focus, Princess.

I took a deep breath and considered what I was about to do. Gabor could kill me if he wanted. I was alone in here with him. Then again, he could kill us all. He was flying the fucking plane.

"How's your hand?" I asked, remembering Camila's teeth clamping down and how patient he'd been.

"Fine," he said, flexing his hand. "My ocelot healed it quickly." His fingers were long and strong, a golden tan like the rest of him. God, how could even his hands be sexy? What was wrong with me?

"Must be nice," I said. "To have self-healing properties like that."

"How's your shoulder?"

"It hurts like hell," I admitted.

The muscle in his jaw jumped as he clenched it. "If you'd like... I could clean it for you and put in a few stitches."

The thought made me squeamish with pain, and I remembered why I was there. Not so a guard could put prison stitches in me. Especially a guard with questionable motives.

"Care to explain this?" I asked, shaking out the contents of Camila's bag onto my lap. Lipstick, prescription bottles, and the tiny ultraviolet yellow glass capsules tumbled into my lap.

"No, Your Grace."

My mouth dropped open and a huff escaped me. "Well, too bad," I said, tossing my hair back. "I think I deserve an explanation."

"Yes, Your Grace."

"Would you please stop calling me that?"

"No, Your Grace."

"Are you trying to irritate the fuck out of me right now, or does it just come naturally?"

"No, Your Grace."

I sighed. "No, you're not trying to be annoying? Or no, it doesn't come naturally? You know what, don't answer that."

Gabor swallowed, studying the control panel in front of him as if it held the meaning of life. "I apologize."

"Look, you do know other words besides yes and no."

"I do."

"Great," I said, holding up one of the little capsules. "Then maybe you could answer my original question because I don't think it's too much to ask for you to tell me why you have a syringe full of whatever the fuck this is."

He finally turned to me, then averted his eyes and swallowed. "I—don't, Your Grace."

"You took it out of Camila's bag, and you certainly seemed to know what to do with it."

"I do," he said quietly. "But it's not mine. It belongs to Her Grace, the heir."

"I could have figured that out. What I still don't understand is why you shot my sister with something toxic."

Finally, he could meet my gaze directly. "It's a tranquillizer."

"Then why does it have this little symbol on it?" I asked, dangling it in front of my face. "I'm not stupid, Gabor."

"It is toxic," he said, his eyes softening for just a moment. "It can be fatal in large doses."

I swallowed, my heart thudding at the thought of Camilla lying out there, so still.

"You didn't—" I choked the words off, taking a slow breath. "She'll wake up?"

Gabor turned to face forward again, the muscle in his jaw the only movement of his stony face. "Yes, Your Grace."

I closed my eyes and let myself exhale. "Right. Sorry. Of course you wouldn't kill the queen." A bubble of nervous laughter escaped me. "What would we do then?"

I knew exactly what we would do then. We'd keep on living under Father's rule. I just didn't know if that's what Gabor wanted. I had thought that maybe he loved her, but I could have read it all wrong. After all, Father had employed him. He'd given Gabor a prestigious position at court, the closest thing to his inner circle without being a politician. He'd taught him to fight, to kill, to fly planes and inject people with tranquilizers, stitch them up, and who-knew-what else.

Camila had given him a pile of laundry.

There was only one way to find out. He was the last guard from the Ocelot Court, the last person left besides me and Camila. I needed to know if I could trust him, and where he really stood. I'd urged her to consider him, and yet, I found my throat tightening as I forced the question out.

"Do you love her?"

Gabor's eyes flicked to me and then back to the control panel. For a second, I thought he wouldn't answer. I didn't want him to answer.

"I love the Ocelot Nation, Your Grace," he said, his voice quiet and steady. "I regret that I have not sufficiently shown my loyalty to the crown."

"You have."

"If I had, you wouldn't have to ask if our queen would wake up after I subdued her."

I studied him, wondering what was going on in that impossible head of his. Was he hurt, or just offended? Either way, I didn't like it. Even if he was incapable of feeling hurt, if he was incapable of letting himself feel anything, I didn't want to offend him. As a hitman for my father, he wasn't allowed to feel anything. He had told me as much when he'd told me he couldn't love me. I respected that, and I wouldn't put his job in jeopardy.

"I'm sorry," I said.

"Don't be," he said, running a hand over the bottom half of his face, seeming to relax a little. "I haven't done a very good job of showing my loyalty on this trip."

"I don't know how you can say that," I said. "You've done everything right, Gabor."

He tugged at the sleeve of the pilot uniform, which was a little short on his long arms, straightening the white stripes on the wrist. "I've been sloppy."

"Want to tell me why Camila has tranquilizers?" I asked, deciding it was pointless to argue about his performance.

"For protection," Gabor said. "For her own safety, as well. I assure you, she gave her permission ahead of time for me to do that, if it came down to it."

She'd told me she'd take sleeping pills on the flight, not be knocked out cold. Did she think I couldn't be trusted with the truth? With her safety?

"So, she told you that she might freak out, and that you could inject her," I said slowly. I thought of her maidservant, who would have helped to dress her and prepare her bath. She would have taken care of the contents of that bag, but when she died, Camila should have given me the task. She'd asked me to help dress her, and yet, she'd kept this from me.

Was she embarrassed by it? Or was it a shifter thing? She'd let Gabor in on it but not her own sister. The sting of it went deeper than I wanted to admit. Did she trust me less than a palace guard? Had it always been that way, or was it only happening now that I'd found Lord Balam and had something of my own? Was he coming between us?

For a long while, we sat in silence, Gabor monitoring the screens in front of him. An awkward charge began to build in the air as I watched him avoiding even a glance to my side of the cockpit. Maybe he'd heard what had happened in the main cabin. Maybe he thought I was disgusting.

At last, I couldn't bear the thought of that any longer.

"About...what happened back there just now..."

"You don't have to explain yourself to me, Princess Itzel."

"It's just... I've never done anything like that. I don't know what you do at your ocelot parties, but humans don't really do that kind of thing. Or at least, I don't. I mean, I haven't. Before."

Gabor didn't say anything, which made me feel even more nervous. I squirmed in my seat, crossing my legs toward him. "I guess you know that. You know my father was saving me for the right man. But maybe I want to decide that for myself. I'm just not sure who the right man is. I don't know if I'm ready to decide that."

I waited for him to speak, staring at him, willing him to say something, anything. If he called me a whore, at least I'd know what he thought of me. I shouldn't care, but I did. A lot.

He remained silent as a stone statue.

I squeezed my eyes shut in frustration. "Want to tell me what you're thinking?"

"I thought Lord Balam was your mate."

"What?" My eyes snapped open.

"You asked what I was thinking. I was thinking that Lord Balam was your mate. Or I had thought that until tonight."

So, he had heard us. At least he'd said it in a somewhat delicate way. Not that it was any of his business. I had offered him more, and he hadn't wanted it.

I sighed, dropping my head back against the headrest. "Human here. We don't have mates."

51

He nodded, the muscle in his jaw twitching. "Right. I apologize, Your Grace."

"Stop apologizing," I said. "You have nothing to be sorry for. You've served the throne loyally, protected the queen, and you've put up with me. That can't be easy." I gave his shoulder a playful squeeze to show I was joking with him, but he grimaced.

"Not as easy as it should be."

I didn't even want to think about what that meant. "Seriously, Gabor. If you're worried about what Father will think, you shouldn't. I'll put in a glowing report for you for every single day of our tour. You've been the best guard a princess could ask for, not to mention you're probably the best man I know."

"I assure you I'm not."

"Okay," I said. "Only you can really know what kind of man you are, I guess. You know yourself and what you've done, and I don't. But I'm not talking about your past. I'm talking about what you've done on this trip. As far as being a good man by action alone, there are two men back there who couldn't hold a candle to you."

"They don't seem to be hurting because of it."

Before I could second guess myself, I leaned across the space between us, sliding a hand along his jaw and pulling his face closer. As my lips brushed his cheek, his eyes closed, and he drew a slow breath. The muscle in his jaw jumped as my lips touched it, but when I moved toward his mouth, he turned his face away, catching my hand.

"Itzel," he said, still facing the window. "Don't."

I slumped back in my seat, my gaze landing on the dead man between the seats. What was wrong with me?

"I'm sorry," I said, jumping up and ducking out of the cockpit. I pulled the door closed behind me, cutting off any more words he might say. I didn't know why I kept pushing. He had told me he couldn't love me, he couldn't be with me, even if he wanted. I had Lord Balam, anyway. Now I might have Shadow, too, in some way. What could I offer Gabor?

Still, my throat felt tight as I crawled onto the couch with Camila and pulled the throw blanket over me. I wished she was awake so I could talk to her. I'd tried to talk to Gabor, but there was too much feeling involved there. I needed a woman's advice. Not that Camila had any experience in this area. What I really needed was my mother, the woman who could have given me wise council about men. But I didn't have a mother. I would have to figure these men out on my own.

EIGHT

I WOKE WITH A START, THE BED BUCKING UNDER me. No, not bed. My hands landed on leather. Fire raged in my shoulder, and my stomach churned from the motion of the plane. Yes. That's where I was. My mind was foggy, my head pounding.

"Balam?" I whispered.

"No, it's me."

I nearly cried out in surprise. I hadn't seen anyone beside me, and yet, there in the darkness not two feet away, was a voice. A voice, and the faint glow of green eyes.

"What are you doing?" I asked, drawing back, my hand going protectively to Camila's sleeping form. Her breath was deep and steady under her spotted coat.

"Watching over you."

"Um, okay," I said. "Thanks, but that's a little creepy."

Shadow stared at me, his green eyes so intense I had to look away. "Why are you getting the amulets if your sister is to be queen?"

"She doesn't have to get them herself," I said, a defensive edge creeping into my voice.

"How will she know she is suited to be queen if she doesn't take the challenges presented on her own amulet tour?"

"She's suited to be queen because she's the first daughter of the Ocelot King," I said, raising my chin. God, my shoulder hurt. A lick of fire seemed to pulse from it with every heartbeat.

"You're the daughter of the Ocelot King," Shadow rasped.

"I'm not an ocelot," I said. "I can't be the queen. So, it's a choice between getting her on the throne, or leaving my father on it. Which would you do?"

"I'd put you on it," he said.

"Not an option," I reminded him with a sigh.

"You do too much for her," he said. "She doesn't own you, Itzel."

"Yeah, she kinda does," I said. "That's how royalty works. And isn't it better to do it by choice than to be forced into it? I'd have to serve my sister whether I wanted to or not."

"Do you?" Shadow asked.

"I do," I said, gritting my teeth. "I'm a subject. I have to obey the laws of my nation just like everyone else. Isn't it better that I take it into my own hands, take back the power of it, by serving her the way I want to?"

"If that's really what you're doing."

"It is," I said, annoyed at his presumptuousness. "Just because I let you fuck me doesn't mean you know what's best for me, or what my life has been like."

"So, tell me," he said, his voice that hoarse rasp that made me shiver.

I pulled the blanket around my shoulders, wincing at the pain in my injury. How could I feel cold when my shoulder felt like a volcano about to erupt with scalding lava?

"It doesn't matter," I said, leaning my head back on the couch. The flight had smoothed out a bit, with only occasional lurches. I wondered how Gabor was doing up there.

"You're the one who doesn't want this to be anything but fucking," Shadow said quietly. "If I don't know what your life has been like, it's because you don't want to tell me."

"You're right," I said, closing my eyes. I'd kept Balam from my heart, too, giving him one purpose in my life—to fuck me. To make me forget Tadeu. I had automatically put Shadow in the same box. These were men who could make me feel things I'd never felt, both unbearable pleasure and humiliation, the thrum of fear and the helplessness of orgasm. But they couldn't make me fall in love. Falling in love was dangerous. I'd let myself do that once, and it had hurt too much. I couldn't afford to be that vulnerable again.

Maybe that was why I felt a connection with Gabor. We might have had different reasons, different ways of going about it, but we were both doing the same thing. We were both keeping our hearts for ourselves.

Shadow leaned down out of the darkness, his nose skimming my neck as he inhaled. A shiver rocked through me, and I clutched the blanket tighter. Half of me hoped he would rip it off and fuck me again, and half of me wanted to crawl away where he couldn't look at me with those piercing green eyes that saw too deeply into me no matter how hard I tried to shut him out.

"Your wound doesn't smell right," he growled.

I leaned away from him. "Thanks."

The plane bucked under us, and I was nearly thrown from the couch. Gabor might have had a pilot's license, but I doubted he'd flown much. He was probably freaking out right now. My sister was still knocked out, and I had no idea where Lord Balam was. I couldn't make him out in any of the chairs in the cabin, and it wasn't big enough to hide in. A dart of fear went through me. Had Shadow gone feral on him in a jealous rage?

Through all this, Lord Balam had become my anchor. He had his faults, and he could be infuriating, but without him I didn't think I could get through it. I wanted to go to the cockpit and check, but I didn't want to leave Shadow alone with my sister, either.

I let myself have one minute of weakness, one minute of self-pity, and then I forced those thoughts away. I needed to be ready for tomorrow. I needed to be strong for Camila. I might need Lord Balam, but Camila needed me.

"Look, Shadow," I said. "I know you haven't had a lot of time to think about this. Your life just changed in ways you didn't ask for. But we're about to be in Africa, so I kinda need you to make a decision."

"What decision?"

"Whether you're going to stay with us," I said. "All Camilla's guards are gone except Gabor. I know you're used to a less structured existence, but we could use your help, if you want to come with us on her amulet tour."

"I will protect you."

"Well, thanks," I said. "But she's the one who needs protecting. She'll be queen. I don't know how she feels about adding you to our party—probably not good. I'll stand up for you and put my foot down with her, Shadow. But I need to know that's what you want."

"I want you."

"Why?" I asked, pulling back a little. "Because I fucked you?"

"You saved me." His hand closed around mine, his fingers rough and calloused.

I found my heart hammering in my chest. He could have meant several things by that, but I didn't want to know. He'd been right when he said I didn't want to know him. In time, if he proved that he would be here, I would. But right now, I couldn't handle more than my own brokenness.

"Okay," I said, trying to pull away. Shadow's grip tightened, refusing to let me.

"I'll come with you," he said. "But make no mistake. I'm there for you, not her."

"If you really want to be there for me, then you'll protect her."

He was quiet for a long minute before nodding. "Okay," he said at last. "I will."

"Thank you," I said, an unexpectedly powerful swell of relief filling me. I squeezed Shadow's hand, lying down and pulling him closer. Without a word, he slid onto the couch with me, throwing the blanket over us and fitting his body to mine. I was used to sleeping beside Lord Balam's thick, sturdy body. Shadow felt skinny in comparison, almost fragile as I wrapped my arms around him and closed my eyes. His fingers found my cheek, brushing my hair back before his lips pressed down on my forehead.

I opened my eyes to find him studying me with a quiet calm, his eyes full of the realness of himself. It was as if I could see into his soul, without any of the blankness that Gabor affected or the bravado of Lord Balam.

I touched Shadow's cheek, so smooth and soft under my fingertips. "You've never kissed me before," I whispered.

"Do you want me to kiss you now?" he asked, his breath warm on my cheek, his green eyes unguarded.

In all the madness and lust of his first night with me, he'd tasted nearly every inch of me, but not my mouth. Today had been more of the same. Frantic fucking. I didn't know this side of him, quiet and watchful, still.

I leaned in, letting my lips brush his soft, warm mouth. Shadow's eyes fell closed, his long lashes curling against his smooth skin, and he moved in slowly. His lips pressed gently to mine, and his fingers tightened on my hip just enough for me to feel the pressure of his body against mine. A tingle shimmered down my body, raising goosebumps along my arms. I sighed, melting into him, awed by the incredible sensation of this soft kiss from a savage man.

When he pulled away, my heart was hammering.

"Goodnight," he whispered, pressing his lips to my forehead again. "We'll take care of your shoulder in the morning."

I nodded against his neck, nuzzling against him and inhaling his scent, so different from Lord Balam's. Shadow smelled wet and fresh, like rain falling in the jungle. I burrowed into his arms, tightening my embrace and flattening my palm against his smooth, soft skin. He rubbed slow, soothing circles on my back until every muscle in my body relaxed. I was halfway asleep when the question slipped into my mind.

"Shadow?" I whispered.

"Yeah?"

"How old are you?"

He hesitated a long moment before answering. "I'm eighteen."

Eighteen. He was my age, not Lord Balam's or even Gabor's. I hadn't thought about it before. He'd looked so dirty and wild that I hadn't really looked closer at the man under all that crazy. He was barely more than a kid, figuring things out like Camila and me. He'd killed for me, lost his home for me, lost his clan for me. For what he thought was right.

And I'd told him I didn't want to know him.

It wasn't true, though. I did want to know him. I just didn't know if I could carry that weight along with my own. I thought I should, though. I should just open my mouth and tell him to spill it all. I would be his family and his clan. But before I could, the soft stroke of his fingers pushed me beneath the surface of sleep.

NINE

I WOKE ONCE WHEN THEY STOPPED TO REFUEL THE plane, but my mind was a blur of pain. I took a sleeping pill from Camila's stash and passed out again. The next time I woke, it was to the jarring sensation of the plane bouncing along the ground. I sat up, gasping at the pain ripping through me. Grabbing my shoulder, I swayed to stay upright. I was pretty sure my arm was going to fall off. It would have been a welcome relief from the agony. With every jolt of the plane hitting another bump, my arm throbbed with blinding pain. The noise of the engine, wheels, and brakes drowned out anything else in the plane.

It took me a minute to see that Camila was gone from beside me. I jumped up, staggering as my head swam. Shadow watched me intently from the chair on the other side of the plane. I stumbled toward the bathroom, the door of which hung at an awkward angle. It seemed like weeks ago that Lord Balam had fucked me up against it, tearing the latch in the process.

"Camila?" I called when I heard water running.

She stepped out of the bathroom dressed in a lavender pantsuit and a string of pearls that matched her dainty gloves and hat. Her face was freshly made up, the clean scent of toothpaste following her out. She could not have looked more different than the yowling wildcat who had torn through the cabin and killed the pilot.

"You're okay," I said, slumping in relief.

"Why wouldn't I be?" she asked, as if nothing had happened. "You should get cleaned up. The Cheetah Nation is very refined."

"I'll try," I said, a wave of dizziness making me sway on my feet.

"No offense, but you stink," she said, wrinkling her nose.

"So I've been told."

"She needs a doctor," Lord Balam said, appearing beside me and sliding an arm around my waist. "She's lost a lot of blood."

"Didn't stop you from enjoying yourself on the flight," Camila said with a look of distaste.

I didn't know how she could possibly know that, and I should've been embarrassed, but I didn't feel up to it. A shiver wracked my body as we made our way to the door of the plane. We stepped out into the bright sunshine of a dusty, windswept tarmac. I wobbled my way down the ladder to the ground, which seemed to shimmer and sway under my feet.

"Welcome to Botswana," Lord Balam said, slipping an arm around me again. The evening was hot and dry, and I saw only a few trees and small buildings around the tin hangar we'd landed beside.

Camilla descended the ladder in her mincing steps, clutching the railing with her white-gloved hand. Shadow came behind her, naked as the day he was born. Lord Balam couldn't fit in any of Camilla's clothes, but he'd tied a couple T-shirts together around his waist to cover himself. Shadow apparently didn't know that was required.

Even though he was the same man, I saw him differently after our kiss and learning he was only my age. He wasn't so scary anymore. He was just a messed up guy who hadn't had the easy life I had. For all I knew, he'd never been required to wear clothes. Maybe he'd grown up alone in the swamp.

Gabor appeared at the top of the ladder, and something inside me calmed at the sight of him looking almost as put-together as Camila. In his black pilot uniform, complete with black tie and white shirt, wearing aviator glasses and carrying Camilla's bag in one hand, you wouldn't know he'd fought a battle nearly to the death the day before. You wouldn't know he'd lost all his guard companions, or that he'd lain on the floor for hours healing from his injuries. That he'd had to drag the princess from under a truck and inject her with tranquillizer while she screamed and ripped into his hand with her teeth. The only thing less than flawless about his appearance was the two inches of black socks showing below the too-short trousers that belonged to our dead pilot.

I must have been delirious with pain and shock to think he'd wanted me to kiss him the night before. In the harsh light of the afternoon sun, it couldn't have been clearer that he belonged with the princess—the real princess. Not the one with the stinking shoulder, matted hair, and too-tight clothes.

Camila snapped her fingers at him and held out her arm, and he moved to slip his hand into her elbow, escorting her toward the hangar.

Before we reached it, four desert camo patterned jeeps roared around the building, surrounding us in a cloud of dust. Lord Balam's hand tightened on my arm as four men with semi-automatic rifles dropped out of the jeeps and barked at us in a language I didn't understand. They were all wearing desert camouflage and mirrored sunglasses that hid their eyes.

"What are you doing flying into the Cheetah Nation's airfield?" the tallest of the men demanded. He had coppery, light brown skin and wore a hat pulled low on his forehead.

"We're here on official business from King Ocelot of the Ocelot Nation," Lord Balam said. "We're here to see Sir Kenosi of the Cheetah Nation."

I gave Balam a sideways scowl. Sir Kenosi was one of the most famous shifters in the world, a man who had probably invented the term "kitty chaser" because of all the fangirls who swooned over his good looks and Forbes-level wealth. We might as well have waltzed into Hollywood and asked to be taken to Zac Efron.

"Hands where I can see them," barked the man. "All of you."

We all held up our hands.

"Didn't they know we were coming?" I muttered out of the corner of my mouth toward Camila, whose hands were visibly trembling.

"Father contacted King Cheetah," she said, her voice quavering. "What is your boyfriend doing? He's going to get us killed."

"Shut up," the tall man said, shoving the muzzle of his gun into Camila's face.

Quick as lightning, Gabor grabbed the muzzle and jerked it down to point at the ground at Camila's feet. The other three men swung their guns to point at Gabor, shouting at him in a foreign tongue. Camila screamed and dove behind me, gripping my shoulders and cowering against my back. Pain rocked through me, and my eyes swam with blackness as her fingers squeezed my injured shoulder.

The man who had held his gun on Camila ripped the rifle away from Gabor's grip and smacked the side of Gabor's face with the muzzle. Gabor's sunglasses flew off, skittering across the pavement. If the guards thought seeing Gabor's eyes would help them read him better, they were in for a big disappointment.

Gabor didn't react, just held his hands behind his head and stared straight at the men. The men who were all focusing on him now, not on Camila, who was sobbing and whimpering behind me. Fucking Gabor. Of course he'd want to take their attention off the heir.

The tall man slammed the butt of his gun into Gabor's middle. Gabor bent double, and the man clubbed the back of his head. He fell to his knees, bowing his head to spit blood on the pavement.

"Stop," I said, stepping forward and holding out my hands. "He's just a guard. If you're after anyone, it's me. I'm the princess. Take me."

The man stopped beating Gabor and looked me over, his nostrils flaring.

"You're infected," he said. "What have you brought here from your country?"

"Nothing," I said. "I got bit by a panther. I need medical attention, not for you to beat my guard. We're unarmed, and we were told we were welcome at the Cheetah Court."

His full lips curled into a cruel sneer. "The Cheetah Court doesn't have time for you," he said. "The king is very busy."

"That's why I asked for Sir Kenosi," Lord Balam said.

"Shut up," the man said. "Get the in the car. All of you. I'll take the princess."

"No fucking way," Shadow said, dropping into that stance with his knuckles on the ground. Fur rippled along his arms. I didn't even see the other man move, but a second later, Shadow was sprawled flat on the ground, and one of the soldiers was standing over him. I lurched toward him, but the tall guy grabbed me around the waist and pushed me into the back seat of the jeep.

"Wait," Camila said, running to me.

I grabbed her face between my hands as the guy hopped in the front seat. "Go," I whispered. "Stay with Gabor. He'll keep you safe."

The jeep started forward, and I pushed Camila away. She stumbled back, and Gabor leapt forward to catch her. I stayed twisted around in my seat long enough to see Gabor get in the back of the second jeep with her. Sagging in relief, I finally let myself turn around.

"Where are we going?" I demanded.

"Don't get your panties in a twist," the guy said, moving the mirror so he could see me in the back seat. "I'm taking you where you need to go."

"You mean kidnapping me."

"I don't know how much you pay attention to current events, Princess, but the Cheetah Nation doesn't have quite the same relationship with humans as your fine country. This is all for your own safety."

"Bullshit."

"Ooh, she's got a mouth on her," he said. "I like that in a princess."

I made a show of peering into the empty passenger seat. "Who are you talking to?"

He was still mostly hidden by the giant sunglasses and camo hat, but I caught a flash of white teeth as he grinned before turning away from me. "Sit back and relax," he said. "The Cheetah Nation welcomes all feline guests with great hospitality. First up, you better get to the clinic before your arm rots off."

"Thanks," I grumbled, sitting back. If he was really taking me to get help, I wasn't going to argue. If he wasn't going to help me, I'd die from this infection anyway, so he might as well get it over with and shoot me first.

"Consider it your first test," he said.

"What?"

"You're here for the amulet. That's what your father said. We're supposed to negotiate, the richest nation in the International Feline Council and the puny little Ocelot Kingdom. You didn't think we'd just hand it over for nothing, did you?"

"No," I said, cradling my arm as the jeep took a sharp turn onto a busy, paved road. I glanced back to make sure the other three jeeps were still following and relaxed a little when I saw them close behind.

"Consider this the beginning of negotiations," the soldier said. "When you pass all the tests, you'll be deemed worthy of carrying the Cheetah amulet to your mating ceremony."

His words sank in, and I realized he thought I was the ocelot heir. I didn't correct him. I was the one who had to pass the test, anyway—not Camila. I tried to stay awake as we swerved in and out of traffic, moving into a sprawling city with towering skyscrapers with glass faces, twisting and elegant instead of simply jutting into the sky. Though it was nothing like the Ocelot Kingdom, it comforted me to be in such a public area. Somehow, surrounded by so many people, I felt safer. They weren't dragging us out to the desert to execute us and dump our bodies.

By the time the jeep pulled into a garage, evening had fallen. I stumbled from the car, grabbing the side to keep my balance. In a second, Lord Balam was beside me. I hadn't even seen their jeep pull up. I clung to his arm, the world seeming to go in and out of focus.

"You're burning up," he said, scooping me into his arms. "I'm getting you to the nearest clinic right now."

A minute later, we were inside a building. The soldiers directed us into an elevator, and a few minutes later, we emerged into a plush waiting room. Two women wearing nurse uniforms that looked suspiciously like Halloween costumes rushed to bring me a wheelchair.

"Balam," I said, clutching his neck. "They aren't real nurses. Look at them."

"They look good to me," he said with a grin, depositing me in the chair. Something wasn't right, but I didn't know what was happening. Why had Lord Balam asked for the richest feline in the world instead of the king? Why weren't we in a palace? Why did the nurses have skirts so short I could almost see their asses and so much cleavage their nipples were about to pop out?

"Come with me," I said, reaching for Lord Balam's hand. "Where's Shadow?"

"He was in the last jeep," Balam said. "He got knocked out, but he's fine."

"I'm afraid this is as far as he can go," one of the nurses said, stopping at a door. "We don't allow visitors in the operating room."

"Then I'm not going," I said, lurching to get out of the chair. My head swam, and I sank back. "Okay, fine. I'm going."

"I'm not going anywhere," Lord Balam said, bending to look into my eyes. He took my face between his hands and gave me a quick, firm kiss. "Go get fixed up. I'll be right here when you get out."

"Promise?" I whispered, laying my cheek in his palm.

"Promise." He kissed me again, then stood back while the nurses wheeled me into the operating room.

TEN

Gabor
Royal Guard, Ocelot Nation

"WHERE IS THE PRINCESS?" I DEMANDED, STOPPING in front of the elevator, where two cheetah guards stood at attention.

"She is your charge, is she not?" one of the men asked.

Irritation flickered inside me, but I knew better than to let it show. An Ocelot guard learned the dangers of showing his cards early—and harshly. Behind me, Shadow let out a low growl, and I began to see my mistake in letting him come along. But he had been unwavering in his insistence that he must see Her Grace.

"I mean Princess Itzel, of course," I said, gesturing at the elevator. "She's in the clinic."

"Rest assured she's well cared for," said the second cheetah guard, a woman with full lips and cold eyes. "Sir Kenosi himself let us know."

"I'm pleased to hear it," I said. "We would only like to visit with her briefly."

"You don't trust Sir Kenosi?" said the male guard. "He said she's fine. So she's fine."

"Bull. Shit." Shadow's words hissed out like a curse behind me.

The female guard's hand landed on the pistol on her hip.

"We are not questioning your master's word," I assured them. "We simply wish to visit with our—"

"Our mate," Shadow said, stepping up beside me and straightening to his full height.

"She's your mate?" the male guard asked me, his eyes narrowing.

"No," I admitted. "She's my princess."

A princess I had been watching for the past ten years with a protective instinct that had changed to something more even while knowing fully the futility of what I could not stop my heart from desiring.

"She's mine," Shadow said. "I won't be separated from her."

"Is that right?" the man asked, his hand reaching for his holster. Before he could make a move, before I could stop what I should have anticipated, Shadow has dropped to all fours and sprang at the man. It happens so fast, far faster than I'd ever seen anyone shift. One second, Shadow was beside me, and the next, he was flying through the air, which was filled with the sound of tearing cloth and scraps of Shadow's clothes as they exploded from his body. He was in his full fur by the time he hit the man.

The woman's gun was out the next second, and she pointed it at my panther companion. And even though he was not an ocelot, and I had no loyalty to his nation, and I knew what he did to Itzel, I swung my fist without a moment's consideration. If Itzel wanted him alive, I wanted him alive. I could never be anything more than a guard to the princess, but he could. I would save Shadow for her, if that's what she wanted. And I knew that it was.

The gun went off before I snapped the cheetah's wrist. She snarled and started to shift, and I knew I was fucked. No matter how much training an ocelot received, it was no match for a big cat shifter. Still, I wouldn't die for nothing.

When she dropped to shift, I hit the button on the elevator. Maybe I could get in, run from the fight like a fucking coward. I would do it to see Itzel, to know that she was safe. I would do anything to know that.

The man Shadow attacked lay dead under him, blood gushing from his ripped throat. But Shadow had collapsed on top of him, a bullet hole leaking blood from his back as his sides heaved with each labored breath.

I grabbed the gun off the floor just as the cheetah emerged from her human form. The elevator doors whisked open, and my chest constricted painfully. Inside were at least half a dozen more guards.

The female cheetah launched herself at me. Pure instinct alone made my hand rise and my finger squeeze the trigger. She hit me, unable to stop her forward trajectory. I fell under the huge feline form. Her claws sank into me, her teeth slicing my shoulder. Pain wrenched through me, but no sound came from my throat.

The guards rushed from the elevator and seized me and Shadow.

"He was trying to stop me," I managed before their fists begin to fall. I squeezed in words between blows, defending myself for as long as I could. "Don't hurt him. I attacked. I shot him. He was defending your guards."

At last, the half dozen of them knocked me to the ground, their numbers alone too much for an injured man to fight off. A foot connected with the side of my skull, and the world blinked out.

I WOKE TO THE JOUNCING OF A CAR OVER A RUTTED road, pain spiraling through me from the beating. I straightened, noting the details of my surroundings in quick succession.

Cuffs on my wrists.

Painful wounds that had begun to heal when I was unconscious but were still intense enough to be a liability.

A jeep with one driver and two male cheetahs in the back seat.

"Is the princess safe?" I asked.

The driver glanced at me with a wry smile. I recognized the man who had beaten me upon our arrival. Sir Kenosi, back in fatigues.

"She's fine," he said. "In fact, she doesn't even know about this little mishap yet."

"Where are you taking me?" I asked, glancing sideways as the car jarred along the pot-holed road.

"We put our own shifters in jail overnight for fighting to let them cool down. I've never had to detain a feline shifter from another nation."

"I apologize for the inconvenience," I said, folding my cuffed hands in my lap. "It won't happen again."

At least I wasn't leaving Princess Camilla unguarded. I knew that despite their differences, Lord Balam would guard her with his life just as I had.

Until this incident, a voice inside my head reminded me.

I closed my eyes and laid my head back on the seat. Lord Balam would be a better guard than me. Hell, even Shadow might, as unpredictable as the man was. But he had a kind of fierce loyalty to the other princess that I had rarely seen. He knew she wanted Camilla safe. I had to believe that was enough. If I were honest, I had to admit a jaguar and a panther were better equipped to protect her than I was.

I had no choice but to trust them to take care of her until Princess Camila came to plead for my release.

If she came.

Sir Kenosi pulled the jeep over on the side of the sandy road where a squat, tan building sat. It was made of adobe, with tiny rectangular windows making slits close to the roof. It looked like the kind of jail that tortured people, precisely what I expected—and deserved—after what I'd done.

I was supposed to be the future queen's loyal and trustworthy guard, not a man whose passions had him going feral and brawling like a common human. No matter the circumstances, I was never supposed to lose control. I was supposed to be an ocelot guard, a royal brute, equal measures dignity and menace.

But my heart had reduced me to this, walking in cuffs in front of an international playboy on our way into a foreign jail. I didn't trust Sir Kenosi, and I didn't like him walking at my back, but I wouldn't let him see my unease. Whatever happened here, whether I survived it or not, I would show only the refinement my nation required. No more mistakes of the heart. Those mistakes were the deadliest of all.

A uniformed black woman sat behind bulletproof glass, watching us warily as we entered. Sir Kenosi spoke to her in another language, one I recognized only vaguely and understood not at all. The woman seemed to relax, speaking rapidly and gesturing to a side door.

After a few more exchanges, the woman took a keyring down from the wall and gestured for us to follow. She disappeared through a door behind the counter, and a moment later, opened the door beside us and gestured for us to follow her back. We walked along a narrow passageway with small holding cells on either side.

Dead man walking. That was the phrase used on the teledramas my little sister had loved so much. That was for criminals sentenced to death.

I didn't know my sentence. Perhaps it rested on the whims of Sir Kenosi, on whether he told my queen what had happened. Or perhaps it rested entirely on the whims of the future queen herself. If he told her, she might fight for me, or she might let me rot here while she continued her trek through the feline nations.

She had once been as predictable to me as my own heart. But considering the number of times I'd failed her so far, each time Princess Itzel drove a spike through the iron walls of my heart, I couldn't predict what my queen would do when she learned of my latest betrayal.

The cells along the corridor stood empty except the last cell on the left. In the occupied cell, a cheetah woman lay sleeping on a bare mud-brick bench. The guard gestured for me to enter the cell to the right. Every instinct in me balked at walking into a cage. But I wouldn't make a scene again. I'd be overpowered in seconds, and I'd only make things worse for myself and my country.

I had to stop acting like a man and start acting like an ocelot royal guard.

I walked into the cell, and the guards closed and locked the barred gate. Without a word, they disappeared down the dirt path between the cells.

I sank onto the stone bench and considered the weight of what I'd done. I knew very little about the criminal justice system of the Cheetah Nation, but I'd attacked guards at the home of one of the most powerful men in the entire world. If they didn't sentence me to death, it was only because of my relation to the throne. And I didn't want to use that to gain my freedom. I didn't want to put another stain on the Ocelot Kingdom's name.

Too late, reality whispered in my ear.

The best I could hope for was that they'd notify Princess Camila, and she'd take pity on me and come to my rescue, pathetic as that made me. Death seemed preferable.

Imagining Her Grace's fury when she found out, I thought it quite possible that she'd leave me here. I had failed her more times than I could count on this trip. She had to do what was best for herself and her country, and I was no longer certain that I was it. How could I expect her to be sure when I couldn't?

I considered my next move. Being a guard wasn't just a job, it was a life. It was as much a part of me as my ocelot. And to be a good guard, I needed to keep my head and my strength, two things that were sorely lacking in an injured shifter. With that in mind, I lay on the stone bench and closed my eyes.

If Queen Camila never came for me, I would live the rest of my life, however long, behaving myself in a manner befitting an ocelot guard. It didn't matter if she knew, if Princess Itzel knew, even if King Ocelot himself knew. I would know. If I could live and die with nothing else, I would keep my honor.

ELEVEN

Princess Camila
Heir to the Ocelot Throne

I stood outside the cell, looking through the bars at the dirt floor and stone bench afforded an ocelot royal guard, as if he were any ordinary criminal. I could have protested his treatment, but I chose not to. He deserved less.

Gabor sat on the bench, his back rigid and his eyes alert despite the deep, swollen bruises circling each one. His clothes were torn and dirty, but he managed to retain the air of ocelot dignity that made our people so imposing. Straightening my shoulders, I commanded my companions. "Leave us."

Lord Balam let out a huff of breath. "I thought we were getting Gabor and leaving."

"We are," I said. "But I would like to speak with my guard alone first."

"Ten minutes," Lord Balam said, turning on his heel and striding off, as if he gave the orders on this procession. Shadow looked from me to Lord Balam's retreating back, wisely choosing to follow the jaguar.

"Come," I said with a flick of my wrist toward Gabor. He snapped to attention and approached the bars. It was nice to see a little urgency in his obedience. He'd been getting rather lazy now that we'd left the Ocelot Nation. You could really tell what a person was made of when you took them out of their comfort zone.

Gabor may have been a formidable presence in the palace, but a few weeks away and his true colors were beginning to show. Pretty soon he'd lose the posture and be nothing but a slouchy roughian like Lord Balam. Perhaps all men were.

"Fighting?" I hissed at him when he stood in front of me.

"Your Grace," he said, bowing his head ever so slightly. His level of respect seemed to be diminishing with our time away from the Ocelot Court as well, so it was nice to see him bowing at least a bit.

"Don't *Your-Grace* me," I said. "You were arrested for fighting like a dirty commoner. What were you thinking, Gabor? You're supposed to be keeping me safe while I gain the amulets, charming and negotiating with their royals, not out brawling in the streets with the servants."

Gabor stiffened even further. "I apologize, Your Grace."

Just once, I wanted him to bow his head in shame when it was appropriate, to bow down to me and kiss my toes like he should. But he was too proud to grovel without a direct order, and I was too proud to order his groveling. He wouldn't even correct me, tell me that he had been neither in the street nor with servants. I already knew he'd fought with some guards in Sir Kenosi's tower. Pride might have made him a loyal subject at home, but it would be his downfall here. And his downfall could mean my downfall. I had to appeal to his sense of duty if I wanted to get through to him.

"I shouldn't have to come to your rescue like this," I hissed. "It's disgraceful to the entire Ocelot Nation for a member of our court to conduct himself in this manner. Need I remind you, rescuing the princess is your job, not the other way around?"

"I was attempting to do just that," Gabor said. "I only asked to check in on Princess Itzel on your behalf. I know how much Your Grace has been worried about her."

My lips felt cold as I drew a breath through them. "I didn't ask you to do that," I said. "I have received an update already."

"You have?" Gabor asked, drawing back just a bit. Just enough for me to see the flicker of concern in his hard eyes, to see them soften for the briefest moment before he put on his emotionless statue face. But he wasn't emotionless. I glimpsed that when I surprised him with that information, and suddenly I knew. He hadn't gone to see my sister on my behalf. That might have been his cover story, but he hadn't walked away like an obedient servant when they refused to let him see her. He'd cared enough to fight with the guards when they wouldn't let him see her. He'd gotten himself beat up—for her.

And even though he was just a guard, the knife of betrayal slid between my ribs with surprising pain. I didn't want Gabor the way Itzel hinted. He was beneath me, and my mate wouldn't be an ocelot. That eliminated him more completely than the sociopathic nature all guards in my father's employ possessed. Still, I should be his first priority. For once, I wanted someone to think I was not only more important because of my birth, but because of my capabilities. But even the guards underestimated me.

"Your duty is to me," I said, matching Gabor's hard tone with my own. "Or have you forgotten so easily now that the threat of your execution isn't hanging over your head from my father's knife? If that's the case, let me remind you that I am every bit as capable of ordering your execution for treason as he is. You did abandon your post, after all. You disgraced our court and used your position to try to gain access to an unconscious member of the royal family. What did you mean to do to her, Gabor? Did you think you'd make her death look like the fault of the Cheetah Nation? Or was it something more untoward you wanted to do to my sister while she slept?"

A muscle jumped in Gabor's jaw, and I knew I'd gotten to him. Yes, he might still look like a statue on the surface, but he was quite capable of losing his temper. He'd done it just the night before, after all.

"I only meant to obtain information on her status, Your Grace," he said, his body rigid as he stood at attention before me.

"That's not your job," I said. "Your job is to stay by my side and serve me every moment that I ask. If you're incapable of doing that because your mind is filled with perverted ideas about a common human, I will be happy to relieve you of all duties and send you home. It is a rare privilege for an ocelot to travel the world. I could grant it to any one of Father's guards."

He swallowed, a glimmer of gold shining from his eyes. "Yes, Your Grace. I am thankful for the opportunity to serve you. I have made a grave mistake, but I hope your infinite wisdom and kindness allow me to prove my loyalty with continued service."

I reached through the bars and patted his cheek. "Oh, Gabor. You don't think I've forgotten what you already sacrificed to serve my family, do you? You have proven yourself to the Ocelot Court. I only want you to remember that before you do something rash like this again. I'm sure you've learned your lesson and won't dare make another mistake like this. After all, you wouldn't want your sister's death to be in vain, would you?"

His jaw gritted back and forth the slightest bit, but the fire had gone from his eyes, which were now as blank as the rest of his face. "No, Your Grace."

"Very good," I said. "Don't forget it again. I might not be in such a forgiving mood the next time. But now that we've taken care of this little misunderstanding, let's put it behind us. I won't speak of it again, and I expect the same courtesy from you. I am your queen, and you will obey me. Your job is not to anticipate what I want to hear about my sister or to try to find out by force. Your one and only job is to keep me safe. Unless I ask for your opinion, you are not to offer anything other than your complete support and agreement of anything I desire."

With a face as serene as if he were in the middle of a meditation, Gabor gave me the answer I desired, the one I'd known would come once I'd talked a little sense into him. He gave a slight nod of his head and answered simply, "Yes, Your Grace."

TWELVE

Itzel
Princess, Ocelot Nation

I WOKE AND SAT UP, ONLY TO BE STOPPED BY AN IV strapped to the back of my hand. I swallowed a lump of panic, trying not to freak out as my last conscious hours came back to me. Sinking back on the bed, I took in the room. It looked like any hospital room anywhere. An adjustable bed with a railing on the side, an IV stand with a bag of clear fluids dripping into my arm, a bank of monitors, and a window. I sat up again, swinging my legs off the side of the bed. The starched sheets slid off, exposing my naked body.

The room swam, but I grabbed the IV pole to steady myself. Apparently, they didn't do hospital gowns in the Cheetah Nation. I scanned the room for anything I could put on, but finding nothing, I made my way to the window without dressing. Far below, I could see a manicured green space with trees, neatly mown grass, and little benches with birds hopping around them, pecking at crumbs. The view comforted me, and I returned to the bed and sank down, already exhausted. My shoulder didn't hurt, but a thick bandage covered it, and my head felt groggy enough for me to know I must be on some strong painkillers.

Just as I lay back, the door opened, and a handsome black man strode in. He wore a tailored charcoal suit that I instantly recognized as designer of the highest quality, fitted to just hint at the sculpted body beneath.

"Glad to see our newest guest is back in the land of the living," he said, giving me a haughty half-smile. "It was touch and go there for a while."

"How long have I been here?" I asked, acutely aware of how naked I was, and how suave and fully clothed he was.

"A few days," he said, pacing to the window. I got the weird sensation that he was checking where I'd been, that he somehow knew I'd gotten up.

"Days?" I asked.

He turned back to face me. "You had major surgery. You'd lost a lot of blood, and there was some deep muscle damage. You're lucky they missed the major arteries."

Something about him—the smile, the voice, the gait—struck a familiar chord, but I couldn't remember much of anything past when I'd left Lord Balam. I studied the man, trying to place him. He had medium brown skin, sensational bone structure, full lips, a wide nose, and short, buzzed hair. An uneasy feeling settled in my lower belly as he stared back at me, as if expecting me to say something.

"Where's my sister?" I asked, my stomach suddenly dropping out. I'd been out for *days*. Anything could have happened to her in that time.

"She and the men are in a suite across the way," he said, gesturing vaguely toward the window. "They'll be pleased to hear that you're awake."

"Are you the doctor?" I asked, scanning his fit build again. He sure wasn't attired like a doctor, but then, I knew less than nothing about medical practices in the Cheetah Nation.

"I'm Sir Kenosi," he said.

Of course he was. That's why he looked familiar. He was a fucking celebrity. And I was naked, injured, and hadn't bathed in days. Now I knew why the guy at the hangar had looked so much like Sir Kenosi. Apparently, the guy liked to wear disguises and go around snatching people who dared enter his country without checking in with him first.

"So that was you," I said. "You're the one who kidnapped us."

"Kidnapped?" He snickered, his lip curling in disdain. "I wouldn't put it like that."

"I would," I said, unable to keep the edge from my voice. Those guys had taken us from the plane, beaten up two of my guys, and thrown us in a car without telling us where we were going.

"You got the best medical care in the world," Sir Kenosi said. "You wouldn't have made it if you'd gone anywhere else. I'd say we saved your life. I believe a thank you is in order."

"Thank you," I said.

"You can call me Sir."

"Sir," I gritted out. "I do appreciate that. But I'm a little confused as to why you did that."

"Does it matter?" he asked. "You're in my clinic now."

"I'm thinking it probably does matter," I said. "There must be some reason you wanted us to come here instead of to the palace."

He snorted. "This isn't the Middle Ages. There's no drafty old palaces here. We're modern people with modern conveniences."

It was true that King Ocelot preferred things very traditional, but obviously, the city we'd entered was nothing like the Ocelot Nation's home. I could see towering buildings twisting into the sky, all shining metal and glass.

"I can see that," I said. "But it still doesn't answer my question."

"Persistent, aren't you?" Sir Kenosi asked, strolling over to the bed.

"You could say that."

"I'm afraid you won't be getting the answers you want until

I've gotten what I want," he said. "You owe my clinic for your surgery."

"Of course," I said. "Send a bill, and we'll take care of it."

"I require payment before you leave," he said.

"Okay," I said slowly. I didn't know why he was making a big deal of it. He obviously didn't need the money. "Then have my sister transfer it to your clinic."

Sir Kenosi hooked his finger under the edge of the sheet and lifted it, his eyes raking over my naked body.

"What the hell?" I barked, slamming my arm down on top of the sheet so hard my IV jerked. I gasped in pain as the needle wrenched in the back of my hand.

Sir Kenosi smirked. "I'll take payment whenever you're ready."

"Fuck you," I growled.

"Whenever you're ready, doll," he drawled again, wetting his lips as his gaze meandered over my shape under the blanket.

"Go to hell," I said. "I'm not a whore."

"Think about it," he said, turning and striding from the room. When the door closed firmly behind him, I let my head fall back on the pillow, my teeth clenched around a howl of fury. After a minute, I'd gotten my anger under control. I didn't have to think about Kenosi's offer. Maybe he was used to girls falling all over themselves to be his little groupies, but I wasn't a kitty chaser and I certainly wasn't a rich-guy chaser. I didn't need his celebrity. I just needed the Cheetah amulet, which meant I needed to get out of this room.

I climbed off the bed again, this time wrapping the sheet around me. Grabbing my IV pole, I started for the door. I needed to find Camila and the guys so we could make a plan and get to the Cheetah Court, whether it was in a castle or a skyscraper. But when I grabbed the latch on the door and tried to turn, it didn't budge.

Thirteen

I POUNDED ON THE DOOR, YELLING UNTIL MY VOICE grew hoarse, but no one came. Eventually, I hobbled back to the bed and sank onto it, my whole body shaking from the exertion, fear, and anger. My heart monitor was going nuts, but no one came to check on me. The next thing I knew, I was opening my eyes to a dark room. A pale light filtered in through the door to the hallway, which had just opened.

I sat up, my heart thundering when a form appeared at the bedside. Before I saw who it was, I lurched sideways against the railing of the bed.

"It's good you calmed down," said a sweet, accented voice. "Don't go getting excited again. We can't have the princess hurting herself."

I relaxed a little when I saw that it was a nurse, one probably no older than I was. "Why is the door locked?" I asked. "Is this a clinic or a prison?"

The nurse, whose nametag read July, gave a deep curtsy as she let out a sweet, tinkling laugh. "It's a clinic, silly. We just want to make sure our patients are safe from any threats, internal or external."

"What does that mean?"

"Why don't we walk over to the condo," she said, clasping her hands together. "You should be strong enough, and you must be dying for some real clothes."

I was, but I was still suspicious as hell, too. Still, I didn't know what better options I had, and I was ready to get out of the locked room, so I nodded. July peeled back the blankets in a brusque, businesslike fashion that reminded me of my sour old maidservant. Damn, if I didn't miss even her right now.

July plucked some suction things from my skin, and the heartrate monitor beeped at her. She shut it off and smiled at me. "Ready to lose your IV and get some real food in you?"

"Clothes first," I said. "Food second."

"Just hang tight, and I'll grab you some."

She ducked out of the room, and I thought about making a run for it in just a sheet, but it seemed impractical, not to mention I was still weak and drugged. When July returned, she handed me a robe and a pair of slippers. It wasn't exactly the real clothes I'd hoped for, but I slid my arms into the soft, luxurious garment anyway. It definitely beat a threadbare hospital gown with the ass hanging open. I secured the belt around my waist, and July removed the IV from my hand, replacing it with a bandage. Her uniform wasn't exactly what I was used to seeing in hospitals back home, either. The white skirt ended at least six inches above her knee, and the top showed just as much cleavage, along with the edge of a lacy, red bra.

"Let's get you out of here," she said, peeling off her gloves and disposing of them in a trash can. "Sir Kenosi has much more comfortable accommodations in the condo, and you'll be able to see your friends again."

That sealed it. I shoved my feet into the pair of fluffy slippers she offered and followed July out. When we left the building, the sky was a deep blue to the east, but a few stars were still visible overhead. Birds sang in the pre-dawn night, which felt damp and heavy as we meandered along the paved walkway through the huge expanse of lawn. From above, it had looked like a courtyard, but it was much larger now that I had to walk across it in slippers.

From beyond the buildings, I heard the faint noise of a few cars passing in the early morning, but mostly, the city was quiet and calm. Breathing in the fresh air brought some peace of mind back. July wouldn't have brought me outside if I was a prisoner. She would have had me escorted by guards. Sure, Kenosi was a complete asshole, but then, he was a celebrity who was probably used to treating women however he wanted and still having them kiss his ass. It wasn't like he'd done anything besides make a lewd comment.

"Why is Sir Kenosi putting us up in his condo?" I asked as we walked.

"Oh, he's very generous," July said. "He'd take in anyone who needed help. And you're not just anyone."

"I'm not?"

"Of course not," she said, giggling. "You're the princess."

Didn't stop him from being a complete perv, but whatever. I had bigger things to worry about than some rich-guy Cheetah with a rock star ego. If I was free, then I was getting out of here as soon as I found the others.

"My sister's okay?" I asked.

"Of course," the nurse said with another giggle. "She was at the spa all day. They're enjoying their visit very much."

"And the others?" I asked.

"Lord Balam is a favorite with the Jaguar King, which means he's a favorite with us."

"What about Shadow? Kenosi knocked him out when we got here. And Gabor, the guard. Is he okay?"

"They're all fantastic," she said, waving a hand dismissively. "Resting up after what sounds like a horrid time in the Panther Nation."

"Oh," I said, breathing a sigh of relief. "That's good."

"Relax, silly," the nurse said. "You have nothing to worry about. Sir Kenosi knows how to treat honored, royal guests.

He wouldn't spare the greatest expense to make sure you're all getting exactly what you need."

"What about the Cheetah King?" I asked. "We were actually hoping to have an audience with him while we're here."

"Of course," she said, a little too enthusiastically for my taste. "Sir Balam has already put in an official request. It just has to go through processing, and you'll be added to the queue."

"Balam isn't knighted," I said, only realizing as I said it that I had no idea what Balam's official title meant. What exactly was a lord?

"Sir Kenosi got him an honorary knighthood while he's here," July said. "It's the highest honor the Cheetah Nation bestows on visiting dignitaries."

"That's nice of them," I said, not sure how to react to all her good cheer. We arrived at the building across the way from the clinic at last. Two guards stood at the doors, each of them dressed in black uniforms with gold trim. A cheetah emblem graced the shoulder of their uniforms, which I assumed marked them as shifters.

"This is Princess Itzel of the Ocelot Nation," July said, calling me by a title I only heard at home if I was being introduced to someone important who needed to be flirted with.

To my complete shock, the guards both bowed.

"Sir Kenosi asked for her to be made comfortable in a private suite after her surgery."

"Of course," one of the guards said, reaching for the door. He paused, a frown creasing his brow as a look of confusion passed over his face. "We just need to confirm your identity, Your Grace."

"Right," July said with a giggle. "Can't have just anyone waltzing in to Sir Kenosi's."

The guard pulled a small black rectangle from his pocket, popped it open, and handed me a Q-Tip. "Please give a sample of your saliva."

"You have my DNA?" I asked, swabbing my cheek and handing it over. They'd done surgery on me, so it was a little late to hold out on giving them bodily fluids. I would have given them a gallon of saliva if it meant I could get back to the others.

The guard slid the swab into a slot in the side of the little rectangle where it came from. "Just one minute, and the results will have you inside," he said. "I apologize for the inconvenience. In the Cheetah Nation, we take your safety very seriously."

"I can see that," I said.

The device beeped, and both guards bowed deeply again. "Welcome to Sir Kenosi's private estate, daughter of Queen Ocelot of the Ocelot Nation," one of them said, handing back the swab. They stepped aside, and sliding glass doors opened to allow us into a spacious lobby with marble floors and ceilings that rose the ten stories to the top of the building, which remained open to the sky. A fountain was placed in the center of the lobby, surrounded by numerous ferns and other plants, and a pool where enormous orange and white koi fish swam. Ambient light shone over the lobby, lighting our way to a glass elevator tucked away in a back corner.

"Wow," I said. "This is impressive. I can't wait to see where King Cheetah lives."

"Our king is very humble," July said. "Sir Kenosi is the wealthiest shifter in all the world. That's why he welcomes visiting dignitaries and royalty such as yourselves. And the king is so busy, you know. He takes meetings with the common people every day, practices meditation, and of course there are laws and plans for his approval. We must not overwhelm him with the day to day minutiae of our guest's accommodations. Not even when the guest is royalty."

"And Sir Kenosi has time for that?"

July gave that unnerving, manic giggle. "Oh no, silly. We take care of all that."

The elevator arrived, and we rose toward the sky, leaving the fountain below. When it opened on the eighth floor, we stepped out into a huge living area with plush chairs and sofas adorned with rich, cream-colored pillows and throws. A thick, luxurious cream-and-dusty-rose rug adorned most of the floor. Large, potted ferns flanked the couch and draped from their pots on either side of the picture windows that looked out over the awakening city.

"This is...really nice," I said.

"Oh, of course," she said. "Sir Kenosi is so generous. He literally saved my life, and the lives of most of the people who work for him. He took us in off the streets and gave us lives like this. He's so amazing, Your Majesty."

"Sounds like it," I said, trying to reconcile her description with the man who had clubbed Gabor and asked me to pay for surgery with sexual favors.

"I'll leave you to get acquainted with your rooms and your maid, but don't worry, I'll come to check on your shoulder every day."

I wasn't sure that my shoulder needed attention every day, but I'd already paid for ignoring the wound the first day, so I didn't argue. July backed away and got into the elevator. As soon as it closed, I hit the inset black square where she'd put her thumb to call the elevator car. A digital display appeared on the wall. "Access Denied."

"Are you fucking kidding me?" I asked, pushing the button a dozen times in frustration, though I knew nothing would happen. I turned and scanned the room, searching for emergency exits. There was an open doorway that led to a small kitchenette area with a table for two, a vase of fresh pink-and-cream roses in the center. Another door opened to a bathroom with pink-and-cream tile, a porcelain clawfoot tub, and delicate ferns decorating the counter on either side of a sink. An enormous mirror covered one entire wall.

The only other door in the room led to a spacious bedroom with a canopy bed topped with cloud-like pillows and bedding. When I sank into it, a moan of pleasure escaped. It was better than my own room at home. I jumped up, wanting to tell Camila. To see her, to share this new experience with her, to marvel that the Cheetah Nation had it even better than we did. But when I walked out of the bedroom, reality greeted me again. I may have been in the world's nicest prison, but I was still locked up.

FOURTEEN

WHEN I HEARD THE GENTLE SWISH OF THE elevator door opening, I jumped up and ran for it. A tall, thin black girl had emerged wearing what could only be described as a stripper maid's uniform. It was slightly more tasteful than a costume and covered a bit more than lingerie, but it was in no way the kind of maid I needed.

"Hi," she said brightly, her eyes widening as I barged past her and into the elevator. I punched at the buttons while she gaped at me, her chin-length hair in relaxed curls around her face, her narrow eyes and high forehead giving her an elegant beauty even in her revealing attire.

"You have to get me out of here," I said. "I'm locked in. I can't get out."

"Why would you want to?" she asked, staring at me like I was insane.

"I need to see my sister," I said. "Is she okay?"

"Of course," the maid said. "I'm May. I'll be your personal maid while you're here. Let's get you ready to go to dinner, and then you can see your friends."

"Really?" I asked. The elevator was clearly not going to move for me.

"I don't see why not," she said. "You're all honored guests here, even your servants."

Servants. She must mean Gabor, maybe even Shadow. The word rubbed me the wrong way, but I bit my tongue and decided to move to safer topics. "Are you all named after months?" I asked.

"Yes," she said with a perky smile. "That's the month of our favor."

"Your favorite month is May?" I asked, narrowing my eyes.

"It's the month Sir Kenosi shows me favor."

"What kind of favor?"

"You know. Gifts, attention, favors..."

"Can you say creepy?" I muttered. I thought about lunging at her, dragging her into the elevator, and pressing her fingerprint to the panel, but I spotted a camera in the corner of the elevator car and changed my mind. If she took me down for dinner, it would be a better chance to run. If I attacked her on camera, I'd never get past the front door.

"I'm here to clean you up," May said, holding up her basket.

"I brought everything you'll need to get ready. Come on, we'll start in the bathroom."

She drew me a bath, and when she insisted I get in, I dropped my robe and sank into the bubbles. After the days I'd had, I couldn't deny it felt amazing. My maidservant at home sometimes drew me a bath, but she never sat there and talked to me while I bathed. I chalked it up to the customs of a foreign nation and listened to May's banal chatter. At last, she drained the bath and gestured for me to stand. She ran a thick towel over my limbs, insisting I not move around too much because I might hurt my shoulder. Finally, she let me get out.

"Now the fun part," she said with a grin, pulling me out of the bathroom. Three women stood in the living area, a massage table set up before them.

I didn't know what Sir Kenosi was trying to do, if he wanted to seduce me into submission with all these treats. I didn't understand what he wanted with me, anyway. I wasn't the heir to the throne. I didn't have another clan's amulet, if he wanted to steal that. I didn't even have money. If he wanted to hold me for ransom, my father wouldn't give him anything, either. It made no sense.

The women all insisted I wasn't too good for his gifts, and eventually, I relented. After the massage, they took me to another floor where we sweated in the sauna and received enough spa treatments to make me collapse with exhaustion and fall into a drugged sleep in the middle of the day. When I woke, I was shaved and lotioned, my nails painted, and my hair carefully brushed and arranged around my shoulders. At long, long last, everyone left except May.

"Here's your wardrobe for the night," she said, laying a garment bag across the plush sofa. "Get dressed, and we'll escort you to dinner."

"Are the other ocelots going to be there?" I asked.

"Sir Kenosi invites only the most honored guests to these dinners," she said.

About fucking time. I had obeyed and played along, and they were rewarding me at last. I couldn't wait to see my sister and get the hell out of this creepy place.

May sighed. "I won't be there. I have to wait ten whole months until I'm in favor again. But you met July. It's her month, so she'll be allowed to attend. You're so lucky to be going."

She looked genuinely downcast as she sank onto the couch. I didn't know what to think of this weird attachment to Kenosi—maybe he'd used the amulets on them the way Father used them on women to make them fall in love. I slid into the dress, a slinky red thing with a slit all the way to the apex of my thighs, the bodice fitted and so low I was in serious danger of falling out of the top every time I moved.

"I can't wear this ridiculous thing," I yelled.

The door opened, and May stuck her head in. "You look amazing," she gushed, coming in to circle me and rearrange my hair. "You're so beautiful, Your Majesty."

"Unless everyone wants to see my nipples in the middle of dinner, I'm going to need a bigger dress."

"Nonsense," she crowed, giggling and slapping my arm. "You look perfect. Sir Kenosi knows your exact size. He sent what you're to wear."

"He better not be making my sister wear this shit," I said with a sigh, stepping into the heels that he'd delivered. They fit exactly, and I had to wonder how he knew my exact measurements. I didn't even want to think about what had happened while I'd been knocked out from the drugs. I would be having some words with Sir Kenosi about that, too.

"Okay, where is this guy?" I said, stomping out of the bathroom. "I'm ready."

"You look every inch a queen," May said, and I could have sworn she almost looked teary with joy as she escorted me to the elevator. We stepped inside the glass cubicle, and she pressed her thumb to the little square that activated the elevator. The car dropped to the third floor, where May stepped out of the car and gestured for me to follow. At last, we stepped out into a long hallway that opened into a huge dining room at the end. I could see a long table backed by a wall of glass that showed the sun setting over the city below.

May grabbed my arm and squeezed. "I'll be waiting if you need me," she said. "Just come back to the lobby."

Before I could ask what she'd be doing in the lobby all evening, she'd stepped back into the elevator. I gathered as much dignity as I could muster while dressed like a hooker and marched down the hall to give Kenosi a serious ass-kicking.

When I stepped into the dining room, every head turned my way. A dozen girls stood around chatting, each of them wearing a designer dress that left as little to the imagination as mine. Apparently, my nipples weren't the only ones on the menu at this dinner.

"Your Grace," July said, gliding over and curtsying before me. "Let me escort you to your seat."

The long mahogany table was set with elegant tapered candles in gold candleholders, and a glittering crystal chandelier hung overhead, casting a soft glow over the silk napkins and silver cutlery at each place setting.

"Have you seen my sister?" I asked, a sinking feeling in my stomach. Even if Camila showed up, it was obvious this was a women's only dinner—except for the tall guy swaggering in wearing a cheetah fur coat and a pair of sunglasses, gold chains draped around his neck. For a second, I thought this must be a pimp coming to hire us out as whores, or a cheesy rapper come to entertain us. Only when he swaggered to the head of the table did I realize it was Kenosi in yet another one of his disguises.

"I see that my favorites all made it to dinner," he said, sinking into his chair and spreading his arms in a welcoming gesture.

"Yeah, I'm thinking a couple of them are missing," I said. "I was supposed to be meeting up with my party here."

"Oh, come now," he said, smirking at me with those full lips. "I can't have everyone in your procession join us for every meal. Trust me, this one is fit only for the future queen."

I opened my mouth, the words halfway out before I realized what he'd said and quickly swallowed them. Everything clicked into place. Why he was interested in me. Why everyone was bowing to me like I was important. He thought I was the heir. I'd played lots of roles as the daughter of the Ocelot King—flirt, ditz, distraction. Tonight, I had a new role to play. If I wanted to protect her from his attentions, tonight I had to be Camila.

Fifteen

As the girls began to find places around the table, Kenosi patted the spot beside him, a grin on his face as he waited for me to obey. Trying to carry myself like a queen, I took the spot next to him. Maybe I could play the part well enough to get my own "servants" back.

"I'm glad you came around," Kenosi said from inside his disguise. I wondered which was the real Kenosi—the violent soldier, the chic billionaire, or the gaudy rapper.

"I'm sorry I can't say the feeling is mutual," I said, giving him my most poised smile.

"Your tits look hot in that dress," he said. "Glad it fits."

"I'm glad you felt at liberty to molest me while I was passed out," I said. "I've seen lots of gossip about you in the tabloids, but no one mentioned you were basically a necrophiliac."

"I'm not picky," he said. "If the pussy's warm, I'll fuck it."

"That sounds more like what I've read in the tabloids," I said, trying not to show my distaste. My decision to play Camila tonight had obviously been the right one. If she thought Lord Balam was crass, she couldn't have handled this asshole. I would probably pay for my deception later, but I was sure as hell going to keep it up as long as I could and hope I could get Camila out of here before he discovered she was the real princess.

"Bring in the quail," Sir Kenosi said, speaking over my head. I turned to see two men in white uniforms standing inside the doorway. When they stepped out, I could see four guards standing outside. I would definitely not be escaping this dinner. I'd just have to put on my big girl panties and pretend I was hanging out with Tadeu and his rough-talking friends at a tavern in the Ocelot Nation. Renewing my determination, I smiled at the server as he entered with a tray set with covered plates of food. My mouth was already watering. I hadn't eaten since they took me off the IV, and the sizzling meat smelled amazing.

"Not her," Kenosi said, flicking his fingers to motion the server away when he stepped up beside me. "She's got some debts to pay before she eats at my table."

"What?" I asked, whirling toward him. "You expect me to sit here and starve while you eat?"

He smirked, his eyes falling to my ample cleavage. "You don't look like you're starving."

My hands tightened into fists, and to my horror, pressure built behind my eyes. Fuck if I'd let this guy make me cry. But damn, that food smelled good enough to cry over. The server set down a plate beside Sir Kenosi and lifted the top off. Not just quail—it was wrapped in bacon. A bundle of grilled asparagus shoots, and creamy mashed potatoes, yellow with butter, the red skins still on. I nearly groaned at the aroma of food all around as the other girls received their food. My stomach twisted, and I pushed my fists into it, determined not to let him know I was even the slightest bit hungry.

"And I thought my father was the monster," I said as Sir Kenosi sliced a delicate bite of quail off with his steak knife. A server tipped wine into our glasses, including mine, but Kenosi didn't seem to notice. His eyes were fixed on me.

"You think I'm a monster?" he asked.

I raised my chin and met his eyes. "Yes."

He quirked an eyebrow. "Yes, *Sir?*"

"Yes, Sir," I said, smirking to show him how ridiculous I found the request to call him that.

"Then it's a good thing I don't run the country." He lifted his glass and turned to the rest of the table. "Tell the princess what a monster I am."

"Oh, no, Kenosi," said July. "I'm sure she doesn't mean it."

Another girl giggled around a bite of asparagus. "She's just playing hard to get."

"Fuck that," I said. "I'm not playing anything. You're the one playing this sick game of his. What's he doing—brainwashing you? I bet every single one of you has the same name."

115

They looked around at each other, their eyes widening like they'd never noticed that he named them all according to when he wanted to see their faces, and presumably ignored them the rest of the year.

"No one's forcing anyone to do anything she doesn't want to do," Kenosi said. "No one's a prisoner here."

"I'm a prisoner," I said, throwing up my hands.

"You're working for your keep the same way as anyone else. There are no spoiled princesses here. Everyone works."

"Yeah, well, I'm not a sex worker." I picked up my glass and downed the wine in four big gulps before he could take it away. I needed the energy after not eating all day. If all I could get was wine, it was better than nothing.

"We all do whatever work needs to be done," Sir Kenosi said. "Your father obviously didn't hire the right tutors for you. Everyone should learn this lesson, Your Grace. A queen must do what needs to be done for her country."

"And what needs to be done for my country is sucking your dick?"

"Right now?" he asked, quirking an eyebrow. "Yes."

"Fuck you, Kenosi," I said, grabbing a quail off the plate beside my empty place setting with my bare hand. The July sitting there gasped, watching in horror as I snatched up my steak knife, gripping it in my other hand in case Kenosi attacked. It wasn't going to kill him, but it would hurt like hell until he healed himself.

He tensed as if about to lunge, watching me with unflinching intensity. I raised the quail to my mouth and took a bite.

I chewed slowly, smiling at Kenosi as juices from the meat dribbled down my chin. He looked disgusted. I was glad. Let the bastard think I was a pig like him. He'd probably eaten like a normal person all day, and here he was, gloating and stuffing his face while I was nearly faint with hunger. I ripped the bacon off the bird with my teeth, savoring it as I chewed.

Kenosi's eyes flicked to the door, and a second later, I was seized from behind, the guard's strong hands yanking me backward. The chair crashed to the floor, and I flailed wildly as they dragged me toward the door. I didn't care how undignified I looked as I slashed with a steak knife with one hand and stuffed meat into my mouth with the other. Fuck all these people, and fuck what they thought of me. They had no idea what I'd already been through. A little humiliation was par for the course. I'd spent most of my life being humiliated. It was nothing after watching the love of my life having his head ripped off by a tiger.

"Let me go," I growled, slashing at the guard's leg with the knife.

He yelped in pain, grabbing for my hand. Crushing my fist in his palm, he stumbled back, trying to get my limbs under control. Another guard ran to help, but I managed to get in one good kick with my heel before he subdued my legs. They hauled me into the elevator, still kicking and cursing. I didn't stop until they flung me out the door into my room.

When they were gone, I stood and smoothed my satin dress. It was the only thing I owned besides a robe and slippers. I had a steak knife to defend myself, a quail bone to gnaw, and a belly full of wine and a few strips of bacon I'd gotten down before they seized me. The wine on an empty stomach made me a little tipsy, but I was happy for the calories. I was not going to starve tonight.

I lay down on top of the feather-soft bed and tried to think up an escape plan. The room was ten stories up, so there was no way I could jump out the window unless I wanted to die. The elevator wouldn't work for me, and there were no other doors. But I had the small knife now, and there were plenty of people who came to the room by the elevator. If I could hold the knife to May's back and get her to take me downstairs without the camera seeing the knife, maybe I could escape. I just had to get her at the right moment, just as she left the elevator, when the camera couldn't see her.

I pulled a chair over and settled in to wait.

Half an hour later, I heard the elevator moving behind the doors. I straightened, clutching the knife next to my hip. This was it. My chance.

The door slicked open, and Sir Kenosi strode out. That sucked for him, but I wasn't about to waste my chance. If he'd come up here, it wasn't for anything good. I dove for him, holding the knife close to my body until I was on him and raising it to strike.

He moved so fast I didn't even see the motion until the next second when my knife was skittering across the floor, and

Kenosi loomed over me, my hands pinned in his grip. He smirked down at me, holding me close enough that I could inhale his spicy scent and see the flecks of gold in his deep brown eyes. "Lesson number three of the day," he said, his voice an amused purr. "Never try to sneak up on a cheetah."

"Let me go," I growled, yanking at my hands.

"You think you can kill me with a steak knife you stole from my table at dinner," he said. "Frankly, I'm offended that you don't think me a more worthy opponent."

"I wasn't trying to kill you," I said, still trying to pry my hands loose.

"You aren't doing very well," Sir Kenosi said, his grip tightening until my bones ached. "I expected a worthy opponent, too. Not a spoiled little girl who can't see beyond her own nose."

"Excuse me?" I said, giving up my struggle to free myself. "That's a little ironic coming from a guy with a new harem of women at his disposal every month."

"I was hoping you'd pick this up on your own, but since you're obviously not smart enough to figure it out, let me enlighten you," he said. "This is a test. Every step you take in my home, in my kingdom, is a test. And you're failing in spectacular fashion."

"Fuck your test," I said. "I didn't agree to any of this."

"I think you did," he said, stroking my hair back with his free hand, cradling the back of my head and pulling me closer, so

I had to look up to maintain eye contact. "You went on your Royal Amulet Tour, didn't you? Isn't that what you're doing here? That's what your father said."

"Yes, but—."

"*Sir.*"

I gritted my teeth. "Yes, Sir. But—"

"But nothing," he purred, pulling my hands against the front of his pants. "You came to our territory, and we cared for you. You want our mating amulet. You perform, and you get what you want. Did you think you'd just walk in and ask nicely?"

"The king invited us," I said, trying not to respond to the sensation of his cock stiffening against my hands.

"The king said you could visit our nation on your tour," Kenosi said, moving my hands to trace the shape of his long cock through his pants. "He didn't say he'd hand it over for nothing."

"You don't have the amulet," I said, my voice sounding a little more breathy than I wanted. I wanted to tell him to go fuck himself, but the scent of his skin was sending prickling heat straight to my core until I was dizzy with it. I wanted to pull my hands away, and yet, the more he made me touch him, I couldn't help the tingle of excitement racing through me. He was huge—longer than Lord Balam, and hard as steel straining inside his dress pants.

"I have the amulet, and I also have you," Kenosi said, smiling like he knew exactly what he was doing to me.

"What does that mean?" I asked, forcing anger into my voice.

"It means that when the king asked if you could come, I said you could come," he said. "Now you're in my debt, and that debt has to be paid."

Sixteen

I remembered Lord Balam's words when he'd explained the Cheetah Kingdom, how he'd said that the king was little more than a figurehead. Now I understood. The king had nothing to do with this. Kenosi ran things. He had the money. He controlled the country. When he said I could have the amulet, he'd give it to me. He might not even tell the king.

"And this will pay my debts?" I asked, letting my fingers wrap around his shaft. A throb of longing went straight to my clit.

Kenosi stroked my cheek, running his thumb across my lower lip, making my mouth water. "You've got a pretty mouth," he said. "Let's see it stretched around my cock."

I nodded, my heart pounding hard in my chest. "Yes, Sir."

I was tempted to race for the elevator when he released my aching hands at last, but I knew he'd catch me and do worse.

This wasn't so bad. I'd given Tadeu blowjobs. I knew what I was doing.

Kenosi ran his hand around the back of my head, sweeping my hair back as he pushed me toward the floor. I lowered myself to my knees, swallowing my nerves. My heart was hammering, and a strange anticipation built inside me. I gulped, unable to tear my eyes from the long ridge pushing against the fabric of his pants. I reached for his zipper, but he grabbed my hand.

"Patience, Princess," he said. "You're getting ahead of yourself. First, tell me what lesson I'm teaching you today."

"Humility," I said.

He tipped my chin up and stroked my lip again. "Part of this is just for my own enjoyment. I like to see a princess on her knees, no better than anyone of low birth."

"You're of low birth?" I said. "That's what this is about?"

Not that it mattered to me. I had no idea, nor did I care, what anyone's station at birth had been. My own was not exactly illustrious. I didn't even have magic. I'd never asked Lord Balam or Shadow about their origins.

"Focus," Kenosi purred, drawing my face closer to his erection. "A queen should always know how it feels to bow before someone superior."

"Now you're my superior?"

"Why else would you call me *Sir*? And how else will you know what others feel when they bow at the foot of your throne?" he said. "A queen must do things for the greater good, not only for herself. Let this be a lesson on how to serve."

I nodded. It was just a blowjob. Nothing to get worked up about.

"Good," Sir Kenosi said. "Now let's put something in that big mouth of yours."

He released my head, a gloating smile on his face as he leaned back and waited. I unzipped his fly, a little lurch going through my belly as I slid my hand inside and felt the heat of his stiff shaft. I undid the button on his pants and drew them down, hating the way my fingers shook. His cock stood up in front of me, gloriously long and brown and flawless. My heart picked up speed and heat pooled between my legs at the sight of it.

My brain knew I was being ridiculous, that I should be stronger than this. But my body wanted to push him back on the bed and sink that perfect monument of male sexuality deep inside me.

Get a grip, Itzel.

I leaned forward, wrapping my hand around his shaft and pressing my lips to the head of his cock. It was soft as velvet, smooth and delicate, so unlike the cruel man who possessed it. My mouth watered for more, thirsty to possess it for myself.

"Come on, Princess," Kenosi said. "Wrap those pretty lips around my cock and suck it."

I ran my hand to the base, marveling at his smooth skin and iron hardness. I couldn't seem to let him go. His musky, spicy scent intoxicated me until all I could think about was burying his cock in my mouth and drinking every drop of cum from it.

I opened my lips, my tongue skimming over the head, drawing a low breath from him. I opened my lips further, sliding him in. I'd just give it a couple quick sucks, just a taste, and then tell him to go fuck himself, I wasn't his slave. Leave him high and dry to serve him right for what he'd done to me.

A drop of saltiness spread over the back of my tongue, and I let out a low moan, nearly melting at the sensation of his soft skin against the inside of my mouth, sliding between my lips, the taste and smell of him invading me. I rose up on my knees, taking him deeper, all the way into my throat. My throat tightened and tears blurred my eyes, but Kenosi cradled my head, pushing deeper.

"Come on, Princess, deepthroat me."

I fought back a gag as he pumped into the back of my throat, tears trickling down my cheeks with the effort of forcing back the reflex. Salty drops slid down my throat, and I gripped his shaft, my mouth suctioned around his head as I cradled his balls with my free hand. He moved faster, murmuring words of encouragement as I slurped at his cock, saliva trickling down my chin with each thrust.

"Good girl," he said, his breath coming faster as he continued pumping my head up and down. "I'm gonna come."

I started to pull back, but he buried his hands in my hair and drove his hips forward, pushing past my gag reflex, cum spurting into my throat. I swallowed reflexively, barely able to breathe. Cum flooded my mouth again, trickling out the corner of my lips and dribbling onto my cleavage as his cock expanded a final time, filling my mouth with thick, slippery fluid.

At last, Kenosi released me, and I fell back, gasping for breath. "Asshole," I said, choking out the word and wiping the tears off my cheeks.

"Don't pretend you weren't drinking that shit up like a milk-shake," he said, grabbing my hair and pulling me back up. "Now, you've got some clean-up to do. I told you to swallow."

"Fuck you," I said, trying to pull away. "I did."

Kenosi pressed me back so I couldn't rise from my knees. "You can get off your knees when you've licked up every drop, you little slut."

I struggled against his grip, but my scalp burned with pain from his tight hold. At last, I leaned forward, humiliation burning through me as I began to lick drops of cum from his cock, balls, and thighs. When I'd finished, I was burning with a rage like I'd never felt, not even when my father killed Tadeu. That had been tinged with shock and unbelievable pain. This was pure, murderous hate.

Kenosi hooked his hands under my arms and pulled me to my feet. "That wasn't so hard, was it?"

"No," I said. "It was pathetically soft and small." I knew I was grasping at straws, delivering the hits of a desperate woman who has lost every shred of her dignity and has nothing left with which to hit back.

Kenosi chuckled. "A good queen knows when to submit to the demands of bigger, stronger nations," he said, stroking my cheek with something close to tenderness. "And a smart woman knows when to obey."

"Then I guess I'm not too smart."

"You'll learn," he said. "If you want to see your friends. If you want to take the throne. That's what your Amulet Tour is for. For you to practice facing the challenges you'll face as queen, maybe not in this exact way, but they'll come in handy one day. You'll see."

I bit back my rage, waiting for him to leave so I could plot a gruesome death for him. Kenosi leaned in like he might kiss me, but I jerked my face away. No fucking way was he getting that from me. There had to be something I could keep for myself.

He chuckled again, releasing me this time and stepping back to pull up his pants. "Very well, Your Majesty," he said. "You've passed a test at last."

"Does that mean I get the amulet?" I asked.

"Don't be greedy," he said. "You've paid off one of your debts. Consider your dinner paid for."

"That only paid for a few measly bites of quail?"

"Let that be another lesson," he said with a grin. "Never let yourself be in anyone's debt. They always get to name the price."

"So, let's take care of the rest. What do you want now?"

"I'll fuck your pussy later," he said. "I want to savor the memory of your mouth a little longer."

"Let me out of here," I growled. "I'll tell your king what sick things you're doing here."

"Go right ahead," Sir Kenosi said, his eyes dancing with amusement. "I can't wait to hear what he says about it."

"Because you know he won't actually do anything about it?" I demanded, my fisted hands squeezing so tightly they hurt.

I was so mad I could barely see straight, but Kenosi only gave a mock bow and stepped into the elevator. "You're getting smarter already," he said. "We'll see what tomorrow brings, my princess."

With that, the door swished closed, leaving me alone in the luxury suite lingering on the threat of more tests to come.

SEVENTEEN

Lord Balam
Curandero, Jaguar Nation

AS THE ORACLE'S VISION FADED, I SAT STILL, waiting for the sting of the magic to sink back through my skin and join my body. My jaguar skin slipped off my arms, and the tattoos that covered my body found their places once more.

I had been marked with them when I was not much more than a boy, but I didn't regret the pain for even a moment. The oracle's visions were as much a part of me as my jaguar. I was equally man, beast, and *curandero*.

That didn't mean I always liked what the oracle had to say. I didn't have to interpret this vision for long, because it had the same message it had given me many times now. Or nearly the same. There was some added weight this time.

I stood and made my way out of the room Sir Kenosi had afforded us for our stay. The moment I stepped out, Shadow scrambled up from where he'd sagged against the wall, his head hung in defeat.

"What did it say?" he asked, his growling voice contrasting with his youthful face. The boy couldn't have grown a whisker if he tried.

I shook my head. "It told me not to interfere."

"Bullshit," he barked.

"Would you like to ask yourself?"

"No," he said, scowling. "I didn't mean that I didn't believe you. We can't just lay around here and do nothing. I know she's in trouble. I can feel it."

His eyes flashed that dangerous shade of green, and I clasped his shoulder. "Calm yourself," I said. "Getting worked up isn't going to do her any good. You're lucky Gabor saved your ass last time."

Shadow drew back and narrowed his eyes. "What?"

"Gabor told them you were trying to stop him from attacking those guards," I said. "Why do you think you're here instead of working your ass off in the broiling sun with him?"

"He told you that?"

I shrugged. "No. One of the cheetahs who hauled him off to jail told me."

Shadow gave me a calculating look, like he wasn't sure if he could believe me. The young panther had some trust issues to work through.

"Why would he do that?" he asked at last.

"I don't know," I said. "Maybe he didn't want to let you die."

"Why would an ocelot royal guard care if a panther died? They killed most of my clan."

"You'd have to ask him," I said. "My guess? He knows how much Princess Itzel cares about you. Don't ask me why."

Shadow's eyes grew serious, but he didn't answer.

"Be grateful she does," I told him. "If Gabor hadn't taken the fall for you, they'd have killed you instead of letting you rest and recover in the clinic."

If only Itzel had an animal inside to heal her when she needed it, we'd have her back as quickly as Shadow. Having a human around—especially one we were all determined to protect— was a liability and a burden. But not one of us was backing down from the challenge.

"I have to find her," Shadow said, turning away.

I grabbed his shoulder. "The oracle told me to trust her," I said. "She may be human, but she's far from helpless, Shadow."

"I know that," he snapped, his back tensing under my grip.

"Our job isn't to run in there and rescue her, if we could even find out where she is," I said. "She might not even want us to.

She's working her own magic, getting the amulet like she wants. If we fuck that up..."

The panther hesitated, still facing away from me, toward the elevator at the end of the hall. "You don't think she wants us to find her?"

"I trust the oracle," I said. "And I trust her."

For a long moment, neither of us spoke. I could feel the turmoil inside the young panther, and my heart went out to him. I remembered the impetuous man I had been at his age.

"You really think she cares about me?" Shadow asked quietly, his back still turned to me.

"Yes," I answered truthfully. "So be worthy of it."

After a moment, he nodded. "I didn't know Gabor did that," he said. "I should be out there with him. What's he doing?"

"Helping build a house for the son of the cheetah guard he killed."

Shadow bowed his head and looked at his hands, his long hair falling over his face. "I killed that man."

"Trust me when I tell you that Gabor has killed plenty of men," I said. "I don't think he minds doing some penance. If he wasn't with the royal party, his punishment would probably be a lot less lenient."

"It doesn't matter," Shadow said. "I can't let another man serve for my crime."

With that, he took off down the hall, not to find our princess, but to do his duty. Somewhere in there, inside that feral shifter, was a good man. If Itzel could forgive him, then I wouldn't hold what he'd done against him, either. As much as I would have liked to claim Itzel for my own, I knew it wasn't in the cards.

She was important, though I didn't yet know exactly how or why. I only knew that I would take what I could get for now, and that I'd remember it as long as I lived. And I knew that I had to protect her, but that I couldn't get in the way of fate. The Amulet Tour was a sacred tradition, and even without the oracle, I knew not to step in and interfere with another nation's quest to gain them.

I'd told Shadow the truth about my reading, but not the whole truth. I hadn't told him about all the other times the oracle had said the same thing. That it had also told me not to interfere with him and Itzel. If it wasn't for that, I'd have murdered the son of a bitch for hurting her the way he had. But I knew I couldn't let my passions rule me. The oracle was wiser than any man. And so, I obeyed.

Now the bastard was growing on me. Shadow's concern for Itzel was clear as the tattoos on my skin. He cared about her and would do anything to protect her. I had to respect him for that, even if he was far too impulsive, and he let those impulses rule him.

I'd told him that the oracle had instructed me to trust Itzel here in the Cheetah Nation. She knew what she was doing.

But I hadn't told him that the warnings were getting stronger. That this time, the oracle hadn't just told me that I shouldn't interfere. When I asked about what to expect in the Lion Nation, it had told me that if we interfered, we would all die.

Eighteen

Itzel
Princess, Ocelot Nation

I BARELY SLEPT, MY STOMACH WAKING ME WITH demands for food almost hourly. By the time the sun rose in the morning, my legs shook with weakness, and I could barely make my way to the bathroom. I swallowed as much water as I could hold and hoped this day's test would include an eating contest.

July came knocking soon after I got out of the shower. She pushed her little cart out of the elevator, calling a cheerful good morning.

"Did you bring food?" I asked, eyeing the assortment of bandages, blood pressure monitors, and other medical supplies. At this point, I would have been happy with some IV fluids.

"No, silly," July said with a giggle, rolling the cart to a stop beside the bed. "I'm here to check your shoulder."

I slumped down in defeat, letting her pull up the bandage to check my stitches.

"Are you a cheetah?" I asked as she examined the wound. Even in my weakened state, maybe I could hold her at knife point if she was human.

"Everyone here is a shifter," she said, dashing my hopes. "This is the Cheetah Nation."

"Right," I said. "Sir Kenosi wouldn't associate with mere humans."

"No," she said slowly, pulling back to give me a strange look. "Humans don't associate with us."

"Ah," I said. "I heard that cheetahs aren't on good terms with their human neighbors."

"We could just conquer them by force, like your people," she said. "But our king is a peaceful, gentle soul. He prefers to let the humans come to terms with our existence in their own time."

According to the history I'd learned from tutors back home, when shifters "came out" to humans, cheetah's had been segregated, sometimes forced to leave their own property behind and live in horrible conditions. Their king refused to fight back or even resist, and humans refused to acknowledge or interact with them at all. Only through dealings with other Feline Nations was a young businessman named

Kenosi able to amass some wealth. He bought land in rural areas and an entire city block where cheetahs could live and work, much to the annoyance of the human population. Instead of catering to humans and trying to appease them, he had developed apps and websites for supernaturals only, and he'd made a fortune doing it.

That was the textbook version of their history. The real version seemed much more complicated. I could see now why the people chose to worship Kenosi's celebrity rather than their pushover king, but it wasn't quite the comfortable living situation history had taught. For one, the women seemed to pull double duty as nurses, doctors, and maids by day and sex slaves by night. The men were guards, cooks, and servers, but if Sir Kenosi was keeping all the women to himself, they must be miserable despite their "comfortable" living.

"Are you happy here?" I asked, not expecting a real answer.

"Oh, of course," July said. "I love my king and our nation very much."

"And Kenosi?"

"He's the best," July said with a sigh, wrapping a blood pressure cuff around my arm.

"You don't mind sharing him with all these other girls?"

"Oh, no," she said, pumping the cuff tighter. "If he was my True Mate, I would. But if we were True Mates, he wouldn't have other lovers to begin with."

"Where's his True Mate?"

"I don't know," she said with a shrug. "Maybe he doesn't have one. Maybe she's dead. Maybe she hasn't been born yet. Most people never find one. It doesn't mean you can't have fun while you're here." She gave me a wink and pulled off the cuff. "You're all set, Princess."

"This is fun for you?" I asked.

"Oh, yes," she said, nodding vigorously. "It's so nice to have a safe place, a good job, food... Not to mention a gorgeous man to meet our more primal needs."

"For one month out of the year," I said. "What about the rest of the time?"

"There are guards, landscapers, cooks, and other men here. Then there are visitors from the other Feline Nations." She gave me a sly smile and winked. "If it wasn't my month, I'd be satisfying myself with *your* guard."

A protective flare rose inside me at the thought, and I was glad that it was her month with Kenosi so she wasn't coming onto Gabor. Not that I could see Gabor caving to desires for the flesh with a random girl, but what did I know? Even if he felt nothing for me, hearing someone have sex all the time had to make anyone need some relief of their own.

"What if you find your True Mate?" I asked. "Isn't that what the amulet does?"

"A lot of cheetahs were killed when we came out to humans," she said. "There aren't a lot left to choose from. On the rare occasion someone finds a True Mate, she leaves Kenosi's bed to be with her True Mate. But in the meantime, he keeps us safe and satisfied. When he found me, I was hiding in a slum, turning tricks for humans with shifter fetishes. If they decided not to pay me, I couldn't eat. And I couldn't do anything about it. I was working for myself, with no protection. If I complained to a John who didn't pay, he could turn me in. If I went to the police myself, they'd figure out why people were ripping me off. They would have thrown me in prison or put me in one of the relocation programs where the human guards did whatever they wanted to the women, and the women never got paid."

"I'm sorry," I said, swallowing the sour taste in my throat. "That sounds terrible."

"It was," she said. "Sir Kenosi saved me."

"But did he?" I asked. "Is this really so much better, or is it the same thing but with nicer trim?"

July threw back her head and laughed. "I like you," she said. "You're funny. Trust me, we're all happy here. If we weren't, we'd leave. It's not like Sir Kenosi would put us back on the streets where he found us, either. He takes care of our people. We'd go live on the pieces of land he bought with his own money and turned into cheetah territory for the entire clan. We're here because we want to be here with him."

"Must be nice," I muttered as she wheeled toward the elevator. I glanced sideways at the knife on the bedside table. As much as I liked July, I liked my freedom better. I grabbed it

141

and charged across the room, knocking her cart aside and diving into the elevator ahead of her.

She let out a cry of surprise, her hand flying to her chest. For just a second, her eyes rounded further, unnaturally, and her pupils stretched vertically. Then she was back to being the smiley, robotic nurse I knew.

"I'm afraid you're going to have to stay here until Sir Kenosi calls you down," she said, looking genuinely regretful.

"You'll have to drag me out of here," I said, gripping the decorative bar that ran around the elevator at hip level.

"I don't want to have to remove you," she said. "But I can if you need me to."

"You just try it," I growled, clutching the serrated knife where she could see it.

She stepped away from her cart, approaching the elevator door slowly. "Now, there's no need for that," she said, holding up a hand like she was trying to calm a panicked animal. "Just put the knife down, and we'll get you in to see Sir Kenosi right away, Your Grace."

"I don't want to see Kenosi," I said. "I want to see the door out of this place."

"Then let's get you there," she said, and the door to the elevator began to slide closed. It took me a second to realize what was happening—that she must have hit the button on the outside.

I dove for the door. Getting stuck in a tiny glass elevator was a hundred times worse than being trapped in a suite with multiple, luxurious rooms. Not to mention that there was no food here, either.

I made it to the door and thrust my arm out before it closed completely. Instead of sliding back open, though, the door pinned my arm. "Hey," I yelled, flailing my arm at July, who stood just inside my rooms. "Get me out here. I promise I won't attack you. Here, you want my knife? I'll pass it through. Just pull me out."

"Pass me the knife," July said, her voice sweet and perky as ever, as if she were asking me to pass the sugar.

I thrust the knife through, dropping it to the floor so she'd know I wasn't going to try to take her by surprise. She picked it up and set it on her cart. "Now open the door," I said. "Please."

"I'm sorry, Princess Ocelot," she said, and she punched the button beside the elevator again.

To my horror, it started to move. Visions of having my arm ripped off at the elbow exploded in my mind. I threw my weight backwards, wrenching at my arm. My elbow stuck for a second, but I twisted frantically, and my arm came free just as the next floor appeared through the glass on the back of the elevator. I crouched in the corner, cradling my arm, breathing through the bruising pain from where it had stuck. Angry red marks circled my arm just above the elbow.

Cursing Kenosi under my breath, I stood on shaking legs. Hunger and exhaustion made me weak, but the adrenaline rush of trying to escape had me wired. Now I was ready to go. I barely felt the pain. I pitied whoever was in the lobby when the door opened. There was no stopping me now.

Nineteen

When the elevator door slid open, I wasn't in the lobby. I was on some sort of walkway, a balcony that overlooked the lobby several stories below. The railing was lined with trailing, leafy vines that hung down toward the lobby, but I didn't see any kind of emergency ladder conveniently stretching to the ground or lying about.

I turned to go in search of stairs, but I found a man standing a few paces behind me. "Your Majesty," he said with a deep bow. He swept an arm toward a wide hallway that led away from the balcony. "I have been informed that you require an audience with the kind Sir."

Kind Sir, my ass.

"If that's how you get out of this place, I'll take it," I said.

"Very well," he said. "Proceed."

He had the same coppery-brown skin and short, kinky hair as the others in the Cheetah court, but I didn't recognize his uniform. Unlike the women, he wasn't wearing expensive lingerie for a uniform, and he wasn't wearing the guard uniform or the white ones I'd seen on the servers the night before. From the way he talked and carried himself, he could have been royalty, but I'd learned that royalty in the Cheetah Nation meant nothing. Money meant everything.

"Right this way," he said, gesturing grandly to a doorway hidden in a small alcove at the end of the hall. He turned the knob and swung the door open, propelling me in. I stopped in my tracks, shocked still by the scene before me.

The *orgy*. There was no other way to describe what was happening. And though I liked to think Lord Balam had opened my eyes, that he'd been my sexual awakening, nothing we'd done could have prepared me for the scene unfolding in the spacious room. The bed was at least ten feet long and extended about twenty feet wide, stretching along half the length of the far wall. Two sofas sat at the foot of the bed. Every surface in the room was covered with writhing, naked bodies in various sexual positions. A woman lay on her back on each of the couches, another woman going down on her while yet another sat astride her face.

When I'd said he had a harem of women, I hadn't gone so far as to imagine this. I had imagined a rotation, not an all-day sex show for his benefit. On the bed, more women lay in tangles, moaning and grinding, licking, sucking, and rubbing. At the head of the bed, propped on a mountain of pillows like the presiding king sat the lone male in the room —Kenosi.

Like everyone in the room, he was naked. Instead of soft curves and rounded angles, Kenosi was sculpted to perfection, each muscle cut with the precision of a marble statue. His pecs were chiseled, each nipple dark and tight against his brown skin. His abs rippled in a perfect eight-pack above a neatly groomed groin where two women enjoyed the dark cock I had sucked last night. His bare legs were sprawled out on the bed, long and muscled with just the right amount of definition.

He saw me watching and gestured lazily. "Come on, Princess," he said. "There's room for more. Climb on my face and let me taste that royal pussy."

"Fuck you, Kenosi," I said, too rattled to think of anything clever to say.

"That can be arranged," he said. "But I like to take it slow. Get you warmed up."

"Like you're getting all of them warmed up?" I asked, throwing an arm in a wide gesture at the room.

Kenosi smirked. "Yeah, like that."

"For what?" I growled. "You can't possibly fuck all these women even if you spent all day doing it."

"I can't?" he asked, quirking an eyebrow. "You underestimate me, Princess."

Holy shit. Could he really fuck a dozen women in a row? I didn't know what was possible, but I didn't think that was. I couldn't go more than two or three times without hobbling around the next day like I'd pulled a muscle. But then, I was a human, and Kenosi wasn't. I had no idea what a shifter could do. The thought sent a flutter through my core.

"Do I sense a challenge?" Kenosi asked. "You're welcome to stay and see if you don't believe me."

"I'll take your word for it," I said with a shake of my head, trying to clear my mind and focus. The adrenaline had worn off, and I found myself so weak I just wanted to sit down so I didn't have to stand another minute.

"Did you come for the show?" he asked. "Because I can make you come for me, too."

"I'm done with your games," I said, anger bubbling through me again. "Just tell me what to do, and I'll do it so I can leave. What do you want? You want to fuck me, right?"

"We're not in the Ocelot Nation anymore, Princess," he said. "You don't make the rules here."

"I'm well aware," I gritted out. "That's why I'm asking what you want."

"I want you to experience powerlessness." He tapped on the shoulders of the girls servicing him. They slid away, leaving him spread out on the pillows, his body nothing short of perfection. His cock stood straight, slick, and—god, just as perfect as the rest of the bastard. "Everyone in power should experience it at least once," he said. "Don't rush the process."

I tore my eyes from his body, so I'd remember that the man

inside that body was a monster. "Like these women?" I asked. "Is that your goal for them, too—powerlessness?"

For a second, his eyes flashed with that glow of gold, his pupils elongating. Fuck. I'd pushed him too far. My heart lurched against my ribs, and I stepped back, wrapping my arms around myself. I watched his fingers, waiting for them to sprout claws and shred the pillows.

Instead, he lifted a lazy hand and gestured to the two women who had been sucking his dick. His eyes were normal, and so were his hands. Kenosi wouldn't lose control like Shadow did. He wasn't a feral shifter, no matter how sick he was. And he wasn't boy the same age as me. He was a thirty-year-old man, and for all I knew, he'd shown me that flash of his cheetah just to scare me.

"Give her the royal treatment, July," he said.

Before I could move, six women were surrounding me. One minute they were on the bed, and the next, they had caged me in before I could so much as blink.

Fuck, cheetahs were fast.

"Get away from me," I warned as one of them stepped against my back.

"It's okay," she purred, her hand dipping into the slit in my dress.

"Whoa there," I said, throwing an elbow. She grabbed it and pinned it behind my back. I tried to wrench free, but her grip was inhuman.

"No fucking way," I growled, throwing a punch with my other hand. The woman there easily ducked the blow and caught my wrist, pulling it down. Their hands were all over me, touching me, binding me. I kicked out, but my legs were lifted from under me until they were supporting my weight, cradling and restraining me. Their hands massaged my legs, my arms. A hand slid between my thighs as I struggled, slipping inside my underwear and caressing my bare skin. I snarled at the woman, but she only moaned and stroked my center, her eyes closing and her head falling back, her lips parted.

"Get off me," I screamed, but they paid no mind. One woman's lips trailed up my arm while another girl tore the strap of my dress with a flick of her wrist. She rolled down the top of my dress, her hands spreading over my full breasts. Moments later, soft lips closed gently over my nipple, a tongue flicking it to life.

I glared at Kenosi, who sat watching from his throne of perversion. "Let me go," I yelled. "Get them away from me."

"I'd enjoy it if I were you," he said. "Open your mind and your knees, Princess, and experience what the world has to offer. So much more than what you've learned in your tiny palace. Relax and see how it feels to be worshipped like a god whether you ask for it or not. They're very good at what they do."

"Your tits are amazing," another woman said, ducking to slide her pink tongue slowly over my nipple. I gasped, a shock of pleasure pulsing between my thighs.

"Fuck you," I growled, kicking out at them. They didn't seem to notice. One of them slid her hand up the slit in my dress again, hooking her finger around the center of my panties and pulling them aside. Her finger tickled my bare skin, and my whole body tensed, trying to squeeze my legs together. The others held me splayed out, though. I was just pissed off enough to be happy that she found me completely dry.

"Bring her to the bed," Kenosi said, and they conveyed my rigid body across the room and lay me at Sir Kenosi's feet like an offering.

I glared up at him, hating him so much I thought my head would explode. "I hope you get a disease and die a slow and horrible death," I said, the words flying out of me like bullets.

"Shifters don't get diseases," he said, gesturing for the girls to go on. They made quick work of my dress, and soon enough, I was as naked as all their beautiful brown bodies. One of them lay beside me, her lips trailing along my cheek.

I squeezed my eyes closed and turned my face away. "Don't you dare think I'll kiss you."

She laughed, a husky sound against my throat, her warm breath sending tingles down my spine. Her lips trailed along my neck, and fuck, all these mouths on me felt...oh god. They felt so good. They offered only pleasure, no pain. Mouths caressed my breasts, my belly. Soft lips closed over my nipples, tugging gently. At last, two mouths moved down my belly, their bodies sinking between my thighs. I bucked, but I was helpless under a half dozen shifters.

Their soft lips kissed my bare mound, then gently probed between my lips. A tremor went through me as one of them tickled my clit with the tip of her tongue. She moaned, dipping deeper, tangling it with the other girl's tongue as they spread my lips and explored my folds. The girl at my neck gave a throaty laugh, her hand massaging the tension from my shoulder as another girl blew cold air across my wet nipple. Suddenly, it was more than my body could handle. Blood rushed to the flesh between my thighs, swelling me with heat. Wetness sprang to life at the sensation of two warm tongues flicking and stroking my pussy.

"You like that, don't you?" Sir Kenosi said, a smirk on his full, beautiful lips. "I can smell how wet your pussy is from here. Maybe next time you won't judge a man for enjoying what feels good."

One of the girls' tongues circled my entrance, and I gasped, looking up at Kenosi with helpless longing. Suddenly, all I wanted, all I needed, was him inside me. I didn't care about my pride or his gloating. I needed more than two small tongues teasing me. I needed a big, stiff cock to fill me and fuck me until the unbearable ache inside me was broken open and released.

"I need you," I whispered, my eyes locked on his. "Sir."

TWENTY

THIS STRANGE LINK SEEMED TO SHIMMER BETWEEN us for a second, as if I were in some kind of echoing tunnel, commanding him in a much more imposing voice. I felt nothing for a beat, as if I were out of my body. A strange shock flickered across his face, a moment of perfect stillness.

And then it was gone.

"It seems the princess would like me to taste her," Kenosi said, rising gracefully from his mountain of pillows. The two girls between my legs moved to either side, holding my knees and watching as Kenosi moved closer. My thighs trembled, and I tried to close them, my mind already beginning to clear. But before I could regain my senses, he was sliding onto the bed, his strong arms caging my hips, his hands sliding around the tops of my thighs and spreading them. With a moan, he buried his head between my legs, his tongue plunging past my opening, the friction of it against my swollen flesh almost unbearable. He slid it deeper and deeper, wriggling inside me like a trapped animal.

I let out a cry of pleasure, and he lifted his head, his lust-clouded gaze meeting mine. In one motion, he shot up my body, burying his cock to the hilt inside me. I cried out in shock, my walls clenching around him as our naked bodies collided. The intimacy not only of our sex, but of our bodies joining together fully, knocked the breath from me.

Kenosi's arms caged me in, his eyes boring into mine. "That's some trick, princess."

"What?" I asked, barely able to breathe past the waves of sensation crashing through me, almost painful in their intensity. Every inch of my skin that was in contact with his ached for more.

As if he could read my mind and wanted to deny me, Kenosi pushed up onto his knees, dragging my hips with him so he could stay buried inside me. "I want to watch this," he said with an edge of gloating in his voice. He wet his lips, watching his thumb skim across my mound and smash down on my swollen clit, smearing my juices across my sensitive skin. I gasped, squirming against him, needing the motion now that he had satisfied my need to be filled.

"Patience, Princess," he said. Another girl crawled over to me, taking my nipple in her mouth and sucking gently. Another took the other side, massaging and flicking her tongue over my nipple. Kenosi knelt between my thighs, gripping my pelvis with an unbreakable hold. He rolled his hips in a smooth, powerful motion, gliding his long, perfect cock out and then burying it deep inside me. A whimper of pleasure escaped me at the soft, insistent suction on my nipples while his cock filled me. My body shuddered with pleasure, my back arching and my thighs spreading in helpless submission. He moved faster with each thrust, an animal growl building inside him with each stroke.

Suddenly he grabbed my ankle and swung it over him, twisting my body so I was lying on my side. Never losing rhythm, he pressed my knees together with one hand, crushing my hip into the bed with his other hand. I gasped at the new sensation, his cock hitting me in ways I hadn't felt before as he pumped into me from the side. My position made my walls squeeze him tighter, and he gave a guttural grunt with each thrust as he pumped his sleek cock into me faster and faster. Heat built inside me until it was almost unbearable, and I cried out for release.

His eyes glowed golden with his cheetah, his breath coming hard and fast. "Tell me what you want, Princess."

"I want your cum," I gasped. "Please, Sir."

"You're about to get it." His fingers gripped me with bruising force as he held my hips and knees still, plunging his cock in one last time. His hips locked to mine as his cum gushed into me in spurt after spurt. My body responded, my walls clenching in rhythmic pulses along his rigid shaft. My whole body shuddered with pleasure as I felt his cock throbbing inside me again and again. Another cry escaped me, and my toes clenched, my scalp tingled, and electricity sparkled through every nerve ending in my body.

When my vision cleared, I saw half a dozen girls circling us, watching with hunger and admiration as I took Sir Kenosi for the first time. Some of them were touching themselves. I didn't know how long they'd been watching instead of engaging with each other, and I suddenly felt painfully exposed. I tried to roll away, but Kenosi held me fast.

"Bring the princess a warm towel," he said to my nurse, who had appeared at some point. "The rest of you are dismissed to your usual duties for the rest of the day."

Sir Kenosi pulled out slowly, and I felt his seed spilling out over my thigh as he withdrew. July appeared with a warm, wet towel, which she gently cleaned me with while I lay there in a quivering ball of exhaustion.

I waited for Kenosi to gloat, but he told July to go. When she had disappeared, he pulled me up the bed, propping us both on his pile of pillows. He drew the sheet over us and slid his arm behind my head like we were lovers instead of captor and captive.

If anything, this felt stranger than the sex. Okay, so he'd fucked me. I'd done that with Lord Balam for weeks before I felt anything. I'd done it with Shadow without meaning, without emotion. But lying in a bed with someone, our naked bodies side by side, made me feel vulnerable in a way that having him between my legs hadn't.

"Did I pass your test yet?" I asked at last, a little seed of bitterness growing in my belly with my hunger.

"Barely," he said. "I don't think you'll make a very good queen if that's the best you can do."

"Ah, so the real Kenosi comes back after you come," I said. "I should have known."

"The real Kenosi just fucked you sideways," he said. "You weren't complaining then."

"If that's all I needed you for, we'd be golden."

He grinned. "What else do you need me for?" he asked. "Does Her Majesty need her pussy sucked again?"

"Her Majesty could use a real meal," I said. "And some real clothes that don't make me look like I'm ready to stand on a street corner. And most of all, I'd like to get back to my sister and the others."

All I could think was that as long as I was here, though, that meant the others hadn't told Kenosi that my sister was the heir. She was safe.

"The food can be arranged," Sir Kenosi said, twisting his body toward mine and running his fingers lightly down my chest and over my sunken belly. "The clothes... I'll have to think about that. I rather like having easy access to that delicious cunt."

"And my friends?" I asked.

"I'm not interested in their cunts."

I gritted my teeth. "When can I see them? I did what you wanted. I sucked your dick. I let you fuck me."

"But you didn't want it," he said. "The lesson is for you to bow down and worship someone else the way you'll be worshipped when you're queen. You didn't come to me wanting me. You have to want me more than I want you. You have to beg me for it."

"I think I did."

His beautiful, full lips twisted to one side. "Did you?" he asked, nuzzling into my neck. "I don't remember that."

"Why do you need me to worship you?" I asked. "You have a whole harem of women to do that, a different set each month. They're all clamoring to get fucked every day. Does your ego really need more?"

"I said you have to want me," he said, rubbing his nose against my earlobe until shivers ran through my body. "Not just fucking."

"Well," I said. "That's not going to happen."

"I bet it will."

"You have a really odd way of trying to make it happen," I said.

He pulled back, a slight smile playing over his lips as he studied me with real interest for the first time since we'd met. "Really?" he asked. "What would you try?"

"Um, first off, I'd try not imprisoning someone and starving them."

"So, if I'd let you stay with your friends these last few days, you'd want me?"

"No," I admitted. "I don't know you. How can I want anything but your body when that's all I know about you?"

He rolled onto his back again, drumming his fingers on his sculpted pecs for a few beats. "You want to talk?"

"That would have been a good place to start."

"Huh," he said. "Women never want to talk to me."

"Maybe that's because you're a colossal asshole who never tries?"

"Possibly," he said, smirking. "Or maybe they just want to fuck."

"Could be," I said. "If you blow their minds in bed, and you're an asshole every time you open your mouth, can you blame them for wanting to keep you in the role of fuck buddy?"

"I never thought of it that way," he said.

"That must be lonely."

Neither of us spoke for a long minute.

"July said she talked to you," Sir Kenosi said after a bit.

"Which one?" I said. "Aren't all your women this month named July?"

"What's that your people say about walking a mile in a man's shoes?"

"I think that saying came from Shadow's people, not mine."

The name of my second lover made a funny knot twist up inside me. I barely knew Shadow, but I knew he'd given up his clan for me. I knew his people had killed my mother, too, though. It was too complicated to dig into with all the things that had happened. Now, I had no idea what had become of him or anyone else from my party. Were they safe and okay? Were they being held captive and tortured?

"It's true, isn't it?" Sir Kenosi said.

"Yes," I admitted. It was true. I didn't know what his life had been like any more than I knew about Shadow's. I knew only what I'd seen in the tabloids, in memes and on posters.

This time, I rolled toward Kenosi, adjusting my head on his arm. "So, tell me," I said. "Make me walk your mile. I can figure out how to be a queen of my own country. What I don't know is what it's like to be famous, or ridiculously wealthy and adored by dozens of lovers, or to be a shifter in the Cheetah Nation."

"Didn't July tell you that?"

"I'm not asking July to tell me," I said. "You want me to want you? Give me a reason. Tell me your story."

A skeptical quirk tugged at his eyebrow. "That works?"

"We'll see."

TWENTY-ONE

I WAS SURE I CAUGHT A FLICKER OF UNCERTAINTY cross Sir Kenosi's face for the first time since I'd met him. "You want to know about my lovers?"

"No," I said. "I want to know about you. How you got here."

"You can read about that in a dozen unauthorized autobiographies."

I pressed my hand over his heart. "No," I said. "I can't."

He swallowed and stared at the ceiling for a long moment before speaking. "I grew up here, same as everyone. In the cheetah village. Basically, the cheetah ghetto where they shoved all the shifters when they found out about us."

"With your family?" I asked, my heart picking up speed.

"For a while." He tapped his fingers on his chest again. "They came to take my mother one night—the humans did. My father tried to stop them, to defend her, and they shot him. My mother shoved me in a box when the men came knocking. She told me not to make a sound, no matter what they did. So I sat there while they dragged her out. They raped her in the street and killed her when they were done."

His voice was flat, his words snapping out with a painful sting.

"Oh my god," I whispered, barely able to speak. "I'm so sorry, Kenosi."

"I had to get a job to buy food," he said. "So, I started working for humans. At first, it was the regular stuff cheetahs did. Shopping for people and bringing their groceries, cleaning their toilets, walking their dogs."

"How old were you?" I asked, sliding my fingers across his chest, interlacing them with his.

"Eight," he said. "It was tough, but lots of kids lived alone in the cheetah section. And there were aid workers from the ICFN who came in sometimes, mostly from the Tiger Nation. They brought food, but better than that, they brought food for our minds. I already knew that money was the answer to everything in this world. I asked for business books, and I studied the people I worked for, trying to figure out what I could give them that no one else was giving them. There had to be a need I could fill."

"And that's where your apps came in," I said.

"That's the interview version," he said with a bitter smile. "What they leave out is the part in between, when I was a teenager. See, when I started to fill out, the jobs people offered changed. Sure, there was manual labor. But it was the women who wanted me to work outside—gardening, mowing, cleaning their pools. I didn't notice the change while it was happening. But then one day one of those rich old pervs wanted me to help her out with a more... Intimate need. You know how some people are about shifters."

"Kitty chasers," I said, nodding despite Kenosi's bitter tone. I hadn't thought of it this way before, though. I'd thought of the shifters having all the power and fame in that relationship, and fangirls chasing after them. But of course it was more complicated, like any fetish. I hadn't thought of the exploitation of those shifters who women chased so eagerly.

"Yeah," Kenosi said. "And I guess that lady enjoyed what I had to offer. Before that, I was lucky to find enough odd jobs to keep myself fed. But pretty soon, I couldn't schedule enough appointments. There literally weren't enough hours in the day to fuck them all."

"I guess it's a lot different when you have control over it."

"What?" Kenosi asked, drawing back to meet my eyes.

"That's probably why you want so many women around you now," I said. "To prove that now you're the one in control."

Kenosi's dark eyes searched mine, like twin pools of black oil. "I hadn't thought of it like that."

I shrugged. "You're rich now. You own everything. You help people out, and they adore you."

"Money really does buy happiness."

"If you say so."

"What does that mean?" he asked, giving me some side-eye. "If you don't believe that, you've never gone without it."

"That's true," I said. "You have, though, and I don't think you're happy. Wealthy? Yes. You have anything you want, after all. If you don't have it, you just snap your fingers, and someone gets it for you. Hell, even a princess. You pay someone enough, they'll lock her up and starve her for you. Women are falling all over themselves for a chance to be the next woman fucked in the famous Sir Kenosi's bed. But under all that, all you really wanted was someone to talk to."

"That's not what I said," Kenosi countered. "I said I wanted you to want me. To beg for it. You said you wanted to talk."

"It's working, isn't it?"

"Is it?" he asked, suspicion clouding his eyes.

"It's working for me," I admitted.

"I'll be damned," Sir Kenosi said. "I can't believe that actually works."

"Well, I'm sure you've never actually had to work for it," I said. "You just flash that million-dollar smile, and they come like flies to honey, right?"

"I have a million-dollar smile?" he asked, showing it off for my benefit.

I rolled my eyes. "There's at least a dozen gifs of it."

"Like I said, there's nothing fame and money can't buy," he said. "Usually I flash the million dollars to get what I want, not the smile."

"That only works because your shifters got fucked over by the humans in this country," I said. "If everyone else wasn't living in abject poverty, I don't think your money would have the same effect."

He chuckled. "You're wrong. King Cheetah is still the king, but no one cares what he thinks about things. When the ICFN comes visiting, they let him weigh in, but if we have opposing views, you know who they side with?"

I didn't answer because I didn't want to admit he was probably right.

"I can get things done," he said. "The king can't. Money means more than titles in this world, not just our nation."

"I don't think it's like that everywhere," I argued.

"Then you're naïve," he said. "You have a title, but I could still order my guards to lock you in a room, and they did what I wanted because they want to keep their jobs. They don't give a rat's ass what title you have. A title matters because someone allows it to matter. Money matters because it gets shit done."

I couldn't deny that having the title of princess did very little for me. But it wasn't because I didn't have money. It was because I didn't have magic. That was my handicap. I came from money, but I was nothing in our world. He came from nothing, but now he had money, so he was someone. He also had magic, but I couldn't debate whether that was more important than money without giving myself away as the unimportant princess.

"Maybe you're right," I said, sliding an arm over Kenosi. "I know I can't understand what you went through to get here."

"No?" Kenosi asked, a tone of mocking entering his voice. "The princess didn't have to pimp herself out for bread money for ten years so she could save up for something better?"

Instead of reacting to his barbed comment, I shrugged. "You're right. I never realized how privileged we had it in the Ocelot Nation. My life was... Damn easy, it turns out. But I do understand what it's like to not be in control of your own life. To feel like a second-class citizen in society's eyes."

When Sir Kenosi scoffed, I snapped my mouth closed, cursing myself furiously. What the fuck was I saying? I had basically just outed myself as not being the heir, right after thinking that's exactly what I couldn't do. Talking wasn't just making me understand Kenosi. It was making me feel closer to him, to forget I was playing a game here. Comfortable was dangerous.

"It took you ten years to make the dating app?" I asked, hoping to divert us from the more personal details.

"Yeah," he said. "At first, it was a kind of secret app that only people here used to find cheetahs. But I always planned for it to go big. I knew there must be people like that everywhere, humans who had a thing for cats, and not just cheetahs. Shifters, and not just cats. And supernaturals in general, not just shifters. The only thing I hadn't anticipated was supernaturals finding each other. The app kept growing. And so did all this." He gestured around at the huge room, the lavish furnishings and giant bed. "The reality shows came next, then the fame, then the women."

"But somewhere inside, you must know they aren't here for you," I said. "Otherwise you wouldn't have asked me to want *you*."

Kenosi narrowed his eyes. "No, I wanted you to want me the same as they do."

I remembered all the times Tadeu complained about the women he fucked getting all attached, and it was my turn to feel stupid. "Well, it's not like I'm going to fall in love," I said. "But I think I understand you, and it's hard to hate you when I understand you. Is that good enough? Or does it just make me a total woman?"

"I don't know," Kenosi said slowly. "I don't guess I actually know women that well, aside from how to fuck them."

"Sir Kenosi doesn't know women," I teased. "Can I get that on record?"

"Never," he said, throwing off the sheet. "Want to get some breakfast?"

About fucking time.

Twenty-Two

Prince Kwame
Lion Shifter, Lion Nation

I STOOD IN THE GRASS, WATCHING THE STORM ROLL toward the savannah. There was something more coming this time. I could feel it. Could sense it.

"What is it, Kwame?" One of the other lions, maybe a grandfather or long lost cousin, bumped my hip with his. I'd been in lion form for so long I didn't know exactly who people were anymore. I knew who lions were. Every day, the knowledge of who they had been in their human form seemed further away.

At first, I'd held on so tightly. I had been sure that I would go back. That I could be human again. I measured time by the moon, so I would know how much had passed when I finally came back to myself. My human self.

But that had slowly faded until only the desire remained. I knew I wanted to be human again, needed it. I could remember why it wasn't possible, but I no longer believed that I would find a way around that.

"Something is coming," I said in the way that we talked, tossing my head toward the bank of clouds, electricity lighting them from within.

He gave me a picture of rain, but I lifted my nose and scented as if I couldn't see it. I could. I knew rain approached, and more than that. Thunder that shook the planes, lightning that split the sky and the trees. But something more. Not with the storm, but it was coming.

I turned and loped toward the shelter where my family lived. My human family. Some of the lions didn't go back, didn't want to remember. After a while, it became easier to live this way, in our skin, and forget what we had ever been. But giving up my human was as impossible as it would have been for me to give up one half of my head.

My mother leapt to her feet when I nosed through the wooden door, which stood ajar.

"Kwame? Is that you?" she asked. She knew it was. She recognized my lion form as well as she'd recognized my human one. She ran to me and dropped to her knees, wrapping her arms around me. I lifted a paw and rested it on her upper back, but it wasn't enough. It wasn't the embrace my mother deserved.

Even in lion form, with so much forgotten, I knew how much older she looked than when I'd last seen her with my human eyes. I wanted more than anything to tell her that she didn't have to worry about me. I wanted to lie, so she could stop growing older with grief. But I could only offer what little comfort my visits afforded. If they gave her any comfort at all. Maybe they only reminded her of what she'd lost— what we both had.

If only there were a way to come back to her. To rejoin my family, to rejoin the human world. Maybe that was what was coming. I could feel a change on the horizon, but I didn't know what it was. Something big. Someone powerful. I wanted to warn her, but I could only make sure that I saw her one more time, in case that someone took them from me. My last connection to the human world, the last piece of my humanity.

I could only hold on a little longer.

TWENTY-THREE

Itzel
Princess, Ocelot Nation

"OH MY GOD, THIS IS THE BEST FUCKING STEAK I'VE ever eaten," I said, slicing off another bite and chewing, my eyes falling closed as the delicious, salty juices spread over my tongue.

"I'm glad you think so," Sir Kenosi said, sounding slightly amused. I didn't care if I looked like a glutton. I was hungry as fuck, and I was pretty sure that I could orgasm from the deliciousness of the steak alone.

"So, if you're not going to let me see my friends, can I at least know what's going on with them?" I asked. "Where are they? Is my sister okay?"

"She is," Sir Kenosi said, slicing into his steak while holding it with his fork.

I was tempted to pick mine up and gnaw on it like a chicken leg, but I refrained. "Have you seen her?" I asked.

"Of course," Kenosi said, sounding surprised by my question.

"And Gabor?" I asked. "He got hit pretty hard the day we got here."

"I remember," Sir Kenosi said. "And he's fine, as well."

"Well?" I asked, lowering my fork and swallowing. "Where are they?"

"They're in the guest quarters," Sir Kenosi said.

My stomach dropped, and I thought my food would make a reappearance when I pictured Kenosi going down to visit my sister. "You didn't..." I stopped speaking and grabbed my wine glass, swallowing a mouthful so fast it made my eyes burn. "You haven't been treating her the way you've been treating me, have you?"

Sir Kenosi had the nerve to throw back his head and laugh. I contemplated whether I could slit his throat with my steak knife while it was exposed, but cheetahs were fast as fuck, so I held myself in check. My hand clenched around the handle of the knife while I waited. "That frigid little prude?" Kenosi said, dabbing at the corner of his eye. "I have no interest in getting frostbite on my dick."

I secretly cheered Camila's poise as I took another bite. I wondered how she was holding up. I knew my sister would be worried sick, probably in a panic that she couldn't see me. She needed me by her side more than ever in this foreign place. Even if the king had no power, she'd had an appointment with him. She had probably thought he could give her the amulet, or order Sir Kenosi to do so. Who was helping her calm her nerves and face her fears in my absence?

"Where do the others think I am?" I asked. "Are you telling them I died in the clinic?"

Kenosi laughed and sipped his wine. "I told them you're in diplomatic meetings, and you're working hard to gain the amulet."

"Oh," I said, sitting back. It was better than him telling them I was dead... Or telling the truth. Shame warmed my cheeks at the memory of what I'd done for this steak. But also, there was excitement with it, a flutter of heat in my thighs at the thought of Sir Kenosi's strong, perfect body kneeling over mine, sliding that big, beautiful, black cock into me.

"So, when do I get to go back to them?" I asked, moving a slice of sweet potato across my plate. "I've done everything you asked. Speaking of, I'm still waiting for that amulet, too."

Sir Kenosi chuckled. "After watching you eat, I was beginning to question whether you were a princess after all," he said. "But with demands like that, my faith is restored."

"Your nation welcomed us and told us they would meet with us on the Amulet Tour," I said, my gaze steady on his. "You knew what we were here for, and you said you'd give it to me.

I'm not making demands. I'm asking for what was promised."

"Then show me how much you want me," he said. "Show me you want me as much as you want that steak."

"Fine," I said. "If it will get me back to the others, I'll suck your dick until it turns blue."

I pushed back from the table and went to Sir Kenosi. He pushed his chair back, too, an amused expression on his face as he slouched down in his seat. For some reason, a picture of my first encounter with Lord Balam swam into my mind. If that whore could suck off Father's diplomats like that, I could give just as good a performance.

I slid my hand behind my neck, drawing my hair over one shoulder, and gave Sir Kenosi my most alluring smile. Licking my lips, I dropped to my knees in front of him. He sat holding his wine glass, swiping his tongue inside his cheek to clear his mouth of the food we'd been eating.

"Go on," he said. "Show me what you've got."

"Patience, Sir," I murmured, peering up at him from under my lashes. I slid my hands up his thighs, pleased to see a slight swell beginning to grow in his pants. Maybe I had started to want him, but he clearly wanted me just as much.

I drew down his zipper, rising on my knees to reach his lap. I nuzzled along his hardening length, kissing him through his pants. He sipped his wine and sat back, watching me reach into his pants and draw out his long, beautiful cock. I dipped my head, letting my lips play along its incredible length. His cock throbbed, and my own body responded, my clit pulsing with pleasure. I inhaled his scent, masculine and slightly spicy, and my heart picked up speed.

Opening my lips, I gently tugged the skin at the head of his cock, flicking out my tongue to taste him. My own juices had dried on him, and the taste of him mixed with the taste of me made my head swim with desire. I sank my mouth onto his cock, moaning in pleasure as my tongue slid over his shaft. My saliva wet him, and he sucked in a slow breath.

"Yeah, Princess," he said. "Suck me like the royal whore."

Instead of bristling, I found my knees weakening and my thighs slickening with arousal. I drew back up, circling the head of his cock with my tongue. A drop of saltiness spread over my tongue, and I had to suppress another moan. I wrapped my hand around the base of his cock, sinking my mouth onto it onto it until it hit the back of my throat. I fought my gag reflex, tears springing into my eyes. Saliva trickled over my hand, and I slurped to suck it back in, but my mouth was watering from the taste of his cum. Wetness dripped down my thighs under my dress, and I slid my free hand down my body, cupping my mound and rocking against the exquisite pressure.

Kenosi's fingers tightened on his wine glass, and he gave a low moan, dropping his head back. His cock throbbed inside my mouth, wetting the back of my throat this time. I fisted my hand in the fabric of my dress, drawing it up further, sinking my hand underneath the hem and between my thighs. Pleasure rolled through me as I clutched

Kenosi's rigid cock, thrusting it into my mouth again and again.

"Are you touching yourself?"

Sir Kenosi's words rumbled through my haze of lust, and I lifted my eyes to his, helplessness trembling through my body as my fingers dipped into my wet slit. I nodded, not releasing his cock from my lips.

Sir Kenosi grabbed my upper arms and hauled me to my feet, spinning me around and bending me over the table. A wine glass toppled, and my chest slammed onto a plate. I cried out in surprise as he grabbed my skirt and gave a tremendous yank, the fabric ripping to shreds as he tossed it aside. He dropped to his knees behind me, spreading my sex open and driving his long tongue deep into me. I gasped in pleasure, my hands curling around the edges of the table as his rough, wet tongue filled my pussy, sliding deeper with each pass.

"I want you," I said, my cheek pressed to the smooth surface. "Fine, you win. I want you, Sir. Now fuck me."

"I give the orders," Sir Kenosi said, standing and gripping my thigh, his fingers digging into my flesh with bruising force. "Now spread 'em for me."

I opened my legs, planting my feet wide. Kenosi grabbed my hands, pulling them behind me, so my chest was flat on the table. He brought my hands around my back and placed them on my round ass. "Open for me."

My cheek pressed into the smooth surface of the table, the heat burning in my face cooled by a pool of Chardonnay, but I obeyed his command, spreading myself open for him. I'd never been so exposed, but when I started to rise, Sir Kenosi pressed his hand between my shoulder blades, holding me down, smearing me in the potatoes on my plate. He dropped his pants, positioning his cock along my open crack. "How much do you want this inside you, Princess? As much as you wanted that steak inside you?"

"Yes, Sir," I said.

"Good girl," he said, sliding the head of his cock slowly back, pressing the rigid head against my knotted entrance. I gasped, my back arching as wetness filled my pussy.

"Now spread that tight little pussy open just as wide, and I'll fuck you so hard your friends ask why you're walking funny. Is that what you want?"

"Yes, Sir," I breathed, sliding my hands down my slick folds. I opened my pussy lips, and a drop of my juices escaped and trickled down my thigh.

"Wider," Sir Kenosi commanded. "I want to see those pink pussy lips stretched around my big black cock."

When I pulled myself open further, Kenosi gave a low growl and pressed the head of his hot cock against my entrance. The pleasure was dizzying, and a wordless cry escaped my lips. My back arched, but he flattened his palm against me, pinning me down again. He held his cock to my opening, slicking it through my juices until I was nearly whimpering with frustration. Then he held himself tight to me and began to press harder, sinking his smooth shaft into me with excruciating slowness.

I released my hold on the edges of the table, pressing my palms flat on the cool surface. I was about to ignite into flame. My hands opened and closed into fists, needing something to hold, but Kenosi kept me face down on the table until he was buried to the hilt inside me.

"Now you can beg," Sir Kenosi said.

"Yes, sir," I managed. "I want you. Fuck me."

He chuckled, his voice low in his throat. "Where are your manners, Princess?"

I squeezed my eyes closed, trying not to scream with the frustration building inside me. "Please," I whispered.

"Please...?"

"Please, Sir. Please fuck me. I need you."

Relief and pleasure coiled through me as he drove into me so deeply I gasped and arched up, a mixture of pleasure and pain rippling through my body. My chest was on a plate, and I could feel food smearing onto my skin, but Kenosi didn't let me up. He began to move faster, positioning himself behind me so he could slam into me with each punishing thrust. His hips slapped my ass as he drove into me harder and harder, ramming me full of his cock with every pass. A wine glass tumbled over, wine spilling across the table, and another crashed to the floor as Kenosi pounded me against the table, knocking it a few inches with each thrust. His hand fisted in my hair, yanking my head back as he drove my hips forward with a guttural grunt. Pain rippled through my scalp and I grabbed at his hand, but he only knotted his hand tighter. My body clenched in pain, and hot cum shot into. me, spurting against my protesting walls.

To my surprise, my own orgasm pulsed through me. His name escaped my lips, and I lay helpless on the table, my cheek stained with wine, waves of pleasure slamming through me.

"I like it when you tighten up for me," Sir Kenosi said, his hand loosening in my hair as he smiled down at me, a gloating expression on his smug face.

"Can't speak," I muttered. "Brain dead."

Kenosi laughed, and for the first time, it sounded genuine and full of humor. He leaned forward and kissed my back, his full lips lingering on the skin just below the nape of my neck. A small chill of pleasure raced through me.

He pulled away then, and a cry of protest almost escaped me. I wanted him there longer, his body against mine as it had been in the bed earlier.

"Well done, Princess," he said, picking up my torn skirt and handing it back. I took it, still too dazed to answer. I couldn't form a complete thought, let alone a sentence. We stared at each other a minute, both of us breathing hard.

"You know, maybe money isn't everything," Kenosi said, zipping his pants. "It doesn't mean much when even the people who want you don't want to be around you."

"I did everything you asked," I said through clenched teeth.

"I know," Sir Kenosi said, turning away. "You wanted me. You even begged. But in the end, you're going to go back to your friends. All the money in the world doesn't mean anything if everyone leaves the moment you unlock the door."

"You're right," I said softly, my heart throbbing against my ribs at the bitterness in his tone.

He thrust his hands into his pockets, his back still turned to me. "I shouldn't have kept you from them," he said. "Go. See your friends. Be with your people. That's where a princess belongs."

"Really?" I asked. And even though my heart hurt for him, it was racing in my chest at the thought of escape. Freedom. My sympathy for him wasn't going to stop me from being another person who walked out on him.

"Go," he said again.

Without another word, without letting him have time to change his mind, I sprinted for the door.

TWENTY-FOUR

MY HANDS SHOOK AS I REACHED FOR THE BUTTON in the elevator. What if it didn't work? What if I was locked in—again? Despite the past hour, when July had changed my bandages and assured me that I was healing well, then let me shower and change into a pair of jeans and a tank top instead of another ridiculously revealing ensemble, I still couldn't quite believe I was going to be able to see my friends.

"I'm glad you've come around to see what a wonderful man Sir Kenosi is," July said, shooting me a shy smile as the elevator doors slid closed.

I grunted in response. It was kinda weird being alone with her now that she'd been up close and personal with my vagina.

"Your friends have been staying here," she said as the elevator stopped on the third floor. "In the servants' quarters."

"Wait, what?" I asked, skidding to a stop halfway out the elevator doors. "They're not servants. Sir Kenosi said they were in the guest quarters."

"Oh, no," she said, giggling and waving a hand to dismiss the idea. "Sir Kenosi wants everyone to contribute in some way while they are here, though. It makes them feel like part of the community."

I didn't see how putting guests to work would make them feel anything but resentful, but then, we weren't in the Ocelot Kingdom. Customs were different here. I tried not to think about what Camila had thought of that. Instead, I hurried down the hallway calling my sister's name. The servants' quarters looked kind of like a nice hotel, with doors opening off a hallway with wall sconces and plush carpeting.

A door burst open, and Lord Balam swept me into his arms, crushing me to his chest so hard I couldn't breathe. "What the fuck, Itzel?"

"You're telling me," I managed from inside his vicelike grip. "Where's Camila?"

"She's fine," Lord Balam said. "A royal pain in the ass, like usual, but fine."

Relief flooded through me, and I relaxed into Balam's arms. To my horror, tears suddenly sprang into my eyes. "Thank all the gods," I said, my voice muffled against his shirt.

"I'm sure Her Highness will be royally pissed if we don't go see her right away," he said. "I just had to see you for a second first. How are you?" He held me at arm's length, surveying my face.

I swallowed back my tears and gave a small laugh. "I'm fine," I said. "More than fine. I'm great. I just want to make sure she's okay. I have to see it with my own eyes."

Lord Balam studied me a moment longer, long enough to make me squirm. I didn't know what he'd seen in his oracle, but he obviously knew something had happened to me. "Okay," he said at last. He pulled me in and planted a firm kiss on my mouth.

When he released me, I followed him down the hall to another room, where he knocked on the door. I started to tell him that she was my sister, and I didn't have to knock, but then I stopped myself. So much had happened so fast that I'd forgotten our argument in my urgency to see her. Before I'd been separated from the group, Camila had been so angry at me that she'd tried to leave me in Florida with Lord Balam. We'd gone after her, but she'd been in ocelot form for the entire trip here. Almost as soon as we arrived, I'd been taken from them. I had no idea if she was still mad at me.

The door opened, and Gabor stood in the entrance. His eyes widened when he saw me, and for a second, everything that had passed between us seemed to sit in the beat of silence. "Princess Itzel," he said, giving a slight bow. "Come in. Her Grace will be pleased that you have returned."

"It's Itzel?" Camila's voice floated from behind Gabor. I glanced from him to the room, then back to the guard. When our eyes met, I was sure there was some hint of guilt.

"They gave us one room," he said quickly. "We slept in shifts. I wasn't... The princess was guarded at all times. Her reputation was never in question."

I'd never seen Camila's stone-faced guard so flustered, and it made me realize with sadness that he probably wanted her in a way that *would* put her reputation at risk. No one would know. We were an ocean away from home. It was the perfect time for her to experience what she wanted before becoming queen. That was probably another purpose for the Amulet Tour, I realized. Or at least something that heirs took advantage of. The amulets were all about mating, after all.

I swallowed hard, picturing them having moments similar to the ones I'd had with Sir Kenosi. Even if Gabor had done those things with my sister, I couldn't blame him. He had needs, too. I'd teased him mercilessly in Florida, hooking up with Lord Balam while he could certainly hear us. Of course he would want to be with a woman, and it wasn't like I'd been around to do it, even if he had wanted me.

I couldn't blame either of them. Gabor was beautiful, and Camila was the sweet one, the innocent one, the pretty one. They were a match. I was the hot mess. I wasn't mate material for an ocelot. Now that I was back with the group, I had to remember my place in it. I was simply an instrument for getting the amulets and getting Camila to the throne. If Father thought I'd been ruined after seducing Lord Balam, well, there wasn't a man in the Ocelot Kingdom who would take me after what I'd done with him, and Shadow, and Sir Kenosi.

Gabor was among the men who would want nothing to do with me—not that he ever would have. It wasn't just that I was human, and he was more than that. I'd already told him how I felt, and he'd told me he didn't—couldn't—feel the same.

I squared my shoulders and addressed the guard properly. "Thank you for your continuing, exemplary service."

"Your Grace," he said, stepping aside and gesturing for me to enter.

I rushed in to find Camila sitting on a narrow bed with a plain, drab comforter. The room looked like a hotel room, too. There was a small bathroom near the door, and a tiny kitchenette area with a coffee pot, sink, microwave, and a cabinet.

"I see you've deigned to visit us," Camila said, crossing her arms and glaring.

I stopped short, blinking at her in surprise. I had been so eager to see her that I hadn't properly considered how she might feel about me right now. She nodded to a small screen that showed an empty, enormous bed with a white canopy.

My heart nearly stopped. "Is that—What is that?"

"It's your room," she said. "While you were living in luxury, being wined and dined by the movie star, we've been taking shifts sleeping on a single bed."

"I... I'm sorry?" I said, not knowing what else to say. Apparently, they hadn't shown her everything. Another thought slammed into me, and I nearly doubled over and lost my steak dinner. What if she'd missed some of the things that happened in that room because it had been Gabor's shift in the room? Had he seen my performance with Kenosi near the elevator? Did he know it wasn't by choice?

In truth, though, I had enjoyed every encounter I'd had with the infuriating, impossible playboy. My face burned at the thought, and I couldn't even look in Gabor's direction.

Color rose to Camila's cheeks, and I realized she thought my blush was an admission of the luxurious state I'd been living in while she stayed in this utilitarian room.

"Did you get the amulet?" she asked through clenched teeth.

"No," I admitted. When Kenosi offered me my friends, I'd jumped at the chance so fast I'd forgotten what it had all been for. Shame burned through me at the realization of what I'd done, and with nothing more gained than what I'd had to start with.

"I can't believe you," Camila fumed, jumping up from the bed. "Here I was, listening to your lover when he said not to reveal my identity to the cheetahs. I bet you were both in on it. Just eating up all that attention, those fancy dinner parties and clothes. But it was all a lie, Itzel. He wasn't trying to impress you. That whole time, he thought you were the heir. He was trying to impress *me*."

"That's not what he was doing," I started.

"Well, guess what?" Camila said, continuing like I'd never spoken. "I'm going to tell him. I'm going to tell him you're just a common human, and I'm the queen. I'm going to tell him that you tricked him all that time. Then we'll see where you sleep tonight."

"That's really not a good idea," Lord Balam said.

"I'm done listening to you," Camila said, rounding on him. "You're not on my side. You've never been on my side. You're on her side."

"Your Grace," Gabor said. "I don't think Sir Kenosi is the sort of man whose attention you want to catch."

Camila planted her hands on her hips, her nostrils flaring and her eyes narrowing to slits. "You're supposed to be on my side, Gabor. You're supposed to look out for me. But I'm seriously beginning to doubt where your loyalty lies."

Gabor's face blanched, but he clenched his jaw and didn't speak.

"Camila," I said. "He's right. You really don't want to go up there."

"I'm done with everyone ganging up on me," she said. "I'm the true princess. If none of you will treat me like it, I'm sure Sir Kenosi will." She pushed past Gabor and Lord Balam, who stood in her path to the door.

"I will escort you," Gabor said, but Camila wheeled around, her eyes flashing.

"You've done enough," she hissed. "You don't have my best interest in mind after all. You're as much a liar as Itzel." She whipped around and marched out.

"Camila," I called, hurrying after my sister. "You can't go up there. Sir Kenosi is a monster."

She almost choked on her laughter, but she didn't slow. "A monster who put you up in the best room in his palace while I slept in the servants' quarters like a commoner." She spit the last word out like it described trash instead of her own sister.

Suddenly a figure towered over me. I hadn't even heard a door open, but Shadow stood blocking my path. He reached out like he might touch me, then drew back, disbelief written all over his face. "Itzel?" he asked in his papery, hoarse voice. "Is that really you?"

"It's really me," I said. "But I really need to stop my sister before she does something dangerous."

"More dangerous?" he asked, without a trace of a smile. "Let her go, Itzel. She won't listen to you. She won't listen to anyone."

"I know my sister," I said. "If I tell her what really happened..."

"Like I'd believe you," Camila called from the end of the hall, where she was stepping into the elevator. I pushed past Shadow and sprinted on my legs, which felt only barely useable after not eating for so long. The lunch had given me strength, but not enough. I barely reached the elevator as the doors slid closed.

Without thinking, I thrust my arm through the crack before it sealed shut. "Camila, listen to me," I panted. "He's not what you think. He's basically made himself king of this country, and all the women are his sex slaves."

"I bet you enjoyed that," she said, hitting a button. Our eyes met, and the coldness I saw there shocked me. The elevator started moving, and I wrenched at my arm, yelping in pain as it was dragged upward. Suddenly the elevator shuddered, and a pair of hands appeared below my arm, gripping the metal sides that held it fast. The metal squealed as it slowly bent, unclamping from my arm. Camila shrieked in fear, and my heart lurched with the instinctual urge to protect her.

But she wasn't my ally anymore.

I fell backward against Gabor's chest as he released the elevator. The doors slid closed around the bent edge, and the car slid upward and out of sight.

Twenty-Five

"She hates me," I whispered. All I could do was sag against the guard, reeling with pain. I barely felt my arm. It was the hole caving in inside my chest that consumed me.

Gabor scooped me up into his arms, carrying me back to the room he shared with Camila as if he were a conquering hero, and I was his captured bride. Except he hadn't conquered me. My sister had. That coldness in her eyes made her look more like a snake than a cat. I'd seen her level diplomats with it, but never me. She'd never looked at me that way.

I had been on her side, had her back through everything since we were kids, even before Mom died. I had loved her and supported her, had built my life around hers. I had grown around her like a tree growing around a fence, accommodating for her weaknesses and hiding her flaws. I had done it all for her, loving her with unwavering fierceness for exactly who she was. If I was her backbone, she was my heart. And now she was cutting herself free of me, and it felt like she was tearing my chest open while I was still alive, spreading my ribcage and letting birds peck out my insides.

"Princess Itzel," Gabor said, setting me down on the bed. "Can I get you anything?"

"No," I said, clinging to his neck and not caring how pathetic I sounded. "Just hold me."

His body remained rigid, but after a second, one hand rested tentatively on my hip. "Your Grace..."

"Stay," I whispered.

His head turned ever so slightly, his face brushing against my hair, and I felt his slow inhalation. His fingers tightened on my waist, and he lifted his head, turning away. "I can't," he said, his voice strangled. "Let me go, Princess."

I didn't think anything could make the pain worse, but I was wrong. I squeezed my eyes closed, feeling the tears wet my lashes. I couldn't watch him go.

I heard the door close quietly, and then the tears came. I curled onto my side, holding the middle of me as if I could keep it from imploding. I didn't hear the door again, but suddenly, Shadow was standing over me. Lord Balam pushed past him and slid onto the bed, curling his body around mine, holding me steady as I shook and sobbed. Shadow slipped over me, melting onto the bed in front of me, curling up to match my position, his knees pressed to mine, his forehead against my damp forehead, his hands wrapping around mine as if to anchor me.

I didn't know if anything could ever anchor me again, though. A month ago, I'd had all the roots a girl could want. I'd had a home, a family, even if things with Father had never been ideal. I'd had a man I loved, one I'd planned to spend the rest of my life with. I'd had a sister I loved, who loved me and trusted me, and a position in court lined up for me that would last a lifetime. I'd had a nation I believed in, one I was proud to help rule.

Now, I had none of that. I'd disgraced Father. The man I'd loved so hard, so innocently, was dead. The dream I'd had of being an advisor looked more unreachable every day. In truth, I wasn't even sure I wanted it unless I could make major changes, reach out to the other nations and help them in a way the isolationist ocelots never had. And worst of all, I'd lost my sister. It was like losing the best part of myself. Without her, I would never feel truly complete. She was my other half—my better half.

I lay there for a long while, crying too hard to be ashamed of my tears. I'd heard crying was supposed to make you feel better, but I always tried to avoid it, not wanting to look weak. But now that I'd let go, shown my weakness, I didn't feel better at all. I felt as if my chest had been hollowed out and scraped raw, leaving an ache as relentless as a toothache.

"Where's Gabor?" I asked at last.

"He ran off after your sister," Lord Balam said.

A fresh tear leaked out at the mention of Camila. I wiped it away, realizing what a mess I must look. "Sorry," I said, sitting up and wiping my face with my tank top. "You really didn't have to stay and watch me ugly cry."

"It's not ugly," Shadow said, sitting up beside me, his long legs folded beside him.

"Then you obviously had your eyes closed and didn't see it," I said, laughing a little. "I swear I'm not usually such a baby."

"Crying doesn't make you weak," Lord Balam said, prying a lock of hair from my sticky cheek and tucking it behind my ear. "It's just an expression of emotion. You're hurt. You cried. There's no shame in it. It just is."

"How'd you get so wise?" I asked, leaning my head on his shoulder.

"Years of being unwise taught me how," he said. "Now, you want to tell us what happened to you over the past week?"

"Not really," I said, running my thumbnail along the seam on the outside of my jeans. "But I guess I should at least give you the basics."

"We all know you weren't relaxing in splendor," Lord Balam murmured, running his palm in slow circles over my back. "And even if you had been, after the last month, we wouldn't have blamed you. There's no shame from us, Itzel. We're here for you."

"But I failed," I said with a sigh. "I didn't get the amulet."

"You will."

I opened my mouth to ask whether he'd asked the oracle, but I decided against it. The conviction in his voice was enough for me. I didn't need to know where he'd gotten it.

"Thank you," I said, taking a deep breath before diving in. I told them an abbreviated version of the story, but even that version had Lord Balam steaming mad. Shadow sat quietly beside me, his arm resting lightly around my back. "How am I supposed to get the amulet now?" I asked. "I've already given him everything."

"Not everything," Shadow said in his low, growly voice.

I turned to him. "Did you not hear my story? I gave him everything, including my dignity. I didn't even ask for the amulet. There's no way he's going to just hand it over for nothing." I jumped up, staggering with the thought that had hit me. "Oh my god. He's going to make Camila take my place. What's better than fucking a princess? Fucking two."

"You didn't give him the other amulets," Shadow said.

I spun to face him. "What do you mean? There's no point trading one amulet for another. I'd just need him to give me the panther amulet instead of the cheetah amulet."

"I didn't mean you'd let him keep it," Shadow said.

"Oh." I stared at him a long moment. In all the chaos since I'd gotten the panther amulet, I'd never even found out what it did.

"The panther amulet is very powerful," Shadow rasped. "It shows a feline his True Mate."

"You think he'll trade his amulet for that?"

"Shifters go their whole lives searching," he said. "To see her, to have her marked as his mate... Most people would do anything for that."

"Come on, then," I said. "What are we waiting for? We need to get up there before anything bad happens. Fuck, I hope Gabor got her in time." I couldn't help being concerned for her, even if she hated me. I couldn't undo the years of worrying about her. I couldn't change the fact that I still worried, still loved, even if she didn't.

"She doesn't listen to him, either," Shadow said. "She's a problem, Itzel. She's reckless, and it puts us all in danger. You wouldn't have been hurt, been put in that clinic, if we hadn't had to rescue her from the attack back home."

"It's too late to do anything about that," I said. "But you're right. She has no idea what danger she's in right now."

"She needs to go home," Lord Balam said.

I felt like a traitor as I stared at him, realizing that my sister was right this time. I wasn't on her side. She wanted to stay, and I knew that she couldn't. We'd never finish the tour if Sir Kenosi got hold of her. She'd be broken not just for this trip, but forever. I had to protect her even if she didn't want me to. No matter what she said or how much she hurt me, I would always want her to be safe.

But plotting to send her home from her own Amulet Tour, to take it over and do it for her, felt like the shadiest thing I'd ever done. No wonder she thought I'd betrayed her. I was obviously capable of that kind of deviousness.

"No," I said. "I can't do that. It's her tour. I'm just a strategist. Now, if we want to get Kenosi to bargain with us, we need the panther amulet. It must be in this room somewhere."

I planted my hands on my hips and scanned the room quickly, searching for a place she would stow something so precious. Had she used it to see her True Mate? Probably not. After seeing what the jaguar amulet did, she probably wouldn't risk it. Even if Shadow had told her what it did—and I doubted he had—she wouldn't trust him enough to believe it.

"Why did you give it to her?" Shadow asked, looking down at his hands dangling between his knees. Even the way he sat was so animal, so primal, as if he could rise from the bed and be in panther form by the time he stood.

"It's hers," I said.

"She took the amulet and tried to ditch you in Florida. Why are you getting the next one for her?"

"That's not what happened," I said, dropping my hands and slumping in defeat. "I overstepped. Camila didn't want me on her tour. She sent me home."

Shadow blinked at me, incomprehension written across his strong, angular features. "But you already got two amulets for her. How can she think you're unsuited?"

I shrugged. "I'm human, for one. And for another, it's not my tour. She gets to decide who goes with her."

"I wouldn't have given the amulet to her," Shadow said.

"Isn't that kind of the point?" I said. "It sounds like you're supposed to trick it from everyone."

"You think Camila's going to be able to trick anyone?" Lord Balam asked.

"It doesn't matter what I think," I said. "It's not my tour."

We stood there in silence for a minute.

"She'll forgive you when she needs you," Lord Balam said at last.

"What does that mean?" I asked, bristling at the insult to Camila.

"You do too much for your sister," he said. "You could have been killed in Florida."

"He's not a killer," I said, gesturing at Shadow.

"I wasn't talking about him," Lord Balam said. "But we didn't know that at the time, either. And you didn't know Kenosi wasn't. You sacrifice yourself for her. Not just your body. Your happiness."

"I'm happy," I said.

He and Shadow wore identical, sober expressions as they waited for me to admit I'd just been sobbing my guts out over her. Still, I was a happy person. At least, I had been. Even a happy person could be sad when their life was spun upside down and turned inside out.

"If she tried to send you home, maybe we should just leave," Shadow said. "Let her get the amulets herself."

"No," I said. "No way. She won't survive it."

"Then she has no business being queen."

I glared at him for a long minute. At last I had to drop my gaze from his burning green eyes. "I'm not going to let her get herself killed," I said. "Maybe you're right about her. But part of what you said is she's a danger to herself. And I'm her sister. It's my job to protect her, even if she hates me for it right now. You don't have to help me if you don't want. But I can't live with myself if I don't at least try to help her."

"We'll help," Lord Balam said, picking up Camila's bag and rifling through it. "Or at least I'll help. I can't speak for the Keeper."

Shadow growled, the sound low and reverberating like a panther was about to leap out of his chest.

"I'll take that as a no," I said, turning to survey the room so he wouldn't see how much his refusal stung.

"I'll help you," Shadow said. "But I can't in good conscience help your sister take over your country. She's more dangerous than even your father."

I narrowed my eyes at him. "What makes you think that?"

"Observation," he said.

Lord Balam raised an eyebrow. "That's saying a lot, coming from you, Shadow."

"I don't want to talk about it," Shadow growled.

"Talk about what?" I asked.

"Nothing," Shadow said. "Let's find that amulet."

TWENTY-SIX

IT DIDN'T TAKE US LONG TO FIND WHAT WE WERE looking for. The servants' quarters were as sparse as they were plain. There weren't a lot of places to hide things, but we found the two amulets wrapped in a silk scarf and stuffed under the mattress. At least she'd hidden them as well as she could and wasn't keeping them on her person.

"Let's go," I said, heading for the door. "As long as Gabor's with her, she should be safe. If they dragged him away..."

I didn't dare complete that sentence.

I punched the button in the elevator, still not trusting it to do as I wanted, but I must have passed Sir Kenosi's tests at last, because I seemed to have clearance to use the elevator as I pleased. I stopped on his floor and asked a guard where to find him. A few minutes later, we were escorted down a hall I hadn't been down before. The guard opened the door for us, showing us an enormous room with floor-to-ceiling windows that overlooked the city, the sun gleaming off the tall build-ings of the skyline.

Sir Kenosi sat at a long, mahogany table with three other men, all of them dressed in black suits. Tablets and pads of paper covered most of the surface, and an enormous screen mounted on one wall showed what looked like a boardroom full of more professionals.

"Where is she?" I demanded.

"Ah," he said, pushing back from the table a bit when he saw us. "I expected a visit from your paramours, but I didn't think you'd be making another appearance, Princess."

"Where is my sister?" I said through clenched teeth.

One of the men at the table cleared his throat. Sir Kenosi rose from the table. "Let us not discuss this in the middle of a meeting," he said. "If you'll wait an hour or so, I'll devote all my attention to the question at hand."

I opened my mouth to demand that he tell me now, but Lord Balam's thick hand closed firmly around my upper arm. "Thank you," he said, giving Kenosi a slight bow. "We would be honored to have an audience with you, Sir."

I gaped at him as he turned and marched me out of the room. When I twisted around to glare at Kenosi over my shoulder, I found Shadow trailing behind us, looking as confused as I felt.

"What the hell?" I asked when the door closed behind us. I

yanked my arm from Lord Balam's grip. "You said you'd help."

"Princess Itzel," he said, inclining his head as if to bow to me. "You would be wise to remember who you're dealing with. Sir Kenosi is the most powerful man in the Cheetah Nation, and we are his guests."

I took a deep breath, calming my simmering anger. He was right, of course. I had done enough political schmoozing to know that. I'd let my anger and panic over Camila's welfare get the better of me. After being so intimately acquainted with Sir Kenosi on almost all our encounters, I had treated him like a lover, not a powerful man of great importance. If he wanted, he could probably toss us all in a real prison, not the swanky room he'd locked me in.

As long as he was in his meeting, I knew that he wasn't terrorizing my sister, so I tried to relax. We sat down on a few of the polished marble benches outside the office. They looked lovely, but they were torture on my ass. A pretty, scantily clad secretary brought us drinks and snacks, which I downed with way too much gusto. I had days of starvation to make up for.

"About this amulet," I said when the woman had left us alone. "What does the cheetah one do?"

"That's something only the cheetah clan knows for sure," Lord Balam said.

"And everyone who has done this tour," I pointed out. "Every king and queen currently on the throne."

"They are bound by shifter law not to share that with anyone."

"Okay, then the panther amulet," I said, turning to Shadow. "I know that Camila has to put it with the others to complete the puzzle, and they'll open for her, showing her the mate of the future heir. But what if she opened yours before that happened? Would it show her True Mate?"

"Yes."

"Then what's to stop her from opening it now and cutting her tour short?"

"That defeats the purpose of the tour," Lord Balam said. "It wouldn't gain the trust or respect of any of the other nations."

"Well, that's a lesson in restraint," I said. "Good thing I don't have to do it. There's no way I could resist."

"There's a curse on it," Shadow said in his low growl.

"What?" Lord Balam asked, turning to the panther.

"An heir did that once," Shadow said. "Afterwards, the high priestess placed a curse upon the amulet. If an heir opens it before it is joined with the other amulets, his or her mate receives a True Mate mark but can never consummate their relationship until they pass into the spirit world."

Lord Balam gave a low whistle, but I just stared with my mouth agape. It was like Shadow had lapsed into another language for a minute—the secret language of supernaturals.

"Um, you're going to have to translate," I said, motioning for him to go on. "Human here, remember?"

"Most shifters spend a lifetime looking for a True Mate," Lord Balam explained. "Sometimes you get lucky and find her right away, but usually it takes decades. A lot of people never find theirs. It might be that the person is dead, or lives across the world, or isn't born until you're a hundred years old. And there's not a beacon shining from your True Mate. You might hate them, or maybe you're already married so you ignore your suspicions. You only really know they're your True Mate when you fuck them."

"Why am I not surprised?" I muttered.

Lord Balam grinned and squeezed my knee. "When you mate with your True Mate, you get a mark, kind of like a tattoo."

"Wow," I said, surveying his tattooed brown skin. "You must have like a hundred True Mates."

Lord Balam laughed. "Don't be jealous. I've never met mine."

"And this curse shows you your True Mate by giving them the mark, but it makes it so you can never fuck them or you'll die."

"Yes," Shadow said. "But only the heir. A normal person like Sir Kenosi can use it. It will only show him his True Mate."

"And who put this curse on it? This high priestess? Should I know who that is?"

"No one knows who she is," Shadow said. "It would be too dangerous."

"She's an extremely powerful sorceress," Lord Balam said. "Basically, the embodiment of the divine feminine. You really don't want her cursing your sex life."

"But she cursed the panther amulet."

"Only if opened by the heir before the appointed time."

"Well, I'll make sure Camila knows," I said. "Not that she'd be tempted."

"Good," Lord Balam said. "It would be hell to know your True Mate and not be able to mate with them. Especially during a heat."

I squinched one eye closed. "Are you saying shifters go in heat?"

He grinned hugely. "You really don't know anything about shifters, do you?"

"Kinda illegal in our country," I said. "Humans and shifters don't mix."

"Shifters are part animal," he said. "They go into heat. Your sister must go through it a few times a year."

I nodded slowly, thinking about my sister's solitary confinement a few times a year when she said she had a particularly bad period and a migraine. She wouldn't let anyone visit but her maidservant. Even I wasn't allowed in.

"Well, this has been an enlightening conversation," I said. "But the real question is, what would happen if I opened the amulet?"

"Nothing," Shadow said. "You're not a shifter."

"Okay then," I said, crossing my arms over my chest. "Good to know."

Before Shadow could make excuses for his attitude, the door to the conference room opened, and Sir Kenosi strode out, looking absolutely devastating in his tailored, slim-cut black suit and tie. Damn it. I should hate the bastard, but just seeing him got my juices all juicy.

We all rose, and he greeted Lord Balam cordially, then me and Shadow.

"Have you been out to the gardens?" he asked, as if nothing had happened between us at all, like I was just another visiting royal from another nation.

When Lord Balam said they hadn't, Kenosi invited us to stroll with him. I had to grind my teeth to keep from yelling at him, demanding to know where my sister was. If I'd learned anything while in Kenosi's clutches, though, it was that he loved the dance, the anticipation. I had to be patient and play his game.

Twenty-Seven

Outside, my first instinct was to run like hell and never look back, but of course I couldn't do that. Not until Camila was free and safe.

Kenosi strolled along the paths that crossed the large expanse of lawn in the center of his complex, leading us to a small, circular grove of palms. It was much smaller than our garden, but impressive for the middle of a city. Tropical flowers of all colors burst from the foliage, and benches made of some kind of finely woven grass lined the path every hundred feet or so. Several noisy birds called overhead as we stepped into the grove and made our way along the pebbled path.

"We have a proposal," I said.

"Do you?" Sir Kenosi said, linking his hands behind his back and watching a butterfly flutter around a small bush with yellow flowers.

"I have done all that you asked," I said. "I am here for the amulet."

"And what do you propose?" he asked. "You're right. You've already given me all I asked. Why should I give you the amulet now?"

"In addition to meeting your demands, we're prepared to offer you a single use of the panther amulet," I said.

Sir Kenosi tore his gaze from the flowers, his eyes bright with interest. "I'm listening. But I thought you were here to bargain for your sister."

"And I thought I'd already fulfilled my end of the bargain for the cheetah amulet."

He turned to Shadow. "What's the panther amulet's power?"

"It gives you a vision," Shadow said. "Of your True Mate."

Kenosi's eyes burned brighter, a bit of gold flickering into his black irises. He stared so intently at my panther protector that I began to get nervous. I could practically see the wheels turning in his head, calculating how he could profit from such a valuable object. He was a shrewd businessman, after all.

"What does your amulet do?" I asked.

"It allows your animal to enter your true mate's body," Sir Kenosi said, letting his hooded gaze pour slowly over the swell of my breasts and down further, sending a pulse of longing straight to my core.

"Let me guess," I said. "During sex?"

Lord Balam gaped at Sir Kenosi so obviously that even I knew that must be a big deal. Yet another thing I'd never truly understand, since I didn't have an animal to go body-crashing during sex. I was used to being left out of shifter politics and events, but this seemed especially unfair. Once again I was left to imagine the kind of intimacy that connection would forge between two people, since I couldn't experience it myself.

"We have a deal?" Shadow ground out, looking far less impressed than Lord Balam. Maybe animal swapping was something fetishy that didn't interest him.

"Alright," Sir Kenosi said with a curt nod. He shook Shadow's hand firmly. "Deal."

"So, where is this amulet, and how does it work?" Sir Kenosi asked.

"Oh, no," I said, holding out a palm and glaring at him. "First, you hand over yours."

The corner of his mouth quirked up. "Very well, Princess."

He slid his hand in his pocket and produced a black velvet box that looked like a ring box.

I reached for it, my heart in my throat. I was actually getting it. I'd negotiated, and I'd earned the third amulet. My heart throbbed with the wish that Camila was here to share the moment.

"For services rendered," Sir Kenosi said, smirking at me like it was just that funny. To him, all I'd done was just another day in the life. I had to remember I wasn't special to him, that what had happened between us was nothing but power plays for him, all part of his strategy.

I eased open the box with my thumb as he and Shadow discussed the hallucinogenic effect of the panther potion, which would take the user on a peyote-like trip and show him a vision of his True Mate. Meanwhile, my eyes were transfixed by what looked like a cloudy, polished ruby the size of a robin's egg. It hung on a glittering golden chain, which was fixed to the small end of the egg-shaped ruby. I could make out the slightest seam where it would open, finer than a single hair.

"Wow," I whispered. It was so different from the stone jaguar Lord Balam had used to pierce my virginity, or even the bullet-shaped crystal Shadow had given me. This looked like million-dollar jewelry compared to their simple amulets.

"Wow is right," Lord Balam said, his strong fingers landing on the curve of my hip. "Can you imagine trading animals in the middle of fucking someone?"

Suddenly, I felt bad for Lord Balam. If he really did accept me as a mate despite my lack of magical ability, he'd be missing out on so much. And what if we made a life together, only to have his True Mate come along? I couldn't hold him back from that.

At the same time, I wasn't going to be the person he killed time with until his real life started. What if we had kids?

Would he just run off and leave me with them so he could have shifter babies with his True Mate?

I pushed the thought away. No one but Camila thought Lord Balam was going to be my "mate." Lord Balam himself had certainly never said anything of the sort. We'd started out with the agreement that it was just fucking. Somewhere along the way, I'd asked him not to fuck other girls, and he'd agreed easily enough. Otherwise, we hadn't discussed our relationship. He'd been pissed at Shadow at first, but that was because he thought Shadow had hurt me. After I'd assured him I was fine, he'd watched Shadow fuck me on the plane without so much as blinking.

I wasn't going to be the girl who made a whole future in my mind with a guy who only saw me as a tight pussy.

"Why would you want to trade animals?" I asked, trying to make it sound like I didn't care, like it was unappealing to my boring human brain.

"Besides the obvious," Sir Kenosi butted in, "You can save your mate in a life-threatening situation."

"Shifters need to let our animals take over to heal us, like you saw on the plane," Lord Balam explained. "If we're injured too badly to shift, an orgasm goes a long way to getting strength back. At least enough strength to shift."

"So, if you were seriously injured, you'd just have sex, and let your mate's healthy cat into you, and it would heal you super quickly when your cat couldn't," I finished.

"Exactly," Lord Balam said, giving my hip a squeeze. That small gesture of approval made me way too happy.

Well, fuck. I was pretty sure I was falling for this man, whether or not he thought of me as more than a way to kill time, or another pussy to fuck, or a common, lowly human.

"I'm going to want to be alone for this," Sir Kenosi said. "You have our amulet. I'll take the panther magic, and you can leave me."

"Oh, no," I said. "First, you tell us where my sister is."

"I don't know what you're talking about," Kenosi said with a smirk.

"Yes, you do," I said through clenched teeth. "You have no reason to keep her. She worked for her room and board in your fine home. Now, our business in your nation is done. We'll be on our way as soon as you release her."

"I have no reason to keep her?" he asked incredulously. "I have the future queen of one of the most powerful, elitist countries in the world in my home. Shouldn't you negotiate a little harder to get her back, Princess Itzel?"

Fuck fuck fuck. He *knew*.

Twenty-Eight

"You know?" I blurted out, staring at him.

Sir Kenosi had the nerve to throw back his head and laugh. "Oh, Princess," he said. "Are you really so naïve? You don't think you can fool a shifter that easily, do you?"

"You led me to believe," I said, gritting my teeth even harder. God, this man was more infuriating than Lord Balam and Gabor combined.

"I did no such thing," he said. "I simply treated you with the respect due. Has no one ever bowed to you before?"

"Is that what you call it? I thought you were torturing me."

He shook his head, the grin still lingering on his perfect lips. "I seem to remember you begging me to fuck you on the table," he said. "Is that the torture you're referring to?"

I glared at Kenosi, not daring to peek at either of my other lovers, even though I'd already told them that Sir Kenosi's bargain included complete submission.

"What about starving me?" I growled.

"My companions and I treated you as we'd treat any princess," he said. "We gave you the utmost respect, just as we did Princess Camila. It's unfortunate that you took that to mean we thought you were a shifter. In the future, remember that shifters can recognize each other by scent. Not a single shifter would ever mistake you for one of us."

"Of course not," I muttered. "I'm a fucking idiot. Of course all that stuff about how I need to know how to serve before I can be a queen was a big fat lie."

"I might have a flair for the dramatic," he said. "But those are good lessons for anyone in power. They might even come in handy for you, Princess."

I was too disgusted with myself to argue. Of course shifters could tell I wasn't a shifter. Of course they never confused me for the heir. How could I have been so stupid? I had no right to feel betrayed. My own stupidity and blind eagerness to protect Camila were the only things that had misled me. It was looking more and more like the best thing I could do was stop protecting her. First she'd begun to resent me for it, and now this. I'd wanted to help her, but I was just hurting her and myself both.

"What I don't understand is why, if you knew I was just a human, you'd go to all that trouble to get me to fuck you? Why me? Was it all just part of your sick game?"

"All of life is a game when you're royalty," he said. "Get used to it."

"I played your game," I said. "Now, the deal was, you'd get to see your True Mate if you gave me the amulet and told me where my sister was."

"She's in the room you were in," he said. "Now, leave me to have my vision."

My head was reeling as we walked away so Shadow could open the panther amulet. I could barely breathe, and the stunned feeling wouldn't leave my brain, my body, my heart. Everything in me was frozen and heavy as lead. I'd foolishly thought it was all for nothing if I couldn't get the amulet. But that was nothing. I'd have left without the amulet if it meant Camila was safe. I hadn't sucked Kenosi's dick for an amulet. I hadn't joined his orgy for an amulet. I hadn't begged him to fuck me for an amulet. I'd done it all so he'd leave Camila alone. I'd done it to distract him from the real treasure—my sister.

Now, I'd done it all for nothing.

"She'll be okay," Lord Balam said quietly as we approached the towering glass and metal building. "When you see your True Mate, your whole life changes."

"How do you know?" I asked, turning to him. "Have you seen your True Mate?"

He paused a second before shaking his head. "No."

I wrestled with my temper. I wanted to lash out, and he was there, but I knew I wasn't angry at him. After a minute, I'd settled myself enough to speak again. "Don't you wonder about her?"

"Of course," he said.

I regretted asking. He'd said it so matter-of-factly that I knew he assumed I would understand that. That I was temporary. I should have been used to feeling expendable, but this was a new area of my life where I'd never felt this way before.

"So, you just go through women while you wait for her?" I asked, not quite able to clip all the bitterness from my words.

"I wouldn't put it that way. Once, in my impulsive youth, I actually married a woman."

I wheeled on him, so surprised I forgot the sting of his earlier words. "You were married?"

He smiled. "Just because I haven't found my True Mate doesn't mean I can't have meaningful, long-term relationships filled with love and passion. I might never meet my True Mate. I choose not to spend my life celibate and alone."

"Hold up," I said, raising a hand to stop him. "Uh-uh. Go back to the married part. Who did you marry? A jaguar?"

"Yes," he said, looking amused. His jaguar tail flicked back and forth behind him. "An advantageous marriage that my parents wholeheartedly endorsed for their upwardly mobile son."

"Why is this funny to you?"

He grinned. "I enjoy watching your jealousy flare. I admit, it's turning me on right now." He took my hand and pulled me closer, sliding it between us and pressing it to the swell in the front of his jeans. I gulped, my heart thumping. God, he was so fucking big.

"Stop distracting me," I said, pulling my hand away. "Where is this wife of yours? I take it you're not still married?"

"No," he said, his smile fading. "She found her True Mate."

"Oh." I didn't know what to say to that. I'd imagined what it would be like to be left by Lord Balam. Not how he'd felt being the one left. "I'm sorry," I said at last. "Did you... I don't know. See her again?"

"Of course," Lord Balam said. "We belong to the same court, live in the same palace, and have a daughter together."

"You have a kid?" I asked, wondering what the hell was going to come out of his mouth next. For all I knew, he'd tell me he was a dragon. I'd made sure we were just fucking, so that's all we'd done. I knew less about him than I did Sir Kenosi.

"Yes," Lord Balam said. "She's just about your age. She also belongs to the Jaguar Court."

"Damn," I said. "It must have sucked seeing your wife around with her new husband all the time."

"It taught me not to make a mistake that big again," Lord Balam said, pulling me back to him. "But that doesn't mean I can't make one this big." He wrapped an arm around my back and pressed his body to mine, dipping his mouth to my throat. His full lips traced my collarbone, and a curl of desire unraveled inside me. I wrapped my hands around his bulging biceps, closing my eyes and letting myself go to the moment.

TWENTY-NINE

"WANT TO GO SOMEWHERE MORE PRIVATE?" LORD Balam murmured against my neck. "What I want to do to you might not be fit for the general public."

A minute later, he was leading me into the room he and Shadow had been using, which was identical to Camila's. I didn't want to think about her right now, though. I wanted to forget.

I threw my arms around Balam's neck, reveling in the way he could lift my curvy body like it was as waifish as Camila's, at the way he could whip me into his arms and crash on the bed on top of me, wanting me as much as Sir Kenosi wanted someone to want him. I didn't have to make Lord Balam beg. I knew exactly how much he wanted me.

"I missed you," I said, wrapping my legs around Lord Balam's powerful hips.

"It's good to have you back," he murmured, rubbing his nose gently back and forth over mine. He rested his weight on his elbows on either side of my head and searched my face, a small smile playing over his lips.

"What?" I asked.

"I've missed fucking this tight little cunt," he said, rolling his hips slowly against mine.

My sheath fluttered in response, and I could barely speak past the breath catching in my throat. "Is that all you missed?"

"No," he said, his deep voice rumbling through his chest and into mine. "But it's what I missed most. I can talk to other people. You're the only one who can satisfy me this way."

"I am?"

He gave me a funny look. "You made me promise not to put my cock in anyone else's mouth, so I figured the rest of her was off limits, too."

"Oh," I said, a flicker of guilt running through me.

Lord Balam paused, raising his head to search my eyes for a minute. "Ah," he said. "I guess you weren't missing me this way."

"I was," I said quickly, locking my feet behind his back. "I just... I told you what happened."

"I know," he said, lifting up to push his jeans down. "I'm not upset that you fucked Sir Kenosi. I don't even mind if you liked it. I sort of hoped you did."

I hadn't told them how I felt about any of it. I'd told them what I did, what Kenosi made me do. I hadn't told them that I'd enjoyed it. That he'd made me want him, made me come, crying his name as I did it.

Lord Balam's thick fingers undid my jeans and slid inside, massaging my mound until wetness slickened my skin. I gasped, trying to squirm away, but he kept moving his fingers, smiling down at me. "You did like it, didn't you?" he asked, sinking a finger into my wet entrance.

I couldn't look him in the eye. "It's just..." I started, then paused. It sounded terrible, but I had to tell him. I couldn't hurt him like that wife of his, no matter how unfair that was to her. "I've never really been with anyone but you in this way," I said, toying with the fur of his cloak. "Yes, I fucked a couple guys to get the other amulets. But I haven't been married. I never even had this kind of relationship with Tadeu. I don't know if I'm ready to choose one man for the rest of my life."

"Are you saying you're done with this?" he asked, driving two fingers deep into me. "If you are, you'd better tell me now because I'm about to be splitting your sweet little cunt in half."

"I'm not done," I said, gripping his shoulders, my nails biting into his skin. "If you're okay with knowing you're not the only one I'm with."

"I have two conditions." Lord Balam pushed my jeans down, positioning the head of his cock against my opening. My juices flowed to meet his bare skin, so hot it made me nearly scream with need.

"Is this really when you want to discuss this?" I asked, my voice choked with desire.

"Itzie, I don't own you," Lord Balam said. "And I'm not a jealous man. As long as you make time for me when I need you, I don't give a fuck who else you want to be with."

"Okay," I said through gasping breaths. "Now fuck me."

I tried to spread my knees, but they were bound by my jeans. I grinded my pussy against his cock, panting for more.

Lord Balam chuckled and stroked my hair back with both hands, watching my face with amusement as I squirmed on his cock. "One more thing."

"What?"

"When I'm inside you, you're mine," he growled. "I won't be a substitute for your dead lover anymore. If I'm fucking you, *I'm* fucking you."

"Yes," I gasped, arching up for him. His hips flexed, forcing his cock past my straining opening with a quick thrust. A squeak of pain left me as he drew back and drove into me again. Each thrust took him deeper until I thought I'd be torn in two. When he'd buried himself to the hilt in me, he began to move faster, each quick thrust both a punishment and unbearable relief. I'd almost forgotten the particular torment of being Lord Balam's lover.

My head fell back, my eyes slipping closed, but I was yanked out of the grip of pleasure when a rasping voice interrupted my bliss. My eyes flew open to see Shadow standing beside the bed wearing nothing but a pair of low-slung sweatpants. "Can I join?" he hissed.

Lord Balam lifted his head and looked down at me. "Your call, Princess," he said. "You said you didn't want to limit yourself."

He was right. I had said that. This was my chance to do anything I wanted, to be free of the Ocelot Court's watchful eye and my father's disapproving gaze. I'd never fantasized about two men inside me at once, but I found the idea suddenly irresistible.

I reached out and tugged down Shadow's pants. His cock was long and hard, just as I remembered it. A shiver of fear mingled with my pleasure, and I took his shaft in my hand, bending it to my mouth. After a few sucks, Lord Balam began to move again.

"Let me roll you over," he purred into my neck. "He can hit you from the back."

The idea sent a jolt of erotic sensation straight to my clit, and I released Shadow. Balam rolled us over, scooting onto the narrow mattress and pulling me astride his hips while he lay on his back, smiling up at me. Shadow pulled my jeans off my feet and peeled my shirt over my head, sucking in a breath at the sight of my curvy, naked body astride Lord Balam's, all bulging muscles and tattooed skin.

"This might hurt a little," Lord Balam said, running his hands over my curves and palming my heavy breasts. "But I promise we'll make you come."

"I can take it," I said, biting back a smile. I glanced over my shoulder at Shadow, arching my back and giving him an inviting smile.

He moved forward without hesitation, climbing onto the bed and positioning his cock against my knotted entrance. A thrill of pleasure at doing something naughty went through me as Lord Balam lifted me off his cock. Wetness dripped down my thighs.

"Oh, yeah," Lord Balam said, dragging a finger through my folds and popping it into his mouth, sucking greedily. "Your cunt smells so fucking sweet."

I bent over him, brushing a kiss over his lips and resting my hands on the bed as Shadow slid the head of his cock into me, wetting it with my juices. He groaned low in his throat, sliding deeper, gripping my soft hips as he pumped into my pussy where Balam's cock had just been. Lord Balam's thick tongue thrust into my mouth in rhythm with Shadow's movements. After a minute, Shadow withdrew, and Balam reached back to grab my ass, spreading my cheeks wide.

A soft breath escaped my lips, and I twisted around to smile up at Shadow. "Put it in my ass."

His cock throbbed, and I felt a drop of his own juices wetting my second entrance as he pushed the head of his cock against the tight knot. I bore down on him, feeling the strain of my tight flesh. He held a hand on my shoulder, guiding me down. The head of his cock forced past the knotted tension, and he let out a sharp, animal growl that shot a current of pleasure straight to my core.

As he sank deeper into me, the strange sensation sliced along the edge between pleasure and pain, and I couldn't help the little gasps escaping my lips. When he was all the way in, his hips pressed tight to my ass, his skin hot against mine, Lord Balam reached for his massive cock.

"Ready for two?" he asked, lifting my hips with one hand and guiding his cock to my entrance with the other.

"Oh god," I panted. "I don't know if it'll fit."

"It will," he said, lifting his hips and forcing the tip into me. I gasped in pleasure at the tight, stretched sensation. It was like I could feel their cocks sliding together through the thin barrier of my flesh. The image sent another wave of wetness over Lord Balam's cock, and a shudder went through him. He guided my hips down until he was buried to the hilt inside me.

Shadow waited, his breaths coming quick and hot against my shoulder. His claws had extended, digging into my skin. Lord Balam's eyes flashed golden, his tail dancing up my leg and wrapping around Shadow's thigh. I couldn't bear the intensity of the sensations rolling through me—the pressure and strain of my body wrapped around these two men, the ticklish softness of Lord Balam's tail, the heat of Shadow, the flash of their cats just below the surface making me shiver with danger.

"What now," I gasped.

"Now we fuck you," Lord Balam said. His strong hands clamped down on my hips, his fingers biting into the soft flesh as he held me tightly, lifting my weight. Shadow gripped my thigh with one hand and my shoulder with the other, bracing his knees on either side of Lord Balam's legs.

"Fuck, your ass is so tight it hurts," Shadow hissed.

Lord Balam slammed my body back down, and both of their cocks sank to the hilt inside me. I yelped in surprise and pain, but Lord Balam lifted me and brought me back down, slamming me onto them again and again. My walls tightened in pain, and I bit my lip to keep from begging for mercy. Once I adjusted to their size straining inside me, Balam stretching my pussy while Shadow's cock pounded into my ass, somehow the pain felt good, pleasure rippling through me with each slippery plunge.

They continued pumping into me, Lord Balam taking over my movements, impaling me onto their cocks until the pleasure was too much, dizzying and unbearable. "I'm going to come," I gasped when I couldn't take it anymore.

Lord Balam slammed me down hard, sitting up to grind his pelvic bone against my throbbing clit with bruising force. Cum exploded into me, filling me with liquid heat. My pussy clamped around his shaft, and I cried out my pleasure with each breath, the overwhelming sensation gripping my body and ripping through me like a storm. Shadow cried out with me, his claws sinking into my skin, drawing blood. I tried to twist away, but they held me pinned between them. Hot cum spurted into my clenched pussy and my ass again and again. Shadow thrust his hips in tiny, rhythmic pulses, making my ass bounce against his narrow hips as cum continued to flood into me. At last, he pushed me forward, and Lord Balam lay back, his arms around me, his tattooed chest rock solid against mine.

Shadow lay forward on my back, his forehead resting between my shoulder blades, his fingers stroking my side.

"Are you okay?" he asked after a long minute of silence.

"I'd rather you didn't maul me every time we had sex, but I guess that's a hazard of fucking shifters."

"Let me clean it," he said.

I remembered Gabor's offer on the plane—the one I'd refused. If I had let him, I might not have ever gotten the infection.

"Okay," I said. We pried ourselves apart, all of us rolling onto our sides to squeeze onto the tiny bed.

Shadow lay facing me, his black hair draped over his shoulder, his green eyes searching mine. "It only takes a minute," he said. "I did it that night in the swamp. That's why your wounds healed so quickly."

So much had happened since then that I'd forgotten all about all the bites and scratches he'd left on me. They'd been there the next morning, I knew that much. But then I'd been bitten and infected by the other panther when I hadn't cleaned the wounds. Everything had happened so fast I hadn't even noticed that all Shadow's marks had turned to scars already.

I nodded, and Shadow dipped his head, flicking out his long, cat tongue to my wound.

"Whoa," I said as his tongue rasped through the cuts. It hurt, but it also felt good, like a healing salve. More than that, it felt incredibly intimate, incredibly right. Was this what Gabor had been offering? If I'd known this was how shifters healed, I would have said "hell fucking yes."

There was no use in speculating now, though. With a sigh, I wrapped my arms around Shadow, nestling back against Lord Balam at the same time. Even though everything that could go wrong on this tour seemed determined to go wrong, I'd found more pleasure and happiness in the small moments with these men than I'd had in my whole life before it.

THIRTY

Sir Kenosi
Entrepreneur, Cheetah Nation

"SIR, DO YOU NEED ANYTHING?"

It took me a moment to register July's voice, to open my eyes. She smiled up at me, all copper skin and ebony eyes. Any other night, I would have said yes. I would have asked her to bring all the girls in to have a little fun.

But not tonight.

Tonight was too important.

I dismissed her, slipped off my shoes, and lay down on the bed. It seemed too big, too empty with just me in it. This time, I wouldn't use pleasures of the flesh to distract me from what was lacking in my life. This time, I would listen to the voices of the ancestors. I would find the most elusive of treasures for a shifter—my True Mate.

I closed my eyes and folded my hands on my chest, focusing the way the panther had instructed. He'd told me I might not see anything, but I wouldn't entertain that possibility. This was a once-in-a-lifetime opportunity, one most shifters never got. If she was out there, I would see her.

I tried to sink into a meditative state. This was one area where the Cheetah King could have done better than I could. He might not provide for his people the way I did, might not protect them, but the bastard could sure as shit meditate like a wise man.

I wasn't so practiced. My mind wouldn't stop moving. It kept coming back to the princess, and not even the right one. The human one, the one whose eyes dared me to break her. I had tried. Outwardly, it might even appear that I'd succeeded. But I knew better. I hadn't even touched the wildness in her eyes, let alone tamed it.

And that just about drove me crazy. Every time I saw it, all I could think about was how I wanted to tame her, claim her. I wanted her to be mine, but she wouldn't. Even when she was begging me to cum inside her tight little pussy, I knew she didn't want me. Not the way I wanted her to. Not the way I wanted her.

I pushed thoughts of the human princess out of my mind and tried to focus on finding my True Mate. If she was out there, I was supposed to see a vision of her. I waited, trying to clear my head.

But again, the image of Itzel slipped back into my mind. Itzel, face down on the table, her face in the spilled wine, her hands in the plates of half eaten food, getting fucked like a dirty slut. Itzel's legs around my neck, moaning as I sucked the sweet nectar from between her thighs. Itzel's full, plush lips stretched around my cock, my hand buried in her hair.

I sighed in frustration. I was not only still thinking about her, but now I was hard.

Shadow had told me to have patience, that it could last all night. So I made myself comfortable, showering and then slipping back into the bed to try again.

I tried. I tried again, and again, and again, until I knew for certain that either the potion didn't work, or I had no True Mate. Because no matter what I did, no matter how hard I tried to drive the thoughts of her from my mind, the only woman I could see was human.

THIRTY-ONE

Itzel
Princess, Ocelot Nation

THAT NIGHT, I TOOK COMFORT IN THE PRESENCE OF one of my amours beside me as the other sat watch. Though the bed was narrow, I didn't mind. After the past week's ordeal, I didn't want any space between us. For the first half of the night, I slept curled in Lord Balam's arms, twining my legs with his and laying my head on his chest.

When I woke with a start in the night, I found comfort in the green glow of Shadow's eyes nearby as he sat up in the dark, making sure no one came for me. Sleep eluded me, so I slid out from under Lord Balam's arm and out of bed. I found a man's shirt in the closet and slid my arms into it, pulling it closed around me as I tiptoed over to join Shadow.

Without a word, he rose from his chair and disappeared into the darkness of the room. A second later, the door opened, letting in a shaft of light from the hall. Shadow gestured for me to go out, following me into the hall and closing the door so we wouldn't wake Lord Balam.

"Do you think Sir Kenosi will let Camila go once he sees his mate?" I asked. "Maybe he won't care about keeping her anymore."

"Maybe," Shadow said.

"Will the amulet have worked yet?" I asked, crossing my arms over my chest and rocking back on my heels. For some reason, I didn't like to think of Sir Kenosi running off with his mate, forgetting me like he'd forget all his Julys when August rolled around.

"Yes," Shadow said in his whispery growl.

"What if... If Camila's his mate, will he be fucking with her head like he did to me?"

"I don't know him well enough to answer that," Shadow said. "But most shifters treasure their mates and would do anything to please them."

"That makes me feel a little better," I admitted, hunching my shoulders and hugging myself tighter. Lord Balam would have comforted me better, but I appreciated Shadow's bluntness. It was refreshing after all the games Sir Kenosi played, the games everyone had played for my entire life.

"I guess we'll have to hope he has a change of heart about imprisoning the ocelot heir," I said. "If he can't be convinced, I'll have to call my father tomorrow."

Shadow tensed, and I remembered again that he was a panther. He was the enemy of our people, my father and my sister. He wasn't old enough to have taken part in my mother's murder, but his clan was responsible. Guilt pulled tight inside me at the thought. I was literally sleeping with the enemy.

"I should try to sleep again," I said.

Back in the room, Lord Balam had risen and insisted that Shadow get some sleep, too. I didn't know how Shadow felt about it, but it was awkward as hell for me to lie down next to him while still thinking about his people murdering my mother. He didn't seem overly eager to tangle up with me, either, so we lay on the narrow bed, both of us trying too hard to respect the other's space.

After an hour of lying awake, frustrated and unable to sleep, I gave in and scooted into Shadow's arms. A sigh escaped him, and he pressed his lips to my forehead in a long, hard kiss before pulling back. He adjusted his body against mine, drawing me close. After a minute, his breathing deepened, as if he'd only been waiting for me to come back to him before he could sleep. I must have been doing the same without knowing it, because I quickly fell into sleep.

I woke to the loud bang of the door flying open.

I jerked upright, pulling the sheet up around my chest. Sir Kenosi stood in the doorway, breathing hard, his eyes narrowed. "You tricked me," he snarled.

It took me a second to realize his eyes weren't on me. I shifted to see Shadow propped on his elbows, his expression alert despite having been woken so suddenly. Lord Balam had leapt from the chair and stepped between us and the angry cheetah.

"What are you talking about?" I asked.

"You lied," Sir Kenosi growled. "You drugged me. I should have you thrown in the shifter jail, and trust me when I say that's somewhere you don't want to go, no matter how much you deserve it."

"It is a hallucinogen," Shadow said, slipping from the bed with that liquid, feline body of his. "I disclosed the effects in full. There was no trickery."

"I tripped my balls off, but I didn't see my True Mate," Sir Kenosi shot back, his eyes flashing molten gold.

"Whoa, whoa, whoa," I said. "Are you seriously going to barge in here acting all indignant that someone tricked you? That's rich."

Sir Kenosi turned his fiery glare on me. "Of course you're in on the deception."

"First of all, I had nothing to do with the amulet. I wasn't even there when you opened it. And second, if Shadow tricked you, maybe it's time you got a taste of your own medicine."

In truth, I had no idea what Shadow had given him, but it was all I could do not to burst into laughter. If Shadow had the balls to drug Sir Kenosi instead of letting him use the amulet, I was so pleased I could have kissed him. Someone needed to knock the cheetah down a peg, and if it was one of my lovers, all the better.

"Sir Kenosi," Balam said. "I'm sure it was a misunderstanding. Perhaps it only works for panthers."

"Perhaps," Sir Kenosi said in a slightly mocking tone. He crossed his arms, narrowing his eyes as he looked between the three of us, seeming unwilling to let it go just yet.

"Maybe we'll give you the real thing if you release my sister like you promised," I said, crossing my arms to mirror Kenosi's posture.

"I don't have your sister," he said, a bit of his usual smirk returning. "I never had her."

"What?" I asked, my heart thudding against my ribs. "Where is she?"

"She demanded a room fit for a princess," he said. "In fact, she wanted the room you couldn't wait to abandon. It was empty, so I told her she could use it and bring her guard along, too."

"You can't just trade us out like we're interchangeable," I said, trying to summon my inner princess and sound as superior as Camila always did. I stood straight and squared my shoulders even though I was still wearing nothing but Shadow's shirt. "Camila's important. I'll have to report this to King Ocelot if she's not freed immediately."

"She's free," he said. "Nothing is stopping her from joining you except her own anger."

"Oh," I said faintly, the knife of pain returning to my chest.

"In fact, I've already met with her this morning," Sir Kenosi went on, a smug smile tugging at his lips. "I hope you'll be pleased to learn that I'm providing one of my private choppers to get you to lion country safely."

"That's very generous," Lord Balam said. "We offer our deepest gratitude."

"Why would you do that?" I asked, narrowing my eyes at Sir Kenosi. "You came in here all angry that we'd tricked you, and suddenly you're offering us transportation?"

"Not only that," Sir Kenosi said. "I'm offering you protection in the form of immunity. Not one nation would dare harm someone as influential as I am."

"What are you talking about?"

"Oh, didn't I make that clear?" Sir Kenosi said with a smirk. "I had breakfast with your sister, and it turns out we have quite a lot in common. For instance, we both believe you should keep your friends close and your enemies closer."

"Still not getting it," I admitted.

"I've done everything I can here," Sir Kenosi said. "To be honest, I've grown rather bored. There's no challenge anymore. I thought I'd spice things up. Be happy, Princess Itzel. I'm not just giving you a helicopter. I'm coming with you."

THIRTY-TWO

I DIDN'T SEE CAMILA ALL DAY UNTIL WE ARRIVED AT the helipad atop Kenosi's tower. I rushed over to her, my heartstrings tugging despite her snub the day before.

"I got the amulet," I blurted out, then slowed when I reached her, feeling stupid. "I just wanted you to know."

"I know," she said, adjusting her sunglasses. "Sir Kenosi told me this morning."

"I don't want to fight," I said, handing her the velvet jewelry box. "I'm sorry that I pretended to be the rightful heir. It wasn't to enjoy any luxuries. I was trying to protect you, and I know it sounds lame, but that's the truth."

Camila worked her lips from side to side, studying me like she wasn't sure she could trust me. "I feel like I don't even know you anymore," she said. "You're so different now."

"I feel the same way about you," I said. But even as I said it, I paused to question what she'd said. Maybe she was right. A lot had happened to me in the past few months. I'd lost my innocence in every way. I'd lost my childhood sweetheart, the dream I'd held onto since my mother died. I'd started casually sleeping with a man, only to have it grow into something real. And now I was sleeping with two men. I'd learned to enjoy some of the darker aspects of my sexuality, too. It wasn't all love and tenderness, as I'd imagined with Tadeu. And now, I was beginning to see some truths about the Ocelot Nation and even my own sister. I couldn't deny that those things had changed me.

What hadn't changed was my love for my sister, my certainty that she would be a better ruler than my father the tyrant.

"Here," I said, shoving the box into her hand. "See, we're all good. I love you, Camila. I trust you. You're going to be a great queen. I wouldn't be helping you get these if I didn't believe that with all my heart."

Camila made a little 'hmph' sound and slipped the box into her satin clutch. She must have gone shopping in the past week, because she wore a new designer dress suit. The others had all replaced their clothes, too. Only I was at the mercy of Sir Kenosi's wardrobe choices. Today, I wore a little black dress that accentuated my ample curves but definitely didn't match everyone else's travel attire.

"You may escort me to the next kingdom," Camila said, raising her chin in her queenly pose, as if she were talking to a guard. She'd rarely spoken to me that way in our own kingdom, but everything was different away from home. Maybe things would go back to normal when we returned. I just didn't know if I wanted that or not.

"Okay," I said. "What do we know about the Lion Nation?"

"We'll discuss this on the way," Lord Balam said, stepping up beside me and guiding me toward the sleek, silver beast crouched on the helipad.

When Sir Kenosi had said "chopper," I'd pictured something noisy where we had to shout over the wind, inhale exhaust, and sit on each other's laps to fit in. I should have known better. The chopper was a luxury machine with an enclosed cabin that could have fit two dozen people. I didn't even have to stoop to walk to my seat, let alone cram in next to someone and yell to be heard.

"This is quite suitable," Camila said, taking a seat in a plush leather armchair and crossing her legs primly. My dress suddenly felt ten times more inappropriate. Camila looked like a princess flying with her escort of guards to visit another kingdom. I looked like a freaking escort her guards brought along to fuck.

Which, ironically, was not all that far from the truth. Except for Gabor, I'd been fucking all three of these men, and I wasn't planning to stop.

After settling in, Camila confirmed my suspicion that she'd gone shopping when she gave me a little cardigan to wear over my dress, so I didn't look like I belonged on a street corner.

I caught the quirk of arrogance at the corner of Sir Kenosi's eye as he watched me, waiting for a reaction. Fuck. Had I just been thinking of him as one of my consorts, a man who wouldn't mind hanging out with the other guys I was fucking? Lord Balam had said he was happy with it, and Shadow seemed to get pretty turned on when he saw us together, jumping in both times to participate. I wasn't sure about Sir Kenosi. I wasn't even sure I liked him. But my body sure as hell knew it wanted more of what he had given me.

"Not a bad ride," I said, shrugging like I wasn't at all impressed. "Not too shabby at all."

In truth, I was trying not to gape. I'd rarely traveled, and my knowledge of helicopters was limited to what I saw on military dramas and reality survival shows.

"Glad it's not too shabby for a pair of princesses," Sir Kenosi said, grinning like I wasn't fooling him one bit. He dropped into one of the chairs and patted the one beside him. "Sit."

I hesitated, torn between wanting to sit next to him and wanting to defy him just to show him I was no longer his puppet. Gabor stepped into the helicopter, scanning us in one quick glance. Our eyes caught, and I remembered my shame at knowing he might have seen what had happened between Kenosi and me. I quickly stepped away from the cheetah, my heart hammering. What was wrong with me?

Gabor might have thought I was forced to do those things, that I hadn't enjoyed them. Knowing that I had made me feel ten times as filthy as the fact that he might have seen me sucking someone's cock—someone he knew was never going to be my husband. With Lord Balam, at least I could pretend I had the intention, since everyone in our court had apparently assumed as much. But with Shadow, with Sir Kenosi? There was no pretending. To Gabor, it probably looked like I was either cheating on Lord Balam, or I was as common as the rumors had suggested and then some. No wonder he wanted nothing to do with me.

I couldn't blame him. I deserved whatever he thought of me. The night before, I'd asked him to stay. I'd wanted him to, would have done anything to have him hold me and comfort me. When he'd refused, I hadn't lain there and cried myself to sleep. No, I'd found not one man but two to take his place, as if he meant nothing more to me than that. As if he could be replaced, and I didn't really care who was in my bed as long as I had arms to hold me and a cock or two to fill the emptiness I felt.

Turning away, I slid into an empty chair next to Camila, barely able to swallow, let alone speak or meet the guard's eyes. Shadow took the seat on my left, Balam sat next to him, and Gabor took the empty seat next to Camila when everyone else was situated.

"Looks like this will be a fun trip," Sir Kenosi said, flashing that million-dollar smile. "If the tension in here is any indication, it looks like I missed some good stuff on this tour."

"Traveling is stressful," Camila said in her sweet, bland way. "The attacks have added to the usual tensions that arise."

"I'm sure that's it," Sir Kenosi said, slouching back in his chair with his legs sprawled out as he surveyed our group one by one. Today, he'd left his disguises at home and wore a pair of simple dress pants and a lavender silk shirt unbuttoned a few extra buttons at the collar. He would look gorgeous next to my sister, I realized. Of course, that was impossible. Our kingdom thought it only right for princesses to marry advantageously, and there was no way they'd let Camila choose a low-born shifter, even if he was richer than a god. My father had married a shifter with zero royalty running through her veins, and after her death, some shifters had blamed Father for marrying beneath him.

If he'd married a high-ranking royal from another feline nation, she would have come to court with a full entourage of guards and ladies who were loyal to her above all else. Though her entire royal guard was executed after the kidnapping, not one of them confessed to betraying her and letting it happen. Still, ocelots were superstitious, and there had been murmurs that if he'd chosen wisely, disaster could have been prevented.

"So, how do the amulets know who you're supposed to marry?" I asked Camila. "And do you have to marry who they choose?"

"They only choose the clan," she said. "I would get to choose who amongst the clan members was most suitable."

"Sounds very clinical," I said.

Lord Balam chuckled. "Trust me, there's nothing clinical about shifter mating. We are animals, after all."

"Some people more than others," Camila said, folding her hands primly and looking about as far from an animal as was humanly possible.

"Do you get any clues before the amulets are pieced together?" I asked. "Or is there anyone you're hoping for?"

"It would be pointless to speculate," she said. "Tradition dictates that I choose the clan the amulets show. It doesn't matter what I want or expect."

"So you'd be happy with anyone?" I asked.

"I'm sure I could find someone in every clan who would satisfy our people." Her eyes moved to Shadow, and a grimace of distaste twisted her pretty face. "Except maybe a panther."

"You should be so lucky," Shadow growled.

THIRTY-THREE

CAMILA TURNED PLEADING EYES MY WAY, obviously wanting me to defend her as I had all our lives. The urge to defend my sister was as much a part of me as my own humanity. No one talked bad about Camila, especially not a man who had never bothered to get to know her. Shadow had hated her from the start for no other reason than I'd given her the amulet.

"What are you saying?" I demanded, twisting sideways to stare him dead in the eye. "I'm sorry that you still feel some misplaced sense of loyalty to them, but in case you forgot, your people would have killed you, Shadow."

"I was the one being disloyal," he said, his head dropping in shame, his hair swinging over his face.

"Yeah, well, what about my mother? Was she being disloyal when panther rebels dragged her from her bed and ate her alive?"

"Bull. Shit." Shadow's raspy voice sent a chill through me.

Blood pounded in my ears as anger pulsed inside me until I couldn't see straight. "What?"

"That never happened."

"Don't you dare defend panthers to me," I said, my voice shaking with rage. I wanted to throw him from the moving helicopter, to rip into him with razor claws and slaughter him the way his people had done my mother.

"Panther 'rebels' are refugees who sought asylum in your country," he said. "When your father wouldn't let them in, they snuck in at night and were shot down by *your* people."

"That's what happens when you enter a country illegally," Camila said, raising her chin and staring down her nose at Shadow.

"I wouldn't know," he said. "I never set foot in the Ocelot Nation. When the boats got close to the coast, your people started shooting. Some of the boats were hit. I was pulled into another boat and pushed into the bottom with some other children. The next day, we started back. We didn't eat for three days, until we got home. A few days after that, I found out that my parents had swam to shore and hidden in the jungle until they were hunted down and shot."

My stomach twisted, and my fingers began to shake. "I'm sorry," I said, feeling about as big as a pile of shit after going off on him. I started to reach for him, but Camila captured my hand, squeezing my fingers in hers.

"It doesn't change what your people did to our mother," she said.

"Panthers never made it anywhere near your precious palace," Shadow said.

"How would you know?" she demanded. "You weren't there, and you said you were just a kid. It's not like your people would tell you they'd eaten our queen."

"They didn't," Shadow growled.

"Fine," Camila said, crossing her arms over her chest. "If you're so all-knowing, who killed our mother? If it wasn't rebels, then who was it?"

"I don't know," Shadow admitted. "I just know it wasn't us."

"How do you know?" I insisted, my eyes narrowing at him. "Do you have some kind of oracle in your clan? You said you have a shaman."

I wanted him to know for sure, to give us answers. In truth, I didn't want it to be his people that had killed my mother.

I didn't want it to be anyone. I wanted her to be alive.

"I just know," Shadow said quietly.

"You're in denial," Camila said. "You can't know, can you? No one from your clan saw something in a magic crystal ball that doesn't exist. You just don't want to admit what you're capable of. For all we know, it was your parents who killed her."

This time, my stomach dropped so fast I thought I'd puke. What Camila said was true. His parents had invaded our country. It could have been them. No matter what I wanted, it didn't change the fact that my mother was dead, and she wasn't coming back. And I was sleeping with someone from the clan that had murdered her, maybe the son of her murderers. I closed my eyes and tried to breathe.

"I'm sorry about your mother," Shadow said after a minute. "I wish I could tell you who it was, or what happened."

"It doesn't matter," I said at last. "I'm sure there are political murders in every country. Maybe it was a panther rebel and maybe it wasn't. I guess we'll never know for sure."

"Maybe we could," Lord Balam said. "I could try. The oracle doesn't always tell me what I want to know. It has a mind of its own, and it doesn't always like to talk about the past. Or the future, for that matter. But I could try."

"Really?" I asked, sitting up straight.

"If you can give me any details first, that would help," he said. "If there's anyone who might have wanted the queen dead. Your father never remarried, so it seems doubtful a mistress would have gone to all that trouble if she wasn't sure she'd be elevated to queen. But if he had a particularly volatile relationship with one, or perhaps one who might have *thought* he'd marry her…"

"My father is not that kind of king," Camila said icily, her fingers digging into the arms of her chair so hard her knuckles went white. "There were no mistresses in the castle when my mother was alive. She wouldn't have it."

"It's true," I said with an apologetic shrug. "My father has plenty of women around now, but he was entirely devoted to our mother. She's probably the only person he's ever loved more than himself."

"His True Mate," Shadow murmured.

"Was she?" Lord Balam asked. "His True Mate, I mean?"

I turned to Camila. "I mean, she must have been, right? I assumed she was, but if it's that rare... Could the amulet have shown him a woman who wasn't a True Mate?"

"Any shifter can have a True Mate," she said, looking uncomfortable. "Not just feline shifters. It's so rare, though, that some people don't even believe it exists anymore. It was something primitive, necessary when we were hidden from humans and other supernaturals. Ocelots use the amulet to find a mate to fall in love with. This True Mate thing is so rare, Itzel. No one has one anymore."

"So, they weren't True Mates."

"No, they weren't. No one is. That's why the panther amulet didn't work for Sir Kenosi, and why it wouldn't work for any one of us here. We don't have True Mates anymore. We have *Furry Finders*, and *Chase That Kitty*, and all the other online dating apps to find someone compatible." She gestured to Sir Kenosi as she named his dating apps, and he nodded slowly, watching me as if he expected me to contradict her.

I turned back to Lord Balam and shrugged. "I'm sorry. I don't know anyone who would have wanted my mother dead. She was beloved by the people—even more so than King Ocelot." I stopped there, not wanting to say something in front of Camila and Gabor. Even now, I had to always remember that ocelot loyals were in our presence. I didn't think either of them would accuse me of treason when we got home, but I couldn't count on Camila to always have my back anymore. I trusted Gabor to protect me, but that was because I was part of the Ocelot Court. If I wasn't part of that, he would owe me nothing. He had basically already chosen his nation and his people over me, and I didn't hold that against him. But I knew better than to say something ugly about the king in their presence.

"I'll see if I can find out anything," Lord Balam said, nodding. He had seen Father's "popularity" with his own eyes, and he'd heard me talk about it enough to read between the lines.

"Thank you," I said, wishing I could hug him. I hadn't even thought to ask him. But then, why would I? I'd never had a reason to doubt the story I'd heard all my life, that panthers had killed and eaten our mother.

"When I'm queen, I'll have twenty guards outside every window in the palace to make sure no one ever breaks in again," Camila said.

I had no doubt my sister would do just that if she could find enough guards who met her standards. If possible, she was even more paranoid than Father about betrayals within her court. After what happened with our mother, they had every reason to be cautious. Now that Shadow had planted a seed of doubt in my mind, I was starting to feel a little paranoid myself. What if it hadn't been panthers? What if one of the guards or another royal had killed our mother? If so, did Father know? He might. A cover-up was the kind of thing he might do—execute the traitor on the spot and hide the assassination, blaming our enemies so no one would realize how easily it could be done. After all, if a guard could get the queen, maybe they could get the king next.

"You must not trust your people very much," Shadow muttered.

Camila glared. "I don't trust *your* people. Who knows when they'll try to invade again."

Shadow glowered.

"Speaking of, where's the panther amulet you stole from me?" she asked. "Are you going to return that?"

"We didn't steal it," I said. "We traded its use for the Cheetah Amulet. He has it."

"You gave it to me," she said, narrowing her eyes at Shadow. "You can't take it back."

I turned to find Shadow leaning almost over my shoulder, his stance that of someone on alert, ready to pounce. "Whoa," I said, pushing him back before he could leap over me and attack my sister.

"I gave it to Itzel," he said, his eyes locked on Camila.

"I'd like it back," Camila said, lifting her chin.

Shadow held her gaze while he reached into his shirt, yanked off the amulet, and deposited the crystal amulet in my palm. Camila's nostrils flared, and I thought she was about to slap him.

"What would happen if I opened it?" I said. "Nothing, right?" I thumbed the smooth surface absently. Without warning, it popped open as if loaded with a spring. Pain seared up my arm, and I yelped and grabbed my forearm. The three men sitting closest to me slapped their shoulders in unison, as if swatting a hornet that had just stung them. Gabor grabbed for the gun in his holster.

THIRTY-FOUR

CAMILA JUMPED UP, HER EYES WIDE. "CLOSE IT," she screamed. "What are you doing?"

"Fuck, I'm so sorry," I said, frantically pressing it to get the top closed again. "I didn't think it would just shoot open like that. Oh my god, what do I do?"

Lord Balam stared at me, his mouth gaping. Kenosi crossed his arms, watching me from hooded eyes. Gabor's gaze was flying around the circle, from me to Camila to the three men seated with us. Only Shadow looked unruffled, a grave expression on his face.

"What the fuck just happened?" I asked him. It was his amulet. Of course he wasn't surprised by whatever magic was still pulsing up my arm like a hot brand. Humans didn't have magic. That didn't mean it didn't affect us.

"So, now you know," he said, looking almost sad.

"Know what?" I asked, glancing around at all the stunned faces.

"You're my mate, Itzel."

"What?" Camila spluttered. "That's not possible. She's a human, and you're—you're..." She trailed off, her face crimson.

"I know," he said quietly.

She turned her wide eyes to me. "Itzel, he's a *panther*."

She said the word like it was dirty, and I didn't miss the way Shadow flinched.

"I know," I said, lifting my chin to her, refusing to back down. Yes, I still had my own misconceptions about panthers to get past, but that was not even close to my main concern right now. Shadow had done nothing but protect us both, even though he and Camila obviously despised each other. He'd protected her—for me.

I turned to Shadow. "You knew?"

He nodded, his eyes downcast.

I took his hand, lacing my fingers through his. "Since when? Why didn't you tell me?"

"I opened the amulet the morning...after," he said.

I knew he didn't like to speak of the night in the swamp when he'd chained me to his bed, but I had to know. "Why then? Don't you usually have a ceremony or something?"

"We don't follow the old traditions anymore," he said. "There is no ceremony. I don't know how long it had been since anyone opened it. A few years, at least."

"But you wanted to open it before you gave it away," I said, nodding.

"No," he rasped. "I already suspected. I felt an unnatural pull to be with you, and I didn't think it was the jaguar potion."

Lord Balam cleared his throat.

"It's not possible," Camila said before he could speak. "Our True Mates aren't human. They can only be other shifters—other *feline* shifters."

"I don't know how it happened," Shadow said. "I only know what I saw. My instinct told me it was right. Maybe because there are so few panthers, our mates have to be something else."

"Princess Itzel was born to two shifters," Gabor said, as if that might explain it.

"What are you saying?" Camila demanded, crossing her arms. "That Itzel is human, but she's magically going to save the panther race by making panther babies?"

Well, fuck. This was what happened when you slept around with shifters. No wonder the different species didn't like to mix.

"Hold up," I said, lifting a hand. "It's one thing to be magically bound to a shifter even though I'm human, and we don't have True Mates. But I am absolutely not going to be anyone's baby factory."

"I don't expect that," Shadow growled, his eyes narrowing at my sister.

My head was spinning with all this new information, and a weird fuzzy feeling was taking over my brain. When I turned my head, light tracers shimmered in the corners of my eyes. "Shadow," I said. "If you knew all that time that I was your mate, why didn't you tell me? You let me be with other men. You don't care?"

"I care that you're happy," he said. "I told you before. A True Mate wants nothing more than to please his mate. When I see that you are happy, I am happy."

I fought to swallow, squeezing his hand to anchor myself. "But why didn't you tell me?"

He dropped my gaze, studying our linked hands and running his thumb gently across my knuckles. "I wanted you to make the decision yourself," he said. "I was going to tell you once... I hoped we would grow close naturally."

I leaned in to kiss his cheek, but dizziness made me almost topple to the floor. His long arms wrapped around me, steadying me. "Thank you," I said, clinging to his neck.

"You should lie down," he said. "It takes a few hours for it to wear off."

"Give me the amulet," Camila said, holding out a hand.

I'd forgotten I still held it clutched in my free hand. I held it out to her, depositing it in her palm. "I'm sorry," I muttered. "Don't open it. It hurts."

My entire arm seemed to be pulsing with fire, as if the sleeve of my cardigan would burst into flame at any moment.

"Well, this is one way to enter the Lion Nation," Sir Kenosi said.

"Drugged is better than infected," I said, laying my head on Shadow's shoulder and closing my eyes. I wanted to ask more, to find out how I could be mated to a shifter, but it would have to wait. I only knew that for now, I was content to be Shadow's mate. His long, ropy arms wound around me, and he pressed his lips to the crown of my head.

When he'd come with us, when he'd fought his own clan for someone he'd only just met, I had wondered. It hadn't made sense to me. Now it did.

If I hadn't trusted him before, that was because I hadn't known. All along, he had been willing to fight for me, to die for me, because I was his mate. Now I knew he would do anything to protect me, and I trusted him completely. I may not be a shifter, but I knew what it meant to them. I knew that he wouldn't betray me, no matter what his people had done.

Panthers may hate ocelots, but he didn't hate me. And I didn't hate him, either. I didn't feel the True Mate bond in the way that a shifter might, but I felt closer to him, none-theless. Trust and compassion had bloomed inside me. I liked that he hadn't told me, that he'd come with me and waited, hoping I'd fall in love with him instead of claiming me or pressuring me into being his alone.

I nuzzled into his neck, inhaling the green smell of him, like dewy grass on a cool morning. My mind wrapped around him, seeing every inch of him, though my eyes were closed. He became so vivid I could see every individual strand of hair streaming down his shoulders, the smoothness of his brown cheeks, every fleck in his magnetic green eyes. I could see the straightness of his noble nose, the line of his serious mouth, the hint of muscles in his slender but strong body. The cut of his narrow hips, the hard muscles in his long arms, the definition in his tall frame. I could perfectly picture each of his dark nipples, his long, smooth cock, his long legs down to each individual toe on his brown feet. I could picture a glowing mark on his bicep that hadn't been there before, a cat's paw with claw marks above it, lit with the silvery-white glow of the moon. I'd never seen one, but I knew instinctually what it was. His True Mate mark. A mark I had given him.

Something snagged at the corner of my mind, but I couldn't quite think of what needed my attention. Shadow's hand caressed my hair, soothing me and sending shivers of comfort and warmth through me.

"I love you," I whispered.

Shadow's arms tightened around me, and his mouth dipped to my ear. "That's the potion talking," he whispered. "But I love you, too."

"How is it working on her?" Camila demanded. "Is she faking it?"

"I don't think she's faking it," Sir Kenosi said.

"How would you know?" Camila asked.

A long pause followed. I could picture Kenosi sitting there across from me, reclining like a king in his leather chair. He'd have a smirk on those gorgeous, full lips, and his lids lowered to give her his superior, hooded gaze from his black eyes that flecked with gold when he grew excited and showed his cheetah. It was like I could see every detail of the men on the helicopter in holographic detail even with my eyes closed. I wasn't drowsy or groggy from the potion, but I didn't want to talk or be interrupted from my mental perusal, either. I didn't know what would come out of my mouth if I tried to speak, so I was glad when everyone lapsed into silence.

Too soon, the chopper dipped, and Sir Kenosi's words cut through the haze in my mind. "The Lion Nation is very traditional," he said. "There are actually many clans within the nation, but this one has the amulet. Lions rely heavily on custom, so you would be wise to follow my lead, even if those customs are foreign to you."

"Of course," Lord Balam said. "We appreciate your guidance. We would like to request an audience with Prince Kwame."

"He has the amulet?" Camila asked.

"Yes," Lord Balam said.

The Lion Court had visited us once when I was a child, but I couldn't seem to remember a lot about them. I had a picture of a tall, extremely thin boy with black velvet skin and eyes to match, but before I could drudge up more memories, Camila spoke.

"Are you sure?"

"The oracle is never wrong," Lord Balam said, stroking his jaguar cloak with obvious pride.

"Our king is very close with King Lion," Sir Kenosi said. "Relations between our clans are excellent. You'll be welcomed with open arms."

Because of his presence. He didn't say it—obviously he was going to be all polite and modest in front of the real princess, the one who didn't know better than to believe it—but I could read between the lines even in my drugged state. He was doing us a huge favor. Like when Lord Balam had offered his assistance, I just couldn't figure out why. Come to think of it, I still didn't know why Lord Balam had come with us. I trusted him now, maybe even loved him. I was in too deep to back out. If he was going to betray me, I was just going to have to suffer that blow. I couldn't help it now that I'd fallen for him.

THIRTY-FIVE

WE CLIMBED DOWN FROM THE CHOPPER IN WHAT looked like a very remote safari camp. There were a dozen mud and brick houses with thatched roofs, some of them large but most only one or two rooms. Around us, shimmering waves of golden grass stretched as far as they eye could see, interrupted only by an occasional small, twisted tree. I inhaled the scent of warm grass in the sun, dirt, the sweat of a hard day's work like I used to smell on Tadeu. The air was so dry and hot I could feel a crackle in it, like some kind of electrical charge, as if it were ready and waiting for us. Shadow kept his arm tightly around my waist, guiding me as we started down a wide dirt path that ran through the tiny village.

A pair of small children with deep black skin and bright eyes jumped up and ran behind one of the buildings, only to take turns peeking at us from around the side of it. A few adults were working outside, but they stopped to stare as we passed.

Sir Kenosi raised a hand and called out a greeting in another language, and they returned it, but they seemed more polite than overly friendly. Despite his boast that their clans had a great relationship, a knot of trepidation tightened inside me. Kenosi was the last man I'd trust.

"Are we walking into a trap?" I hissed to Shadow.

"If there's anyone here more lost than you, it's me," Shadow muttered.

I turned to Lord Balam, but he only shrugged. "One way to find out."

Of course he wasn't going to stop this. So far, he hadn't stopped anything that had happened. He seemed willing and eager for everything that had happened. He'd gone looking for Shadow in the swamp with me. He'd hopped on the plane to Africa with me. I loved his willingness to go on any adventure. I couldn't fault him for it now.

Only the ocelots seemed concerned. Camila hung back from Gabor, clutching her tiny purse with her gloved hands, her face ashen, her eyes darting around. Gabor walked straight and stiff, his hand hovering close to his holster.

Their suspicion calmed me slightly. I wasn't the only one getting nervous about this.

When we were almost to the end of the small street where the largest house stood, two women in brightly patterned wrap dresses emerged, big smiles on their faces. They greeted Sir Kenosi first, embracing him and speaking rapidly over each other. I didn't have to know their language to see that he was a friend to them. Relief sank into me, and I relaxed a little.

Not a trap.

I swayed on my feet, suddenly fascinated by these bright, cheerful women. They reminded me more of birds than lions. Their wrap dresses were lightweight to combat the heat, and they both wore their hair shorn with patterns worked into the short length left on their scalps. A coil of gold wound around one of their necks three times, while the other wore gold bangles around her wrists and several gold hoops in her nose and lips. Both wore an assortment of gold, seashell, and bead earrings.

Suddenly, they were greeting the rest of us, and I realized I had no idea what to do. I had zoned out on the beautiful women, not paying attention to anything else. I really hoped I'd have time to sleep off the rest of this potion trip before I met the king.

"They don't speak your language," Sir Kenosi said, turning to us. "Do you speak French?"

"A bit," I said, suddenly wishing I'd paid more attention to the tutors instead of escaping to the stables to play with the servants.

Lord Balam and Camila greeted the women fluently while Shadow shook his head. He and I stumbled through the introduction, and then we were led into the large, spacious house. Stepping out of the blazing sun was a relief, though I had to blink a few times to adjust to the unlit interior of the house. It was made up of one big, open room, though there were spaces at the back sectioned off with colorful sheets of fabric. Four doors stood open around the house, letting the hot breeze shift through the interior.

A circle of at least a dozen people sat in the center of the room, most on straw mats on the packed earth floor, but two of them elevated on carved stone chairs. Damn it. I definitely wasn't going to get a chance to sleep this off before meeting the king and queen. It was nothing like my entrance into the Cheetah Kingdom, though. This place was as far from Sir Kenosi's as I could imagine.

The women asked a question about staying, and Kenosi answered with words that meant small. Then we were at the edge of the circle. The king had small, narrow eyes, a wide mouth, and a high forehead marked with a series of raised scars that started at his eyebrows and rose to his hairline. A feeling of *deja vous* swept over me, and I had a vague memory of these people visiting the Ocelot Court when I was a child, years before our mother died, when our father hadn't yet alienated the entire IFCN.

As the two women who greeted us skirted the circle and took their places on either side of the king and queen, more of that visit came back to me. Those women were princesses. Plural. Unlike ocelots, lions had multiple children, though I couldn't quite remember why. Camila had whispered it to me back then, and I knew it had something to do with their shifter ability.

That fact had impressed me most about the lion visit, followed closely by my fascination with the king's ritual scarring. When my five-year-old self couldn't contain her curiosity, I'd asked their son Kwame, who was probably in his late teens and had a set of his own scars, but who was far less intimidating than the king. Kwame had told me, but I'd refusing to believe someone would voluntarily receive dozens of cuts that would mar his face forever.

For the rest of the trip, Kwame had teased me with stories about how they'd gotten the scars. A father-son hunting trip had gone wrong when they'd fallen on a porcupine. A lion had attacked his father, and Kwame had heroically defended him, getting scratched across the forehead before defeating it. They'd been struck by lightning while holding up a metal utensil—and on and on.

I searched the group for Kwame, that teenage boy who hadn't been too proud to tease a kid, probably because he had kid sisters of his own. I could imagine him now, thirteen years older, with the same inky black skin and eyes as his father, the same tall, whip-thin build, the same spark of humor in his wide smile. But I couldn't tell which of the men around the circle was the boy I'd met back then. All the men had scars, though not as many as the king. They each wore a simple strand of gold around their necks and loose tunic-style shirts with beading across the chest.

We stood before the circle of people, waiting for something, though I wasn't sure what.

"How you have grown, little golden child," Queen Lion said. "How is your family?" She spoke slowly enough that I could understand her French, but she wasn't speaking to me. I wasn't the golden child—Camila was. I remembered the lion princesses' fascination with Camila's white skin and blonde hair when they'd visited, and how left out I'd felt when they braided her hair and put beads in it like their own. That might have been the first time I realized that I was less desirable than my sister for reasons beyond her magic.

"They are well, Your Majesty," Camila said with a prim curtsy. "It is a pleasure to visit your fine kingdom. Thank you for welcoming us so graciously."

Back then, my sister had sucked up the attention of the princesses, and I had gone off to pester Kwame with more questions. Now, she performed the role she'd been born to play while I stood there high on panther potion in a slutty dress. Some things never changed.

Instead of answering, Queen Lion glanced sideways at her husband.

"You are looking well, Lord Balam," King Lion said. "How is Lady Zuleima?"

Fuck. Was that his ex-wife? Or his daughter? If I hadn't felt like a token piece of ass on this trip before, I certainly did now. I didn't even know my lover's child.

"And you look quite strong and healthy yourself," Balam said with a deep bow. "I see your family is as beautiful and plentiful as I remember. How are your herds this year?"

King Lion smiled, his narrow eyes crinkling at the corners, and inclined his head slightly before turning his gaze to his cheetah guest. "Sir Kenosi, you are looking as fine as ever. How is your king?"

"You look like a million bucks," Kenosi said, a grin on his face. "And your family looks like twelve million. My only question is, when are you going to let me marry one of those daughters?"

King Lion laughed, a big laugh that came up from his belly, waving a hand at Sir Kenosi. Clearly it wasn't just their clans had an excellent relationship. As the king began to address Gabor, I caught the pattern of their speech and address. They were addressing each of us in order of our status. Camila, being the heir to a shifter throne, was of the highest status. I, being a human, was lowest in the hierarchy of shifters.

Only after her husband finished addressing all the men did Queen Lion turn her unreadable gaze to me. While King Lion seemed friendly and welcoming, I couldn't read his wife as well. She had only given Sir Kenosi the smallest smile, otherwise remaining solemn, even cold, as she studied us each in turn.

"And you must be Princess Itzel," she said. "You have grown into a handsome woman since I've seen you. How is your king?"

My mouth opened, an answer to her question rising automatically to my lips. But no one else had answered the questions, so I steered my response to match the others. "You and your family are even more beautiful than I remember," I said, bowing deeply as the others had.

Fuck. I was supposed to ask a question, but I knew nothing about these people. All I could think to ask was, "Which one of your handsome sons is the patient Kwame I remember from your visit?"

There was a beat of silence, and I knew I'd fucked up. Why hadn't I asked about the weather?

"Prince Kwame is a lion now," King Lion said. I was relieved to see that his eyes were warm and sympathetic as he addressed me. Suddenly, a lion was lunging at my face, a snarl furrowing its nose, its long fangs exposed and gleaming.

I lurched backwards, a cry caught in my throat, but Lord Balam's strong arms caught me. "Forgive her, Your Majesties," he said to the monarchs. "She didn't know."

"Didn't know what?" I asked, glancing around the circle of sober faces, trying to shake the hallucination of the lion from my mind. "Aren't you all lions?"

Queen Lion folded her hands calmly in her lap, her inscrutable black eyes fixed on me. "Our eldest son spends his time in this world in lion form," she said. "I'm afraid there is no way for you to see him in human form."

"Why not?" I asked, my confused thoughts tumbling over each other. "Forgive my ignorance, Your Majesty. I'm not well acquainted with shifter politics."

"Not politics," Lord Balam murmured. "It's their nature."

"Lion shifters can only use their human form in the spirit world," Queen Lion said, her eyes as sad and old as time itself. "I'm not long for this world, and for that, I am glad. For soon, I will be with my beloved son again."

I blinked at her, trying to unravel her meaning. "He's..."

"I'm sorry to disappoint you, Princess Itzel. But Prince Kwame is dead."

Thirty-Six

"I messed up," Camila wailed, flapping her hands like a bird and sucking in shallow, quick breaths. "Oh, god, Itz, I messed up so bad. I forgot the proper etiquette with them, and I had to go first, and I just panicked. I made such a bad impression. What am I going to do?" She broke off with a hiccupping gasp, her blue eyes wide as she scanned the savannah where we had gone to walk after the painful introduction to the Lion Court.

I knew what I should do. I should comfort my sister, tell her she hadn't messed up, that she'd done fine. That she couldn't be expected to know how to greet foreign dignitaries in their country. And then I should fix it for her, tell her how to make it better. I should calm her the way only I could. So why did I feel like grabbing her shoulders and shaking her, telling her to get herself together?

"At least you didn't bring up their dead son," I said, crossing my arms and staring out across grassland, trying to make out a lion in the shimmering mirage of heat. But though my head was still woozy and tumbling with strange thoughts, I hadn't seen anything since the snarling image had leapt at me from thin air.

Camila rounded on me, her eyes narrowed to slits. "You're not the heir to the ocelot throne," she hissed. "You would do well to remember that, Itzel."

"Oh, trust me, I remember," I said. "No one lets me forget for a second. Don't think it escaped me that they greeted me last."

"Who cares when they greeted you or what you said?" Camila said, throwing her hands up. "You're not even a shifter!"

"So, I don't matter," I clarified. "That's what you're saying. That's what you're all saying, all the time. I'm getting really, really tired of being treated like the ugly stepchild of the group just because I happen to be human. It would be nice if my sister didn't have to remind me, too."

Camila blinked at me like I'd slapped her, but she quickly hid the hurt with a cold stare. "You really have changed. You used to care about me. A few months ago, you would have been devastated if I made such a blunder. Now all you care about is yourself."

"No," I said. "I'm just starting to care about myself, too."

"You never lacked that," Camila said, a bitter edge to her voice. "Running around with Tadeu instead of doing your lessons so you could make a good impression where I didn't.

A brilliant answer from you today might have shown our kingdom's class and smoothed my rough start. And how can you say you've been ignored? Lord Balam and Shadow can't keep their hands off you."

"I think I've done a pretty good job picking up the slack on this trip so far," I said through gritted teeth. "I can't always be there to save you. I make mistakes, too."

"See, there you go making it all about you again," Camila said. "You used to think about me, too. Ever since Lord Balam paid attention to you, you think you're all that. And now that delusional panther is making your head even bigger."

"Shadow has nothing to do with this," I said. "And neither does Lord Balam. Except maybe they've made me start to believe someone could value me despite my lowly human status."

Camila gawked at me. "Itzel, you can't be serious. You can't actually believe you're the mate of a shifter."

"Well..." I said with a shrug. Was it crazy? Was Shadow?

Camila let out a short, sharp laugh. "Wow, Itz. You really are naïve. At least Lord Balam has a title. Shadow is an unhinged nobody."

"I'm a nobody," I said. "So why can't I be his mate? We can be nobodies together."

"Itzel," she said, putting her hands on my shoulders. "You're tripping on potion. Shadow is not your mate. It's impossible. He's either delusional, or he's playing you."

"Why would he do that?"

"To get to the Ocelot Court," she said. "Obviously. At least Mom had to be kidnapped. You'd just invite him into the palace, wouldn't you?"

I tried to step away, but she held fast. She'd never used her shifter strength on me. It was nothing compared to the other big cats, but it was more than I had. "Let me go," I growled. "You don't want to believe anyone could actually like me for myself, do you? Is that it? You can't believe anyone would like someone with no magic and no throne waiting."

"I'm sorry Shadow drugged you," she said. "Just another reason I'm leaving him here. I don't trust him, Itzel. He's dangerous. He should never have come along at all."

"Funny. He says the same thing about you."

Camila drew up as if she'd just been doused in ice water. "You believe him? And not me?"

"No," I said. "I just find it ironic."

"Well, it's my decision," she said. "So, it doesn't matter if he trusts me. He's dismissed from the rest of the tour."

"You can't just ditch him in the middle of Africa," I said. "In case you forgot, he's here because he protected you against his own clan. If he hadn't warned us, none of us would be here."

"How convenient for him to make you think that."

I rolled my eyes. "He didn't set up some big plot against you. He didn't even know you had the amulet."

"How do you know he's telling the truth?"

"I just do," I said with a shrug. Maybe it was the drug, but I knew Shadow. Though we'd barely talked, I understood him in some deeper, fundamental way. I knew what he was about, and it wasn't trickery.

Camila crossed her arms. "Not good enough."

"We can't leave him," I repeated. "I won't."

I didn't think I'd ever openly defied my sister, refused her order so blatantly. It was both freeing and terrifying, like I'd just leapt from the helicopter with no parachute. I was already falling now, though. It was too late to go back.

Camila's jaw clenched. "You can thank him for services rendered in the way I'm sure he wants. Then he's not our problem anymore."

"He's not a problem," I said. "He's a person."

"Fine," she said. "If you'd choose a crazy swamp creature over your own sister, that's your mistake. It's better that I know where your loyalties lie now rather than after I've taken the throne."

With that, she turned, flicked her hair over her shoulder, and strode back toward the house. Did it really come down to this? Abandon Shadow in the middle of nowhere after all he'd done for us, or abandon my sister after coming so far and getting half the amulets? It was an impossible choice, and yet, it was never really any choice at all. I couldn't survive alone in the Lion Kingdom, either.

I stood watching her go, torn between letting her go and running after her, begging her to forgive me, and saying all the placating words. She was right about one thing. I had changed. I wasn't the sister who would sit back and be called expendable, who would take whatever scraps I was thrown and make the most of them. I wanted more now. I wanted my own life, and I wanted a say.

If she wouldn't let me have it, maybe I didn't belong on her tour, either.

THIRTY-SEVEN

I LAY IN THE GRASS WATCHING THE SKY GO FROM blue to white to crimson and orange. Insects sang and buzzed, but I didn't move. Only my mind moved, reeling like the birds high overhead. Thoughts of Camila, of her accusation that I'd changed, mingled with the discussions I'd had with Sir Kenosi over whether money or title came with more power. Shadow's proclamation that I was his mate was shaded by the petals of doubt Camila had dropped. Lord Balam's mysterious motives, the fact that he'd protect me from Shadow one moment, and the next, he'd stand back and watch as Shadow fucked me with no indication that I wanted it.

After a while, I closed my eyes and dreamed. A lion stood over me, its body at least twice as long as mine, muscled with unimaginable power. I gasped, wanting to scramble away but not daring to move, to breathe. It lowered its head and snuffed at my arm, the one the magic had burned. Then it was gone, but I was pinned, unable to move.

"My *cherie*," a voice whispered, though there was no one there. It was as if the swaying grasses themselves spoke. "I never imagined my mate would be the incorrigible little ocelot princess."

A cold breeze swept up my neck like a breath from invisible lips. I tried to roll over, but my body was pressed to the earth. I struggled, but nothing happened. I was as trapped as I had been under the lion's stare. My legs were parted, and another sigh swept through the prairie.

"Are you Kwame's ghost?" I whispered, going still.

"Can you see me?" he asked. The cold shimmered over me, and my dress was pushed up.

"No." I struggled to free myself as I searched the dark, starry sky for a sign of him. There was nothing, only the cold pressure moving over me, insistent but without substance. I didn't know how it could pin me to the ground while he had nothing to brace against when I reached to push him away, bucked to get him off. It was like a person made of air, a person with no substance but with the ability to pull aside my panties and circle my clit until I whimpered and squirmed harder. It was as if one point of pressurized air was drawing a circle around my sensitive bud, burrowing between my folds.

"What I wouldn't give for one taste of this succulent flesh," his sighing voice whispered in the night. "To suck the honey from this sweet cunt."

I tried to close my knees, to squeeze my legs together, but they were held open, splayed wide. My pussy lips were spread open to the night air. Cold suctioned between my legs, and I gasped, arching up despite myself. A rumble sounded through the savannah, but I couldn't tell if it was thunder or the ground itself trembling beneath me. Coldness coiled around my limbs, and I shivered, but it only increased. Cold pressure teased my opening, worming inside me like snake made of pressurized air. I pictured Kwame as I'd known him, a young man about my age, his teasing smile. If I pictured that, maybe I wouldn't scream myself awake from this nightmare.

The cold shaft of air filled me, harder now, thicker, pumping into my dry flesh with quick, sure strokes. I cried out, trying to free myself, though there was no pain. There was nothing there, no friction to cause pain, nothing forcing into my resistant flesh. The violation felt deeper than that, as if he were plundering my soul instead of my body. He had me pinned like a moth, spread wide and helplessly fluttering against him.

"Stop," I gasped. "Please, stop."

"Come with me," he said. "Come with me into the spirit world. We can be together forever."

"No," I said, louder now, my panic giving me strength. "I'm not ready to die. Let me go!"

"You won't die," he said. The snake of cold air thrust into me faster, harder. I struggled, squirming and bucking to free myself, but it kept on, pounding into me relentlessly until I couldn't help my body's reaction to the stimulation. Wetness slicked my walls, and the cold invasion went deeper, aching as it strained against my depth. Cold spread through me, tingling from my core and through my limbs. I gasped despite myself.

"Say yes," his cold breath whispered against my neck, sending a shiver through me.

"Then let me go," I panted.

"If you'll come with me," he whispered. "If you come, I'll give you the amulet. We can be together in body there, not only in spirit. Don't you want to be with your mate?"

I started to say Shadow was my mate, but I didn't want to anger this ghost. I didn't know what he would or could do to me, or why he'd picked me, or why he thought I was his mate.

What if Camila was right about Shadow? What if he was tricking me? Just because I'd pictured a mark on his arm, this didn't mean he had it. I'd seen his body a dozen times, and there was no mark. Even if there had been, that didn't prove that it was my mark. He could have found his True Mate a long time ago, maybe even lost her in the conflict with our people. Maybe he wanted revenge. Some people never met their True Mate, or he was already dead. That's what he'd said. So maybe this ghost really was mine—or I was his.

"I don't know," I said at last. "How will I get back here?"

"You're living," he said, as if that answered everything. "Don't you want to see your mother again?"

"Mom," I gasped. My heart erupted in my chest. I wanted that more than almost anything. I had missed her every day—her kindness, the way she looked at me like I was just as good as the shifters, the way she combed my hair, her smell. More than that, I missed her for the things only a mother could do. She hadn't been there to help me with the embarrassment of my first periods, to advise me on my first love when I fell for Tadeu. I missed what it felt like to know someone was always on my side. So, I'd replaced her with my big sister, believing she was like our mother because Father had said it so many times. But maybe she wasn't the kind and gentle soul I'd always believed.

I wanted to know if Mom was. Had I built all that in my head, idolizing her out of grief instead of picturing the reality of who she'd been? I wanted to ask her other questions, like whether she had ever loved Father, and if not, had she resented us because we were a product of their forced marriage? Had the panthers really killed her, and if not, what happened to her after she disappeared from the palace in the night?

"Your mother is there," Kwame said. "All of the dead are there. Anyone you've ever loved who has died is in the spirit world."

"Tadeu?" I asked.

"Every spirit," Kwame confirmed. The cold invasion slipped from between my legs, but I remained splayed on the ground, my skirt around my waist.

"How will we find them?" I asked, trying to ignore the exposed feeling.

"When a living person enters the spirit world, all souls notice," he said. "They'll be watching you every moment until you leave. Every one of them. Your mother, this Tadeu... They will come running to see you."

"Really?" I whispered as the point of cold pressure shivered up my thigh, over my hip, exploring my body. I wanted to scream, to shove it away and end this violation. It skimmed up, tracing the outline of my curves, tugging down the top of my dress, circling my nipple like a tongue. I squirmed, a strange heat that was both desire and disgust building inside me. "Let me go, and I'll go into the spirit world with you."

The cold pressure instantly ceased, and I was free. I began to swim toward the surface of consciousness, trying to find my way out of the dream, but I couldn't seem to wake up. I could see the stars above me, like diamonds scattered across a sea of black velvet, and feel the cold breeze over the grasses making goosebumps rise along my arms. I sat up and pulled up my dress, then stood and pulled down the skirt before hugging my cardigan closed around me. My breath shook as I inhaled, taking in the scent of the dry grass.

The lion lay so still I almost stepped on it. I bit back a scream, leaping backward. It lifted its head, a growl rumbling through it.

"Well, fuck me," I whispered, backing up another step. "This is worse than the dream."

The lion's eyes flashed the color of copper, burning in the night. It looked at me a long moment, then lay its head down again, its eyes closing. I turned to run, but before I could take a step, a cold snake of pressure whipped around my arm, pulling me back, anchoring me to the spot.

I squeezed my eyes shut. *I'm dreaming. It's just a dream.*

"Come," he said, pulling me back. "The spirit world is waiting."

And then I was tumbling through darkness, nothing to anchor me but a current of air squeezing tight around my wrist.

THIRTY-EIGHT

Prince Kwame
Shifter Prince, Lion Nation

I WOULD LIVE AGAIN. I WOULD HAVE MY HUMAN form again, in the human world. I had waited all these years, and now it had come. The thing I had been waiting for—the person. Not only someone powerful, but someone important. My mate.

A moment of regret tugged at my heart, that I had to deceive this way to make it happen. But my mate would be happy when she realized. She would be happy that her mate was not trapped in the form of a lion.

I did not know exactly how this magic worked. I only knew that I must convince her to stay with me here, or to bring me back as a man. I could not return to my world into that lion body one more time. Not with my mate at my side. Not to see her fear and disappointment that she was stuck with a fearsome lion as her mate.

If only she would choose to take me back in human form. If only I could see my mother again, my father, my sisters. To join their laughter. I had missed that the most. Lions didn't laugh. But humans—humans laughed. To laugh again, that was a dream. And now it was within my reach. How could I convince her?

I would give her everything she desired. I would give her the mother she had lost. The amulet she sought. I would give her the mate she deserved, the one she'd come for. Not the one who took advantage of her helpless state as I had shamefully done on the grass. It hadn't seemed real. Just a little play.

But now I knew how real it was, and how wrong I had been to go about our first mating that way. I would make it up to her when we could both be human. I would enjoy having a human body back for that more than anything. To feel her body with the presence of mine, not just my spirit form. To take a woman again in my raw, solid, man form. And not just any woman. My mate.

My *True Mate*.

I had found her. How lucky I was, to have found her. Or unlucky, if she would not have me. It could be a curse more terrifyingly unfair than death itself, to find one's True Mate when it was too late.

We still had one chance. She might not understand the True

Mate bond yet, but I did. I knew that she would need me in my human form every bit as much as I did.

I would not let it be too late. I would do whatever it took—anything—to be with her. To give her a real man as a mate. Even if she hated me for it, I would give her what she needed.

THIRTY-NINE

Itzel
Princess, Ocelot Nation

I OPENED MY EYES, EXPECTING TO FIND MYSELF finally awake from the dream and back in my body, clear-headed and potion free. But I wasn't lying in the grass or curled in the hammock they had offered me for the night. I was lying on an enormous bed, the towering posts made of ornately carved black marble. The mattress was soft as clouds. Beside me lay a man.

I jumped up and backed away, rubbing my wrist where the cold still lingered. The man propped himself up on one elbow and smiled at me, revealing straight white teeth with a gap between the front two. He looked like I remembered but older—shorn hair pinched into little twists, dark black skin, scarification tattoos on his forehead, and keen, bright copper eyes. While I took him in, he sat up and swung a pair of very long legs over the edge of the bed.

"It is you," I said, my tone accusing.

"Prince Kwame," he said, pressing a palm to his chest.

"Please tell me this is part of the hallucination, and I didn't just arrive in the underworld."

"Welcome to the spirit world, Princess Itzel." He stood and gave a small bow. He was incredibly tall, at least six and a half feet, and still as thin and wiry as I remembered. "Now we can be together in the flesh."

"I'm not dead, am I?"

"Of course not," he said, looking offended that I'd ask.

"Are you really going to give me the amulet, or is this going to be another place where I have to do a bunch of humiliating challenges, and then you try to get out of giving it to me, anyway?"

Prince Kwame had the decency to look ashamed as he shook his head. "I don't have the amulet. It belongs in the world of the physical, the world of substance."

"You lied to me," I said, my hands balling into fists. "You don't even have it?"

"I didn't lie," Kwame said, holding out both hands, palms up. "I said if you came here, I would give it to you. My mother has it. If you return with me, she will give it to you. I swear on my... Honor." He faltered on the last word, as if forgetting he had nothing to give up. He was dead.

"That might be worth more if you hadn't just ghost-fucked me."

To my surprise, he reached out and took my hand, then bent to kiss it. "Thank you, my queen."

"Um. You know I'm not *that* princess, right? Because I'm told shifters can tell. But I don't know about... Ghosts, or whatever you are. Sorry." I winced at my babbling, so unlike me. He had me flustered with his gentlemanly manner after the little encounter in the grass. I had expected someone more like Kenosi or even Lord Balam.

"If you are my mate, you are a queen in my eyes," he said. "A prince must die to become a lion shifter. I'm sorry this is the only way we can be together."

"You mean in the spirit world, or by using trickery? Because if the amulet isn't here, I came here for nothing."

Kwame's eyes softened, and he gave me a wounded look. "You came here to be with your mate," he said. "And to see your mother, my queen."

"Is there an actual queen here?" I asked. "Of the spirit world?"

"There are many queens here," he said. "But none that I care about."

"Ah, right," I said, nodding. "All the queens who have ever died are here."

"Yes," he said. "And you can meet them all, if you like."

"I'd like to see my mother," I said. "How does that work? How do we get around here? I don't suppose there are cars driving spirits around."

"No," Kwame said with a laugh that was both deep and bubbling, like a spring welling up from deep underground. "Come." He took my hand and pulled me toward the wall. "When you are here, you are living. Every spirit will be watching you, wanting something from you. If you want to see someone, you only have to think of them. They will be overjoyed at the chance to meet a living person. It so seldom happens here."

"I just think of someone, and they appear?"

"More or less," he said. "More powerful people can summon you if they wish. But usually, a mutual desire to see each other is enough."

Kwame stepped through as if the wall were nothing but air. I balked, expecting to smack my forehead against it, but instead, I moved through without so much as a hair on my head being disturbed.

We stepped into a large yet cozy room with a stone wall opposite us, a fireplace burning in the center of it. Brown leather couches and chairs sat facing the fire, and a thick woolen rug covered the floor. A woman sat on the sofa, a stack of thick leather tomes on the end table beside her and a lamp burning beside them. For one horrifying moment, I was sure that if I looked too closely, I'd see someone else. But it was her. It was my mom.

"Mom?" I whispered, not daring to hope but not able to stop myself. My heart was pounding so hard I couldn't even think. Could she hear me? Speak to me?

"Itzel." She shot to her feet and rushed at me.

"Mom," I cried, dropping Kwame's hand and leaping toward her. I crashed into her arms so hard the breath was knocked out of me. Relief crushed me with painful force when my arms circled her, clinging tightly to her solid form. For a second, I'd been sure my arms would cut right through her, that she'd be nothing but an illusion.

"It's you," I said, relishing the bruising force with which we both held on. "It's really you. I never thought I'd see you again."

"I hoped I wouldn't," she said, detangling herself and holding me away. "At least not yet." Her eyes were sad as she searched my face. She looked exactly as I remembered her— exactly as she'd been before she died. Kindness pooled in her big brown eyes as she stroked my wavy black hair, so much like hers, behind my ears. "You shouldn't be here."

"Neither should you," I said, sliding my hands over hers, not wanting to let go of her in case she disappeared when I did.

"What happened?" she asked, sorrow weighing on her strong features. "How are you here?"

"I'm not dead," I said. "Prince Kwame said I could come to visit and then go back."

"I know you're alive. Did he tell you the rules of moving between worlds?" she asked, her voice tight with fear.

"No." I turned to confront Kwame, but there was no one behind me. Damn it. I'd known it sounded too good to be true, but I hadn't been able to resist seeing Mom and Tadeu. I could tell from Mom's voice that had been a mistake.

"You're in grave danger," Mom said, grabbing both my hands and squeezing. "You must get back. If anything happens to your body while you are here..."

"I'll never get back," I finished, swallowing hard.

Fucking Kwame.

Mom's lips tightened, her eyes soft with concern. "You must go back at once."

"But I just got here," I said. "I've barely seen you. Mom, I have so much to ask you."

"As do I," she said. "But your life is more important. There is one thing I must tell you. Beware of the men in your life."

I drew back in surprise. "Which men? Kwame? Shadow and Balam? Can you see us in our world? Do you watch over us?"

"All men," she whispered. "Now, go. Find Kwame and go."

"It was worth it to see you even for a minute," I said, throwing my arms around her again.

"It was," she agreed softly. "You've grown up so beautifully, Itzel."

"How do I get back?"

"Kwame is a bridge," she said. "That is someone who moves between worlds. He can take you back."

"Where is he?"

"We'll find him," she said, gripping my hand. "I don't know how much time we have. Where did you leave yourself in the human world?"

I swallowed hard, my throat aching with the effort. "Out in the open," I said. "With lions."

Mom shuddered, her fingers going cold in mine. "You have to get back."

"Is Tadeu here?" I asked, feeling greedy for wanting more but unable to keep myself from the thought of him. If I wanted hard enough, would he appear, too? Could I apologize to him, be with him for even a moment, long enough to make peace?

"I don't know," Mom said, shaking her head. "There are many here."

"I have to see him before I go."

"You don't have time."

"I do," I said, a flicker of anger going through me. If everyone in the spirit world knew I was here, and he saw me leave without even attempting to contact him...

No. I wouldn't leave without seeing him.

I pulled my hands from Mom's and pressed the heels of my hands against my eyes as if I could push the tears back into my eye sockets. According to Kwame, I could bring Tadeu here with just my thoughts. My love, the man whose death had set all this in motion. He'd opened my eyes to what my father really was, to the monster ruling our nation. If it hadn't been for his death, I might have lived in comfort in the castle while my sister went on her tour. I had vowed his death wouldn't be in vain.

I called to him, my chest aching with the need for his wide, smiling face and his rough humor. He had taught me that even a mere human could have value. He had taught me about love, about life, and how it felt to be a woman. I'd planned to elevate him in status, to show our world that humans could have important roles in our government, too.

Suddenly, I felt his powerful, bright energy connecting to my own. I'd found him! My heart swelled with love and excitement, and my eyes opened, laughter coming through my tears at the thought of seeing him again. The man I'd loved all my life was here. I could feel him.

And then something yanked tight inside me, as if I'd been drawing him to me and then he'd stopped short. Something had interrupted our connection.

"What's happening?" I asked, turning to Mom. "Is Kwame stopping me from seeing Tadeu?"

Mom shook her head, her eyes sad. "No," she said. "Tadeu is stopping it."

"What?" I demanded. "Why?"

"I don't know," she said. "I don't know what has come and gone in the human world. I only know what is happening here."

So, she could tell he was refusing to come to me, but she didn't know why. Relief and shame washed through me at once. She didn't know that Tadeu blamed me for his death, but I knew. I'd seen it in his eyes the moment he was killed. It hadn't hit me fully, though. Not like this. I didn't know he hated me so much that if he got the chance to see me again, even after death, he'd refuse. My heart wrenched, and my stomach churned with so much hurt I thought I'd be sick.

"You must go," Mom said, laying a gentle hand on my arm. "I'm sorry, but you can't stay here, Itzel. It is too dangerous."

"Wouldn't I feel it if something happened to my body up there?"

She shook her head. "No, and it's not only that. You are in danger here. If the spirits here can find a way to you, they'll swarm a living soul with demands. If they are strong enough, they will take what they want, whether you give it freely or not."

"Take what?" I asked, my cheeks warming at the memory of Kwame's ghost pushing into me.

"Your life," she said. "Your life force. They will drain it away."

"How does that help them?" I said. "They're already dead."

Mom shook her head, her eyes wide and serious. "Prince Kwame didn't tell you? Itzel, if a living soul is strong, she can bring back someone from the spirit world when she returns."

FORTY

"WHAT?" I ASKED, SPINNING TO MY MOTHER, MY eyes wide. "I can bring you back? As in, bring you back to life?"

"Not me," she said gently. "I lived my life. I'm at peace here. Bring back someone young, someone who can still make a difference in your world."

"But I don't need anyone else," I insisted, my heart twisting inside me as I clutched her hands. "I need you, Mom."

She shook her head, tears pooling in her eyes. "Not me," she said again.

"Why not?" I demanded, balking when she tried to pull me from the room. I understood now. I understood why Kwame had dragged me here and what he wanted. If I brought him back, his mother would give me the amulet. He'd told me as much. I just hadn't realized I'd be bringing him back to life. Or that I'd be choosing him over my mother.

"Itzel," Mom said. "Think clearly. I know you are emotional right now, but you must think of your country, your world, in this moment. Not only the people you have lost, but those the world has lost."

I took a deep, shuddering breath, trying to accept the fact that my mother didn't want to go back. She didn't want to return to us. Maybe she'd never wanted to be our mother at all.

"Why not you?" I asked, refusing to let her push me away so easily. "The world lost you. You could make things better. You'd be a queen again. You have influence." If she wasn't the woman I remembered, if I'd built that in my head after she died, she was going to have to tell me straight.

"I'm sorry," she said. "It's not safe for me there."

"And it's safe here? Mom, you're dead."

"And you're not," she said. "It's your turn to live. You must do it now, before it's too late. Surround yourself with strong people you can trust, Itzel. That was my mistake. I chose one man who loved me above all else, and that was my downfall. You need more than that. You need loyalty on every side, but you need them to be accountable to each other. Never trust one man with your whole safety, no matter how much he loves you."

As she spoke, she dragged me through the wall, and we were back in the bedroom where I'd woken with Kwame. He sat on the edge of the bed, his earnest smile ready for me.

"Mom," I said, turning back to her and taking her hands in mine. "Come back with me. There's so much I need to know. You can teach me."

"Is my mate leaving me so soon?" Kwame asked, looking wounded.

"You didn't tell her the rules of the spirit world," my mother said, her formidable dark eyebrows drawing together. "You think you can trick my daughter?"

"N-no," Kwame said, his smile melting. He looked almost... scared. He may have been a prince, but my mother was a queen. And even though she'd come from nothing, not even the staunchest proponent of keeping royal blood pure had ever dared say anything derogatory to her face.

My mother's only answer was a fierce frown that made even me feel sorry for the Lion Prince.

"I only meant to spend more time with my mate," Kwame said.

"By bringing her to the spirit world forever?" my mother asked.

"I didn't think..." Kwame broke off and shook his head. "It was the only way. I have to be with her. You don't understand. She's my True Mate."

"Sorry to disappoint you," I said. "But I don't think I'm your mate."

"Of course you are," he said, drawing back with a look of surprise. As if to prove it, he rolled up his sleeve and showed me a mark like the one I'd seen on Shadow. "You marked my arm when we mated."

Shadow had said the same thing. I didn't know either man well, but I knew Shadow better. I knew he'd held me all night when I needed it. Was that a trick? What about everything he'd said on the helicopter? He'd told me he loved me.

Still, what did I know about shifter mating marks? That pawprint could belong to anyone. I didn't even have a paw, for fuck's sake. I wasn't a cat.

I turned to my mother, but she just nodded, her lips pressed together.

"He's my mate?" I asked, my mind reeling.

Then Camila had been right. Shadow had lied to me.

"How is that possible?" I asked. "I'm not a shifter."

"Sometimes it's more complicated than that," she said, sounding tired and resigned. "You have shifter blood running through your veins."

"Take me back with you, my queen," Prince Kwame said. "If you must go back, it's the only way. We have to be together. I cannot bear to know you are out there and not be with you. I'll—I'll—." He broke off, looking stricken, like he'd just realized he couldn't say "I'll die."

How long had he been dead?

Before I could ask, my mother was nodding. "You must go, Itzel. You must go now."

"With him?" I asked, a knot the size of a pineapple forming in my throat. I couldn't just walk away from her. I'd spent nearly half my life wanting her, needing her, and being unable to have her. Now I had a chance to take her back, to make her live again. I couldn't give that up for a man I'd barely met.

Mom was already pushing me toward him, though. "Go," she said again. Tears leaked down her cheeks, and she turned me toward her, holding my face between her hands. "It's not safe for you here. I'm sorry, Itzel. I would like you to stay, to see you longer. Believe me, I would like nothing more than to spend another day with my daughters. But not like this."

"Then come," I said, gripping her hand. And even though I knew she was strong, and her grip was firm, there was something fragile about it, as if I might squeeze too hard and my fingers would disappear through hers altogether. If she vanished on me, I thought I'd be the one to die.

"If you choose me, I can't stop you," she said. "A living soul is stronger. But you'll be making a huge mistake. Please trust me. If there's one person you can trust, one person you know is always on your side, you must know it's me."

"I do," I said, closing my eyes against the tidal wave of tears that threatened. It was so painfully unfair I could hardly breathe knowing that I was leaving my mother here, that I was leaving Tadeu here. I could force him to come back with me, give him back his life. If I did, maybe he'd forgive me.

"Are you sure?" I whispered into her ear. "Mom, I need you so much."

"I'm sorry," she said, drops of hot tears falling on my shoulder as she embraced me. "I'm so sorry, *mi vida*. You must get your sister to the throne."

"If you are returning to the world of the living, you must go now," Kwame said. "With or without me, my queen. Your time here is over. If you don't go now, you will not be able to go at all."

Mom pulled back, grabbing my shoulders with both hands. "You must get rid of your father. He's a dangerous man— more than you know. Promise me, Itzel."

I sniffed and wiped my face hard, mopping up all the snot and tears that had come as I said goodbye to my mother. In all the years since I'd lost her, I'd wished that I'd at least had a chance to say goodbye. But it turned out that there was never a right time, a right way, to lose your mother. Words were inadequate, especially in a rush. This decision was impossible, and yet, I had to make it. I had to choose someone I had just met over my mother, as if his life were more important. I might as well be killing my mother all over again, and I didn't know if I could do it.

But I had to do it. She was right. It didn't matter what I wanted. In some twisted way, all of Sir Kenosi's games, his lessons, had prepared me for this moment. I might not be a queen headed for the throne, but I was a princess, and sometimes, a princess had to do the impossible. Sometimes, a princess had to do what was best for everyone but her. Sometimes, she had to listen and trust the people who had been there first, had to follow their advice even if it meant tearing out her own heart.

Even if it meant sacrificing her own mother.

All I could do was wrap my arms around her one more time and choke an inadequate promise into her hair. "I promise," I said. "I love you."

"Go," she said, crushing me to her one more time. "Don't ever come back here."

"I won't," I said, swiping the tears that wouldn't stop. "Please don't ever forget that I'm doing this because you asked me to. Not because I don't want to take you with me."

"I know. Thank you."

Kwame's hand closed around mine, but I hesitated. One last time, I reached out for Tadeu, aching for a chance to explain. This time, I didn't have to search at all. He was right there. But he didn't let me tug on him this time. The sense of his presence was immediate, but the door to him slammed in my face instantly, as if he couldn't stand to even feel me in his world.

I choked on a sob, turning to the one pair of arms that still opened to me. Prince Kwame pulled me in, and I pressed my face to his chest, too wrecked to be upset that he'd basically brought me here to trap me, thinking I'd die and live in the spirit world with him forever.

Just as the strange sensation of moving between worlds gripped me, I realized something. My mother hadn't known my father for most of his reign. They had ruled together during her life. If she couldn't see our world and watch over it, how did she know what he was like now?

I lifted my head, desperate to ask one more question. "Mom," I gasped, even as my body felt like it weighed a thousand pounds, as if I'd sink into the earth any second. I reached for her, and her cold fingers linked with mine, as if she couldn't bear to let me go, either.

"You said Father is dangerous," I said. "How do you know that? What did he do?"

I was already falling, and her fingers slipping from mine when she answered. "Itzel. Your father killed me."

FORTY-ONE

WHEN WE ARRIVED BACK IN OUR WORLD, I JERKED upright, sucking in a breath. The lion beside me sighed, and Kwame appeared over it in human form. He laughed, spreading his hands and staring down at them in the starlight as if he'd never seen something so incredible. Before I could even dry my fresh tears, someone had leapt at us out of the darkness.

I screamed, scrambling away as a shadowy form slammed into Kwame, knocking him to the ground. Growls and snarls ripped from the figure, animal sounds coming from a man.

Shadow.

And more than that, four lions prowled nearby in the moonlight. Four real lions. No wonder they'd told me I had to get back.

Rage rippled through me, and I jumped to my feet. "Stop fighting," I yelled, kicking at them. This time, I didn't have a gun. I had no way to stop them as they rolled over in the grass, fists and claws flying. I only knew that both of these men had lied to me, tricked me. Shadow hadn't just told me he was my mate. He'd used that lie to gain my sympathy, to come between me and my sister. I knew he hadn't killed my mother now, but I didn't know why he'd lied to me. I wanted a chance to find out, though, and I'd never get it if he got himself killed.

And though I resented Kwame for making me choose him over my mother and Tadeu, my mother had confirmed that I was actually his mate, and that meant something to me even if I didn't know exactly what. It was romantic, somehow, to have a mate, even if it wasn't infused with magic for me. I'd given up my mother for him, and I hadn't done it so he could be killed.

I had to save him, to get the amulet if nothing else. His mother wouldn't very well give me the thing if I had just gotten her son killed again. Besides, my mother had told me he was important, and I believed her.

When I couldn't find anything around to use as a weapon, I threw myself on the two men. I had put myself in mortal danger plenty of times lately. I was the expendable human, and if throwing Kwame's mate into danger would make him stop fighting, I'd do it, even if that mate was me. If my mother could give up a chance to live again for Prince Kwame, if he was that important, then I could risk it, too.

Claws raked down my back, and I arched in pain, crying out.

A second later, someone slammed into me from above as another person threw himself into the fray.

"Break it up," Lord Balam snarled, ripping Shadow from Kwame. Shadow twisted around, catlike, and sank his teeth into Lord Balam. Kwame leapt back onto Shadow, snarling about his mate. Lord Balam hurled Prince Kwame across the grass, his body landing with a thud. Shadow barked that I was his mate, slashing at Sir Kenosi as he ran in to grab me.

I rolled away in the grass, fighting back sobs of pain. Strong arms scooped me up, and his smell, like dried grass in the sun, enveloped me. I pressed my face to Kwame's chest as he whisked me away from the fight, leaving my three lovers snarling at each other in the savannah.

I didn't care. Prince Kwame had been there in the spirit world. He knew I was his mate, and he knew what I'd given up for him. I was going to make damn sure he never forgot it. But for now, I could only wrap my arms around his neck as he carried me inside the royal house.

"What happened?" came a low, familiar voice out of the darkness. I hated that I couldn't see anything in the interior of the house. As cats, they could probably see everything, but I could make out nothing but Kwame's flat, hard chest against my tear-streaked cheeks. But I knew that voice, a voice that had traveled the halls of my father's treacherous kingdom all my life. The kingdom I had believed was mine, that I would return to, until that moment.

"Lay her here," Gabor ordered, and though he was only a guard, and Kwame was a prince, the lion obeyed. I was lain on the floor, and I felt Gabor's strong hands turning me, pressing me face down on the packed dirt. Gabor, who served my father with unwavering, unquestioning loyalty.

I remembered the days after my mother's death, when a dozen guards were executed for failing to protect her. My father had ordered those executions, murdering twelve innocent men who had given up everything, given up the chance at living for themselves so they could live for their country and serve the king with blind devotion. And he'd killed them, twelve men who might have been as good as Gabor, for the simple reason that he had to make it look like an outside attack.

That was when Gabor had been promoted, brought into the palace and trained and brainwashed to believe my father's lies. And now... Now I felt something for him that I didn't feel for anyone else. Not Kwame, my mate, or Lord Balam, my first lover. Not even Tadeu, my first love, or Shadow, whom I also could not trust. What I felt for Gabor was so much more complicated, and yet, so simple. He would always be my father's. He would never be mine.

It didn't matter that his hands were agony on my skin, holding me steady with relentless pressure, as gentle as a lover's and as hot as the devil's. He held me down as Kwame's tongue swiped over my wounds, drawing a ragged sob from my throat. I wanted to scream at Gabor to do it himself, that I wanted him to heal me, to taste my blood, not this kind stranger who had done nothing to earn my fury but who had gotten it nonetheless. Kwame's healing tongue finished its job, and Gabor lifted me into his arms without a word, conveying me to a hammock and shifting me gently into the swaying sling.

"Gabor," I said, sliding an arm around his neck. One day, if I kept asking, maybe he would stay. Maybe I could rewrite history, rewrite reality, and one day, one night, he would tell me he felt the same.

"Itzel," he whispered, not using my royal title this one time, as if the rules had changed in the darkness. His fingers stroked my hair back, and after a second, his forehead touched mine. He moved his head slowly back and forth, his skin brushing mine, the gesture so innocent and yet so painfully intimate it stopped my breath.

"Where is my guard?" Camila's voice hissed through the night. "Gabor?"

Gabor stilled for a beat, and then he was gone, a cool rush of air taking his place as he hurried to my sister's side. Prince Kwame had stood back respectfully, not fighting for his mate as he had when Shadow had tried to claim me. I didn't protest when Kwame slid into the hammock beside me, his long body stretched the length of the hammock. He wrapped an arm around me, murmuring words of comfort to me, apologizing for hurting me and assuring me I'd heal quickly.

I hardly heard him. I'd spent my tears for the evening, but my heart was a shell. It wasn't just the wound, the gashes torn along my back. The last few days had destroyed me. Everything I'd always known had been ripped from under my feet, sending me tumbling into a freefall. Camila didn't trust me. My mother was gone, and I'd had one chance to bring her back, and instead, I'd brought back this supposed mate of mine.

I wanted to sob so hard I turned myself inside out. But all I could do was lie there, as silent and empty as the night world once the men had come in from fighting. There was no fight in me anymore, either. I knew I should want to overthrow my father this very day, not waiting the six more months for Camila's coronation. For tonight, though, all I wanted was everything I couldn't have. The mother I hadn't saved. The sister I'd lost. The man who had married himself to my father's service. And most of all, I wanted to be anyone but the daughter of a monster.

FORTY-TWO

I WOKE TO THE SOUNDS OF SHRIEKING AND laughter. Since I was not exactly a morning person, the last thing I wanted to do was get up and face a bunch of bright and chipper people—especially when the weight of the night before came crashing into me. I pulled the hammock tight around me, aware that I was alone in it now, unlike when I'd fallen asleep. If only I could block out the noise, the people, the past. But the delicious aroma of fried onions and spices and something sweet called to me, and my stomach twisted, keeping me awake from within even if I could have drowned out the noise.

Finally, I gave up and clambered from my hammock. My back hurt, but not nearly as much as it should. Someone had peeled off my shirt replaced it with a soft, pink thermal top and black cotton shorts with pink clouds printed on them. Judging by the tightness of the fabric across my chest and hips, I had to assume they were Camila's, though I didn't know why she'd bothered to have someone dress me. And how they'd managed to do it without waking me, I'd never know, but I didn't have the energy to question it. Probably the panther hallucinogen or Kwame's saliva. I had stopped trying to understand shifter magic.

Without stopping to find more clothes, I stumbled out from behind the fluttering curtain that sectioned off the sleeping area. The moment I emerged, the chattering of two dozen voices ceased. Everyone turned to look at me, pausing around the feast laid out on platters in the center of the circle where they sat. After a second, Prince Kwame rose from a seat around the huge circle and loped over to me. He took both my hands in his.

"Good morning, Princess Itzel," he said, a smile twitching at the corners of his lips.

"Good morning, Prince Kwame," I said, curling my toes against the cool dirt floor.

A bright, gap-toothed smile broke over his face, making the raised scars on his forehead bunch and his eyes squinch almost closed. "Let me introduce you."

"Actually, I met your family yesterday," I said, wincing at the memory of my blunder.

"You're my family now," he said, tucking my hand into his and pulling me across the room. I knew I should protest, tell him I couldn't have an audience with the queen while still in pajamas, but I decided it didn't really matter. Camila would be scandalized, and Gabor would probably think I represented our nation with a marked lack of decorum, but none of it bothered me.

I scanned the faces, finding many new and unfamiliar ones as well as the lion royals. Then there was Sir Kenosi, wearing the same sort of tunic as the other lion clan members, and Lord Balam, stoically watching his lover approach on the arm of another man. And Shadow, his long cascade of black hair hanging down his back, his green eyes bright as he watched me. There was so much I needed to say to them all, but him in particular. Gabor sat next to my sister, her face placid and calm even though I knew she was fuming with humiliation that I'd come to breakfast in such a state.

For a minute, I wanted to let her be furious at me. I wanted to let her biggest concern be my attire. To let her keep believing our father loved us, that he'd mourned our mother with us. For a minute, I wanted to let her keep living the lie we'd lived for half our lives.

Before I could find a way to pull her aside, the queen was on her feet.

"My daughter," she said, holding out a hand in a welcoming gesture. Instead of her cold expression from the night before, she wore a smile that covered her whole face. Her eyes squinted almost all the way closed as she stood and held out her arms to me.

I was too stunned by her transformation to move, but Prince Kwame conveyed me forward into her arms. Queen Lion enveloped me in a full body hug like the ones my mother used to give me. Only then did I realize she was talking to me. That she'd called me her daughter.

"I hear that you are in need of this," she said, stroking a glass bead on her necklace.

"Oh, yes," Camila said before I could answer.

"Th-thank you," I managed.

"Thank you for bringing my son back to me," Queen Lion said, pulling back to take my face between her strong, worn hands. Even the lines around her eyes seemed to have faded since the day before. Tears glistened on her lashes as she smiled at me. "I can never repay you."

"We are forever in your debt," King Lion agreed, appearing behind his wife. "No matter what happens, if you ever need our assistance in any matter, you don't even need to ask. Not only are you our daughter now, but you have returned our son to the land of the living."

He enveloped both his queen and me in his arms. Prince Kwame joined the embrace, stepping behind me and wrapping us all in his long, ropy arms. Laughter sounded all through the big house, and the queen's tears fell freely. When the king pulled back, tears ran down his face as well.

"You have a second family," said one of the princesses, standing to join our small group. "It can never replace your first, but you're our brother's mate, which means you're our sister now."

I wanted to tell them that I wasn't sticking around to make a home there, but this didn't seem the time. The queen undid her necklace and carefully removed the beads, at last pulling out a sleek yellow-and-orange bead. She handed it to Kwame, wrapping her arms around him and holding him so tightly I wasn't sure she'd ever let go.

Camila rose gracefully from her mat on the floor and cleared her throat. "Your Majesty," she interrupted in her soft, sweet voice. "I am the heir to the Ocelot Throne, as you know. I am collecting the amulets."

"Of course," Queen Lion said, the joy beginning to drain from her face as a bit of her queenly resolve returned. "You're a part of our family now, too."

"A royal marriage in return for the amulet is a tradition we are happy to continue," Camila said.

Wait, what? My gaze flew between my sister and the queen and then to my other lovers. My father had assumed I would marry Lord Balam—or he had certainly hoped I would before Lord Balam got tired of me and left me a ruined woman. Though Lord Balam and I had never made that commitment, quite the opposite in fact, I didn't want to be the one leaving him any more than I wanted to be left by him. He'd already seen his wife find someone else. Now he had to see me do it. Kwame pushed the bead into my hand as if solidifying the fact.

"Cooperation is not a question this time," King Lion said. "This is more than a marriage of alliance. My son has found the rarest jewel—a True Mate." He said the words with reverence, as if I were a goddess or something. The way Kwame was looking at me let me know he shared the king's estimation.

"Thank you," I said, bowing slightly. "I am truly honored to be a part of your family as well as my own. As Camila's escort, I must finish her Amulet Tour with her. I would be happy to visit the Lion Kingdom as soon as it is over."

"Oh," Queen Lion said, more of her smile slipping away. "I see. Of course. Preparing to join our nation is a big step. A few delays are unavoidable. We only hope you will return quickly. Preparations for a royal wedding are in store." Her smile returned, and she took both my hands in hers and squeezed.

Okay, then. This True Mate thing was a bigger deal than Shadow had let on. Suddenly, people were planning my wedding, and I'd only met Prince Kwame twice in my life. I didn't even know if I liked him. But then, that's how arranged marriages worked. You didn't have to like each other. You just had to spend the rest of your life together.

"Delays won't be necessary," Camila said. "I'm happy to leave my sister here to enjoy her True Mate if you are able to provide me with one female escort for the remainder of my tour."

"Yes, yes, take anyone," Queen Lion said in a rush, as if afraid Camila might change her mind.

My heart twisted in my chest like my sister had skewered it on the end of her knife when she slipped it in my back. I shouldn't have been surprised, and I really wasn't. I shouldn't have hurt, but I did. Every time, it was like the first time, the sting so fresh and raw it nearly brought me to my knees. My sister didn't want me there.

"Good," Camila said. "Then it's settled. Thank you for your hospitality, and I hope this marriage will create a bond of trust between two great nations."

She bowed to the queen, who returned the gesture, though not as deeply.

Camila bowed to the king and then to Kwame before turning to me. If I married Prince Kwame, I would be the next Lion Queen. I saw that knowledge click into place as she met my eyes. She'd never considered that I could be anyone of importance, certainly not someone of an equal title. But not every feline nation considered humans inferior. Prince Kwame and his family seemed nothing less than overjoyed to have me as their family. Of course they did. The king and queen themselves were mere humans, unable to take a lion's form until they died.

It occurred to me then that this wouldn't be my last amulet tour. Prince Kwame would one day have to take this journey, and I might very well accompany him. As my gaze moved around the circle, I had to swallow past a knot in my throat. If I married Kwame, would I have to give up these men, only to see them again when Prince Kwame was ready to take the throne? He'd have to bargain for the amulet from Lord

Balam, the *curandero* of the Jaguar Nation. From young Shadow, whose trickery I might never understand. From Sir Kenosi and his twisted games. And from Queen Camila, who had taken each amulet from my hand as if I owed it to her.

What if I wouldn't give it up this time?

FORTY-THREE

ONE DAY, I WOULD NEED CAMILA'S ALLIANCE. ONE day, I would need to ask her for the Ocelot Amulet, would need to give her something in return. Maybe I would remind her of this moment, when the queen had given the Lion Amulet to me, and I handed it to her instead of keeping it.

But I knew that in her mind, she had already earned it. She hadn't gone into the spirit world and given up her mother for it. She'd traded it for a marriage alliance.

One bead for one human sister.

For all I knew, she'd planned it all along. Maybe that was why she'd brought me with her at all. When she held out a hand to me, palm up, I hesitated before delivering the bead with shaking fingers.

"I hope it's worth it," I said.

Camila looked as if she didn't know what I was talking about. "You may help me prepare my things for our journey to the Tiger Kingdom," she said. "We must take our leave so that we can collect the remaining amulets and return in time for your wedding."

Maybe it was knowing all those eyes were on me, or maybe it was the princess training that was ingrained in me despite my best efforts, but I couldn't argue with my sister there in front of the whole Lion Court. So, after promising Queen Lion that I would come celebrate with them afterward, I followed Camila back to the sleeping quarters.

The others in our party trailed behind.

"Itzel," Lord Balam said, a troubled frown creasing his forehead. "Can I talk to you a minute?"

When our eyes met, I had to look away. What would happen if I refused this arranged marriage? Would the Lion Court turn on me, consider me a traitor, as the Ocelot Court would if someone dared defy a royal order? Would I be executed? Or would they chase down my sister and take the amulet by force, as the Panther Kingdom had tried to do?

"Yes," I said. "But I have to talk to Camila first." Time for a goodbye was the least I owed Lord Balam. In truth, I owed him a thousand times that. But I couldn't give him what he deserved right now.

I tugged Camila behind her curtain without waiting for an answer. I pulled it shut, trying not to crumble from the ache in my chest when I saw the eyes of the men I was closing out.

"Camila, you need to take me," I said. "When you go to the other kingdoms. If something happens to you..."

"That won't be necessary," she said, opening her bag and nestling the cheerful bead in next to the polished stone jaguar, the panther crystal, and the cheetah's ruby. "I've negotiated brilliantly for the Lion Amulet, haven't I?"

"I promised Mom," I blurted, not knowing how else to break through her poise.

"When?" she asked, her hand flying to her throat.

I realized how long it had been since we talked, and how very strange it would sound to her if I tried to explain the night before.

"Okay, this sounds insane," I started. "Just listen to what happened before you say anything."

I quickly ran through the night before, skipping the weird ghost sex and going straight to the part where Kwame tricked me into going to the spirit world, how I saw Mom for just a minute, and what she'd told me about Father. When I finished, Camila stared at me a long minute. "What—is wrong—with you?" she hissed out through clenched teeth.

I took a step back, not sure what I'd expected, but it wasn't this.

"What do you mean?" I asked.

"You got to bring one person back from the dead?"

"Technically," I said. "But I didn't know that when I went."

"And you thought you'd bring back some guy you just met instead of our mother?" Camila asked, her neck beginning to

329

redden. "What is your problem, Itzel? You've always been common, running around with that nasty little stable boy and all his friends, and I looked the other way. I was still going to let you be my advisor. People might whisper, but no one was going to make a big deal of it. They wouldn't dare. But this? Are you really such a whore that you'd sacrifice your own mother so you can add one more dick to this dirty little harem you're collecting?"

"What?" I asked, stumbling back as if she'd slapped me.

"Or is it because he's the prince?" she asked. "Maybe I was a little slow to think that one through, but you weren't, were you? You knew that if you got him thinking he was your mate, he'd do anything for you, even elevate you to queen. You've always been ambitious, but I never realized you were so cut-throat you'd kill your own mother for a throne."

"I didn't," I said, my hands balling into fists.

"You might as well have," Camila said. "You could have saved her, but you chose someone else instead. Someone you could fool into marrying you."

"I'm not fooling anyone," I said. "And I'm not the one who set up this marriage. I didn't ask to marry Kwame. You traded me for the amulet."

"You know, at first, I thought Shadow was trying to trick us, but now I see that it was you. When you didn't need him anymore, you found someone else to believe he's your True Mate. How'd you do that, anyway? Put that mark on them?"

"I didn't," I said through clenched teeth. "And I wanted to bring Mom back. She told me not to. She told me to bring Kwame. It was the only thing that could have gotten you the amulet."

"I don't even know if I can trust you anymore," she said. "I always thought you'd do what was best for me. But obviously you were looking out for yourself first all along."

"That makes two of us," I snapped, finally unable to stand there and take her insults. "And if you're so upset about me marrying Kwame, maybe you should let me out of that one. That's not who I'd choose to marry, anyway."

"Oh, no," she said. "You'd choose to keep running around with your fan club, making them all think they're the one. I knew you were just a human, ruled by your baser instincts, but you really have made a scandal of yourself. I'm glad Father's not here to see it. Now I just have to make sure Gabor keeps his mouth shut."

I swallowed hard, wondering if that's how he saw me, too. But I was too mad to hold my tongue. "You know, that's pretty rich coming from someone who has to lock herself in her room when she goes in heat. How's that for baser instincts?"

Camila's face raged a flaming red, and I knew I'd overstepped. I wasn't supposed to know about shifter customs, let alone speak of them. But fuck it. She talked about my humanity all the time. Everyone did. How come it was okay for them to insult my common human nature, but I couldn't criticize their shifter nature? I didn't choose to be human any more than they chose to be shifters. I couldn't help my nature any more than they could help theirs. So yeah, I was going to be petty and pretend that it was okay for me to do wrong since I'd had wrong done to me.

"You will never speak to me again," Camila said, and she turned and marched out of her sleeping area.

Okay, that had gone badly. I hadn't even told her about our father, which had been my main concern. Before I could get myself together, the curtain opened, and Gabor slid through. His eyes cut to me, but he went to Camila's bag and picked it up. I hadn't even considered saying goodbye to him, but of course he would be leaving with Camila. He was her guard, not mine. Still, the thought of never seeing him again made my heart clench with an unbearable ache.

"Gabor," I whispered.

"Your Grace," he said, the muscle in his cheek twitching. So much had happened that I'd barely seen him on this trip, and yet, my feelings had not faded. When his eyes lingered on mine, his gaze drinking me in, a rush of warm goosebumps swept over my whole body, and my breath caught in my throat.

"You're leaving," I managed.

"Yes." He stood with Camila's bag in his hand and a thousand unspoken possibilities on his tongue. I knew he would never voice them, no matter how badly I ached for him to say the words I needed to hear.

Before I could think better, I strode across the space between us and wrapped my arms around him, pressing my cheek to his solid chest as if I could memorize the rhythm of his heart. It beat within me, too, the same broken beat, the stutter-step when our bodies collided. Instead of pulling away, Gabor's arm wrapped around me, and he pressed his nose into my hair, inhaling my scent without pretense this time.

He dropped Camila's bag and threaded his fingers through my hair, tugging my head back. My heart stopped beating entirely when his gaze swept over my face and settled on my lips.

"Kiss me," I breathed, my whole body swooning into his, my limbs turning to liquid with one look.

"Itzel," he said, his voice barely a murmur. "I'll never love another woman. A guard is married and mated to the throne he has vowed to protect. I am bound by that oath. You know that, don't you?"

I nodded, tears clogging my throat. I didn't know why he was telling me this now, but I knew it. Guards couldn't have families, couldn't marry. It was a liability to the throne. And they couldn't leave their post. They had promised their lives to protect it, and the only way to quit the job was to give their lives. Having a guard leave his post, possessing all the knowledge and skills Father had given him, was unthinkable. Gabor had sold, if not his soul then his physical being, when he'd taken the job. The only freedom from the ocelot crown was death.

Tears spilled down my cheeks, and Gabor cupped my face between his hands, swiping them away with his thumbs. He lifted my face and gently brushed his lips against mine. Everything in me melted at the tender gesture. Hot tears flooded from my eyes, and I choked back a sob, collapsing against him. He held me tightly to his chest for a minute, letting me cling to the front of his shirt even as I wet it with the proof of my heartbreak. At last, I heard a rustle behind me, and Gabor tensed. I had to let him go. I didn't want to, didn't want to let him walk out of my life, but I couldn't make him stay. I couldn't make him sacrifice for me, couldn't stain his reputation.

Sucking up my tears as best I could, I released him, though it felt as if my heart were being slowly shredded as he stepped back.

"I wish you great happiness, Princess Itzel," he said. He stooped to pick up Camila's bag and then hesitated to give me one more searching look, as if he expected me to have the answer. When I didn't speak, he strode past me and out of the room.

FORTY-FOUR

I turned to see Shadow standing in front of the fluttering curtain. We stared at each other a minute as I tried to think of what to say. Ask why he'd lied about me being his mate? Tell him I knew his people hadn't killed my mother?

"You're marrying the prince?" Shadow asked.

"I don't know," I said. "I guess so. That's the way it works, right?"

Shadow's scowl turned fierce. "You really mean to choose a mate for the political gain of your sister?"

"I didn't choose anyone," I said. "You chose me. You said I was your True Mate. Humans don't even have mates."

"But you do."

I sighed. "I don't know what's going on, Shadow. I don't know why you and Kwame both think I'm your mate. But my destiny was decided the moment I was born. I was never going to be anything but a political pawn. That's what princesses are in our nation."

"You're not in your nation anymore," Shadow said, his green eyes blazing with intensity. "This is your life, Itzel. When will you stop living it for her?"

The answer that rose to my lips out of habit, out of eighteen years of saying it, was that I'd never stop living for Camila. But then the reality of my situation knocked the air out of me like a fist to the gut. Camila was leaving me here. She meant for me to marry the Lion Prince, to live here as a princess until his parents passed, and he took the throne. I wouldn't be living for her anymore, anyway. I'd probably only see her every few years, when the clans in the International Feline Council of Nations joined for a conference. Camila had just thrown me out of her life. She didn't care who I lived for now.

So, maybe it was time to start living it for myself.

Before I could answer Shadow, the curtain curled back, and Kwame stood in the entrance. "My queen," he said, glancing between me and my panther lover. "Is everything all right?"

Here goes nothing.

"I don't want to get married right now," I blurted. I'd decided to take the reins on my life, and I wasn't going to back out so soon. But I remembered what my mother had said. I'd promised to get Camila to the throne, so that's what I had to do, one way or another. And that's what I would do, no matter what it took. My father had killed her, and she had asked for only one thing in revenge—to get him off the throne. A promise to my mother came before anything in my life.

Sending Camila to the Tiger Nation with only Gabor and one human woman from the Lion Nation wasn't going to get her anything but dead. If I wasn't going to live my life according to her dictates, that meant I was free. I didn't have to stay here and marry Kwame. I had to do what I'd always intended. I would see my sister to the throne whether she liked it or not.

Kwame licked his lips and glanced back toward the group of celebrating royals. Then he stepped closer, letting the curtain drop behind him. His coppery eyes searched mine. "I know what you gave up for me to live," he said. "I know my mother is hasty, but I will do anything to make that up to you. I will give up just as much. You gave me back my life, and I pledge that life to you."

"Oh," I said, drawing back in surprise. I'd expected him to be angry or even hurt. I definitely wasn't expecting him to be... Nice.

"I am Itzel's mate," Shadow growled, pulling up his sleeve to reveal the luminous tattoo.

Kwame's eyes narrowed, and he turned, sliding up the sleeve on his tunic. The exact same mark glowed on his skin. His frown deepened, and he focused on me. "How is this possible?"

"You tell me," I said. "I don't know anything about it. And honestly, it's not my top priority."

Kwame reluctantly pulled down his sleeve. "What is on your mind, my queen?"

As I looked back and forth between them, I realized that even if it didn't make sense to me, this was nothing short of a miracle. I had two men here who wanted nothing more than to serve me in whatever way I wanted.

For the first time in a long time, I didn't have to think about what someone else's needs above my own. I knew exactly what I wanted.

"I want to talk to my sister," I said, straightening. "But first, I need to explain things to your parents, Kwame."

"They will understand," he said. "They've gotten what they wanted most in the world. They want only for you to have the same."

I nodded grimly and looked from one of my mates to the other. "I may not understand how I'm the mate of both of you, but I'll do my best to learn when this is over. For now, I can only thank you for sticking by me and promise I'll do the same for you. I may not understand it, but I know how important it is to the feline people."

Shadow frowned at Kwame, but after a second, he seemed to decide something within himself. He gave the lion a respectful nod and turned to me. "What do you want us to do?"

"Kwame, come with me to talk to your parents," I said. "Shadow, go out and make sure the helicopter doesn't leave without me."

FORTY-FIVE

AFTER OUR AUDIENCE WITH THE LION ROYALS, I walked out into the blazing sun with Prince Kwame at my side. The shiny beast we'd ridden in on, now crouching in the golden grass like some kind of spaceship, had just started up. My heart did not race at the thought of what I had to do. I was sure in my resolve.

Lord Balam jogged back to me from where he'd been standing near the chopper.

"Are you going to the Tiger Nation with my sister?" I asked without a greeting. I knew I only had minutes to pull this off.

"Are you?" Lord Balam asked, a frown darkening his inked brow.

"I don't know," I said. "I'm about to find out."

"I agreed to escort you on the Amulet Tour," he said. "That's what I intend to do."

"Thank you," I said, my throat suddenly tightening. He could have walked away. He probably should have walked away. But he hadn't. Through it all, every wobbling step of the way, he'd been by my side. He'd been my strength. And now it was time I was my own strength. I had to get Camila on the throne. I would save her even if she was too proud to save herself.

Lord Balam hesitated, his tattooed face serious as he watched me, his lips parting as if he were about to speak. But then he clamped his mouth shut and gave me a quick nod. That said everything. He was with me, and for now, that was all I needed.

I turned in search of Sir Kenosi, the man I'd spent so much time with, the man whose story I knew better than anyone's. Still, his reaction was the one I could predict the least.

He was nowhere to be found.

"Where's Sir Kenosi?" I asked.

"He's on the helicopter," Lord Balam said. "If we're going, we'd better go."

Together we ran for the helicopter. As the propeller moved faster, dust swirled up from the golden grasses. A dozen kids had run out to watch from afar, thumbs crammed in their mouths, eyes rounded with wonder. Shadow stood next to the open door, watching us approach. We crouched low and leaned into the wind, the sand burning our cheeks until we stood at the entrance. The stairs had already been pulled in. The chopping sound of the blade circling was so loud I could barely shout over it, but I saw my sister there in the seat closest to the door.

"Camila," I yelled. Instead of looking down at me from her seat, Camila shifted her position so her shoulder was turned, her back toward me.

"Are you really going on with just one guard and a female escort?" I asked, bracing my hands on the doorframe.

"Please close the door," she called to Gabor. "It's loud out there."

Before he could obey, I braced my hands on the floor to heave myself in. Lord Balam's strong hands clamped around my waist, and he lifted me in as if my curvy figure were as feather-light as Camila's.

"I believe we've gone over this," Camila said with a sniff. "The rest of my tour is none of your concern. And I asked you not to speak to me again. Gabor, get rid of her."

Gabor took my elbow and steered me toward the door. Though his touch was gentle, laying his hands on me was the wrong thing to do. In seconds, Kwame and Shadow had leapt through the door. Shadow scooped me away from Gabor while Kwame manhandled the guard. I knew Gabor was armed, but he didn't reach for his gun. He only stood bracing his arms against Kwame's chest as the lion went for his throat. Kenosi sat back watching, but he wore a headset, and I knew he was communicating with the pilot.

"This is your last chance," I said to Camila, who shrank back in her seat. "I have strong, loyal supporters. Mom said to surround yourself with them. They'll get you to the throne."

Camila straightened, her blue eyes as cold as Father's. "Did I not make myself clear enough? Shall I spell it out for you? I've been trying to get rid of you for the last two stops. I will not have a would-be usurper close to my throne. Why is that so hard for you to understand?"

"It's not," I said, grabbing her arm and pulling her to her feet. "But I'm not a usurper. All I've ever wanted to do was see you on the throne. And I'm going to make sure you get there."

"What are you doing?" she demanded, trying to wrench free. "This is my helicopter. Get out!"

"Actually, it's Sir Kenosi's," I said.

"Let me go," she cried. With a shove, she knocked me flat, taking me by surprise with her shifter strength. I was so used to thinking of her as helpless, but she'd always been stronger than I'd given her credit for. Stronger than me.

I jumped to my feet and stared at her, breathing hard. Maybe she had shifter strength, but I wouldn't have her destroyed by doing what had to be done for the amulets.

"I'm sorry," I said. I looked over her shoulder to where Gabor stood, his face clouded with uncertainty. I wasn't sure if I was talking to her or to him.

"Get out of here right now," Camila said, stamping her foot and pointing to the ground outside.

Instead of obeying, I flicked my eyes to Lord Balam, who leapt into the helicopter, his muscles rippling under his jaguar cloak.

"I'll bring you the amulet," I said to Camila as the chopper began to rise. "I need to keep you safe. This is the only way."

With that, I threw my entire weight at her. Her slender form may have held hidden strength, but it was no heavier than a human's. She went flying, toppling from the chopper and hitting the ground outside. She gave a shriek that ripped into my very soul, and tears burst into my eyes.

After leaving my mother, this was the hardest thing I'd ever done.

Gabor leapt to the door, then turned back. Our eyes met, and for an instant, he wore no mask. I knew that no matter what he did for her, he agreed with me. He knew that the only way to keep her safe on her tour was to keep her from performing the tasks necessary. He didn't say goodbye. His face said everything I'd needed to hear, everything he'd never said. Then, without a word, he turned and jumped, disappearing out the door as the helicopter climbed.

A sob wrenched free of my throat, and I fell to my knees. I had given up everything for the amulets so my sister wouldn't have to. But giving up my virginity, or my dignity, or even my mother, couldn't have hurt worse than giving up my best friend, my sister, the heart that beat inside my chest.

As Sir Kenosi rose from his seat to pull the door closed, I reached out, as if I could take back what I'd just done. But my fingers only touched the smooth, warm surface of the door.

"Goodbye, Camila," I whispered.

And then Lord Balam was lifting me, and Kwame was asking what I needed. Shadow's hand stroked back my hair, and Sir Kenosi instructed the helicopter's operator where to go.

I realized in that moment that I hadn't lost everything. I wasn't alone. Just as I had given up everything for Camila's bid for the throne, these four men had given up everything for me.

That's when I knew the truth. It didn't matter whether or not they were my mates. Each of these beautiful, terrible men was mine.

Optional Ending

If these books pushed your limits or made you uncomfortable, I suggest this as a good stopping point to the series. The next book features material that may be more than most readers can handle, including violent dubcon and extreme taboo.

Please note the warning, as I'm not kidding about the rest being nasty AF. If you think you can handle it, continue on!

Epilogue

Shadow
Keeper, Panther Nation

THE OTHERS SLEPT, BUT I SAT UP, KEEPING WATCH even when the only dangers to us lay in peaceful slumber. Itzel's body curled against mine, her head on my chest, her lips parted in sleep.

My mate.

I had never entertained the possibility that I might find a woman to be my mate, let alone a True Mate. But here she was, cradled in my arms. And even though I knew Kwame thought she was his mate, too, he hadn't made a fuss. In the end, he probably wanted exactly what I did—to see his True Mate happy.

It didn't matter that she somehow belonged to both of us. I'd already shared her with Balam. Seeing her with him didn't diminish my love for her. There was no jealousy in me when it came to her. Jealousy was selfish, and what I felt for her was unbound by selfishness. I would have shared her with the whole world if it brought a smile to her face.

I leaned down, pressing my lips to her forehead. She gave a sigh and nestled closer. Somehow, in this ridiculously extravagant helicopter over the Arabian Sea, mated to the human daughter of a king who had executed my parents, I found a contentment I hadn't known since childhood. The odd assortment of shifters with royal titles didn't intimidate me. Though I was nothing more than a poor panther orphan, with my True Mate in my arms I felt like the richest and most important man in the world.

Too soon, the helicopter began to descend. Sir Kenosi straightened in his seat and picked up the headset he'd used to communicate with the pilot.

"Thank you for taking us," I said. "For letting us use your helicopter."

The cheetah's eyes flicked to my mate, who stirred restlessly as the chopper began to descend. I understood that look even if he quickly covered it with a casual grin.

"Anything to be rid of those cold-blooded ocelots," he said with a shrug.

Itzel sat up, stretching her beautiful body before sagging against me again. "I left her," she said dully. "I left Camila."

Right where she belonged, I thought as the helicopter lowered. I knew nothing about the other nations, but the

Lion Nation probably had some sort of transportation. Camila would probably find a way home—or come after us.

I hoped she had to suffer a little on the way. Itzel had done far too much of that for her sister already. From now on, now that we'd gotten rid of the biggest obstacle on the trip, maybe things would go a little easier for my mate. Maybe her turn to suffer was over.

Ahead of us, what looked like a lush green jungle spread out in all directions. A gorge cut through it, probably cut during one of the earthquakes that had wracked the world for the past several decades. A river ran through the gorge, and dotting the edges, I could just make out small grass huts.

"Camila will be fine," I told my mate.

"Maybe not when she sees this," Kenosi said with a grin, picking up a quilted bag from the floor next to a seat.

"The amulets," Itzel said, a hand flying to her mouth.

"Will she come after them?" I asked.

"She's probably already on her way," Itzel said. "Oh god, what have I done?"

I pulled her in to comfort her, but this time she struggled free and jumped to her feet.

"You did the right thing," Balam said in his deep, thick accent.

Itzel turned to us, her eyes rounding. "She'll be coming here with only one guard after all."

The helicopter gave a slight lurch before settling, and Kwame reached out to steady our mate. "She will be fine," he said. "My parents will make sure of it. She's the sister of their future daughter-in-law. They will give her every protection and comfort."

"You don't understand," Itzel muttered.

"If she comes after you for revenge, we'll protect you," I said.

"Welcome to the Tiger Nation," Kenosi said as the door lifted. We all stepped out, and the hair on the back of my neck raised. I dropped to all fours, my panther out before I could question it with my human mind, convince myself that there was a logical explanation for the watched feeling.

"Whoa, what the fuck," Balam said, burying his hands in my fur as if to hold me back.

"He's right," Kwame said, glancing around. "There's something here. Something not of this world."

"What is it?" Itzel asked.

In answer, a massive tiger streaked from the trees. Itzel screamed. Kenosi shot across the space between us with unearthly speed, slamming into the tiger. But it was at least twice my size, even in my panther form. Without effort, it flung Kenosi's body aside.

All around me, I heard ripping cloth as the other men shifted. I leapt, but the tiger was already sailing through the air. In a single bound, it cleared my form and slammed into Itzel, knocking her to the ground. I threw myself at its back at the same moment that Balam and Kwame dove in, now fully shifted. But it was too late.

It was too late for all of us.

The tiger closed its powerful jaws around Itzel's neck and ripped her throat out.

YOU WERE READY FOR THAT CLIFFHANGER, RIGHT? 🙄 You were warned!

TO FIND OUT WHAT HAPPENS NEXT, GET BOOK 3 here: http://books2read.com/felineroyals3

FREE OFFER

Join the B-Team newsletter to get a bonus, deleted scene from Book 1 from a male point of view! https://www.subscribepage.com/p5b7l2

You'll also be the first to get future bonus scenes, exclusive content, and news!

www.ingramcontent.com/pod-product-compliance
Lightning Source LLC
Chambersburg PA
CBHW020527020726
47494CB00006B/1668